HOW
DO YOU
LIKE
ME
NOW?

Holly Bourne is a bestselling author. She is passionate about gender equality and mental health. *How Do You Like Me Now?* is her debut adult novel.

HOLLY BOURNE

HOW
DO YOU
LIKE
ME
NOW?

HODDER &
STOUGHTON

First published in Great Britain in 2018 by Hodder & Stoughton
An Hachette UK company

1

Copyright © Holly Bourne 2018

The right of Holly Bourne to be identified as the Author of the
Work has been asserted by her in accordance with the Copyright,
Designs and Patents Act 1988.

A CIP catalogue record for this title is
available from the British Library

Hardback ISBN 9781473667723
Trade Paperback ISBN 9781473667730

Typeset in Plantin Light by Palimpsest Book Production Limited,
Falkirk, Stirlingshire

Printed and bound in Great Britain by Clays Ltd, St Ives plc

Hodder & Stoughton policy is to use papers that are
natural, renewable and recyclable products and made from
wood grown in sustainable forests. The logging and manufacturing
processes are expected to conform to the environmental
regulations of the country of origin.

Hodder & Stoughton Ltd
Carmelite House
50 Victoria Embankment
London EC4Y 0DZ

www.hodder.co.uk

To Lexi,
for the phone call.

Month One

Olivia Jessen

Six month bump alert. The belly has popped people, the belly has popped. #BumpSelfie #Blessed

81 likes

*

Harry Spears

I liked it so . . . I put a ring on it.

Harry Spears and Claire Rodgers are engaged.

332 likes

*

Andrea Simmons

Poo explosion! But look at that cheeky face . . .

52 likes

Comments:

Olivia Jessen: Oh no, Andrea. I've got all that to look forward to.

Andrea Simmons: I'll give you a nose peg at your baby shower!

*

Event invite: Olivia Jessen's super-secret baby shower.

16 attending

*

Tori's WhoTheF*ckAmI? Official Fan Page

Alright my f*ckers! Who's coming to the London show tonight? I can't believe it's sold out! I love and adore you all. See you at seven. I'll be the one on stage with the microphone, wondering how the hell I got so lucky in life.

2434 likes. 234 comments.

★

I look out at a sea of earnestness.

There are too many faces to make anyone out individually, but there is a collective look. A collective glow. Their eyes are dewy; their hands are clasped.

They hang on my every syllable.

I'm getting to the good bit. The bit I know they've been waiting for. The bit I've been building up to. I walk across the stage in my designer heels and smooth down my designer dress. I look exactly how a successful woman should look. Groomed, plucked, highlighted, contoured . . . but not in an obvious way. I look right out at them. At their anxious, eager faces. And I say:

'That's when I realised it.' I raise one threaded eyebrow. 'Sitting there, cross-legged in that fucking tent in Sedona. Chanting bollocks with a load of wankers, wearing a rosary necklace for God's sake. That's when it hit me . . .'

I pause.

The audience stills. You could float a boat on the expectation filling the air.

'I was trying to *find myself* how everyone else finds themselves,' I say. 'I was having a nervous breakdown exactly how everyone else has a nervous breakdown and I was healing myself how everyone else tries to heal themselves. And I said to myself *NO MORE*.' I hold out my hand like I'm signalling stop. I pause again, waiting for the beat. '"Just who the fuck *am* I?" I asked myself. "What do *I* want?" Because life isn't a paint-by-numbers. You cannot find yourself along an identikit path. And, actually, even after my quarter-life crisis, even after this whole year of self-discovery, I was still twenty-five and doing exactly what had got me into this mess in the first place. I was doing what I thought I *should* be doing rather than what I fucking *needed* to be doing.'

A stray whoop. The audience softens into gentle laughter. I laugh, too, and it echoes around the walls, bounces out of the various speakers.

I nod. 'Exactly.' I pause to let them settle. I clop back to the other side of the stage. There is a hush. I blink slowly, trying to remember that moment. Trying to invoke the triumph I felt. Six years ago. On that day, that incredible day. The day where everything started going right for me.

'So,' I tell them. 'I opened my eyes, I uncrossed my legs, and I walked out of that stupid meditation yurt and never looked back.'

The applause is overwhelming, like it always is. It takes about five minutes for them to calm down, like they always do. I make my own eyes go dewy to show my appreciation, like I always do. Then I get around to telling them the rest of my story. The story they all know already. Because all of them have my book clasped in their hands, waiting for me to sign it afterwards. Waiting to have their moment with me. To tell me about their own messy twenties, their own terrible boyfriends, their own shitty jobs, their own smacking disappointments. And to tell me how my book, my words, my story helped them through. *Still* helps them through.

It's crazy really. I sometimes forget how crazy it is.

We don't sell many books despite the queue that snakes around multiple corridors. They all already have their copies. Battered copies with crippled spines and Post-its to highlight their favourite parts. I sign for over three hours – my grin stapled on, trying to keep my energy up for all the women who've waited so long for this moment.

This moment with me.

Like I'm special or something.

So I smile and smile and I high-five them when they tell me of their own adventures. I hug them when they cry. I lean in and listen carefully as they whisper their secrets. My publicist hovers, twitchy, and asks if I'm OK. If I need a break. If I want some water. I smile at her and say no. I'm OK. I'm fine. I'm managing. But thank you.

Every single person asks the same questions:

'So, when is your new book coming out?'

'What are you working on now?'

'Do you have a new project coming out soon?'

'I'm so impatient. How long do I have to wait?'

My smile goes tight and I tap my nose and say, 'Wait and see' and 'Watch this space.'

Then, of course, they also want to know:

'So, are you still together?'

'The guy you met at the end of the book? Are you still with him?'

'Are you still in love?'

They ask the way a child asks their parents if Santa Claus is real – their eyes big, wide with a mixture of excitement and fear. I know why they're excited and I know why they're scared. They're excited because if I can find him, they can find him. If I can make it work, they can make it work. If magic is real for me, it is real for them. I am the reflection of everything they want in their own lives. I'm essentially the Mirror of Erised.

They're scared because I could also be their albatross. If I can't make it work, who can? If magic doesn't work for me, it most certainly won't work for them.

I nod and simper and coo and look all bashful. I repeat the phrase over and over. 'Yes, we're still together. We live together now.'

Oh, how that makes them happy. They gasp. They demand photographs. They swoon, they sigh. Their eyes grow bigger and wetter and they are so relieved. It makes my own eyes water and I blink like crazy to stop it. Because they make me remember Us. The Us we were. The Us that we were when the story they clutch finishes. I can remember it so clearly – maybe because I've been forced to talk about it non-stop for six years . . .

'Are you OK?'

'Huh?'

I blink and look up at the face of a woman standing over me. Her entire body jolts with nerves; her fingers tremble on her copy of my book, which has over one hundred Post-its glued in.

'Sorry.' I smile and take the book off her. 'Now, what's your name?'

'Rosie.'

'Oh, that's a lovely name,' I say. It's what I always say.

'Thank you.'

I sign her book with the message I always write:

Dear Rosie,

Live the life you fucking need to live.

Love,

Tori xx

She's crying.

'Oh wow, thank you,' she stutters through her sobs. 'Can I . . . can I take a photo?'

I hand her book back. 'Of course, of course. Are you OK?'

She laughs a little and says, 'I'm fine, it's just so amazing to meet you.'

I hold out both arms warmly. 'Come here for a hug and a photo.'

Rosie hands her phone over to my publicist and is so

overcome with emotion she forgets to even ask if it's OK for her to take the picture. Then she clatters around to my side of the table and quivers next to me. I pull her in, putting my arm around her. She's hot and sweaty. Her dampness sinks into the crisp fabric of my dress, but this moment is worth more than my dress.

'Smile!' my publicist says, holding up the phone.

I smile with my good side facing towards the camera – chin down to give me better jaw definition, eyebrows relaxed so my forehead wrinkles don't show. There's a flash and Rosie giggles and steps back to her side of the table, retrieving her phone and checking the photo.

'Thanks so much for coming.' I hand her book over.

'No, thank *you*. Thank you so much for writing it. You don't understand. When I was twenty-three, I was such a mess . . . then I found your book and . . . it changed my life . . . it really did.'

I am tired of smiling, but I need to smile at this because it's important to her. 'Wow, I'm so touched to hear that. How old are you now?'

'Twenty-five.'

She's only twenty-freaking-five. They just keep getting . . . younger.

'Well I'm so glad you enjoyed it.'

I'm looking past her now, to the next person. Because it's gone ten and I've got the wedding tomorrow. But, just as I reach out to take the book off the next shaking fan, Rosie discovers the courage to say one more thing.

9

'Hey, sorry. But, can I just ask? Rock man? The man from the book? You are still together, aren't you?'

Rock man.

The man who found me on the rock. Who found me on top of a vortex in Sedona screaming *'fuuuuuuuuuck'* and throwing my rosary beads off into the skyline, and somehow found that endearing.

Tom . . .

The man who could've been anywhere else in the world that day, but whom a thousand gusts of fate somehow blew to Arizona too. *Sedona* too. Climbing up to the vortex too.

My happily-ever-after.

The one you're always rewarded with in stories where a character decides to be brave.

'Yes,' I confirm, feeling like my smile might snap. 'We're still together.'

She lets out a little squeal and a yelp, arms flailing in the air. Then she blushes. 'Sorry. I'm fangirling.'

'That's fine.'

I'm looking past her again because, in the nicest possible way, she is taking too much time now. There are still at least fifty women waiting not-so patiently any more. Rosie doesn't read my vibe. My response has only given her more confidence. She is conducting the conversation that she needs. In her head, we are friends now. Already great friends.

'And you're still blissfully happy?'

I close my eyes for a second longer than I should. When I open them, my smile is still there. It has to stay on. For the next fifty people it has to stay on. I give Rosie my dimples and my charm and my glowing, golden happiness. My wisdom. My serenity. Everything she expects. Everything she has paid for in her ticket price.

'Of course,' I tell her. 'We're still blissfully happy.'

★

The adrenaline starts to ooze out of me in the taxi home. I feel each muscle clenching and releasing. The cocktail of performance hormones steadily filtering out of my tight stomach, unravelling my intestines inch by inch. I lean my head against the blackened glass and watch London twinkle outside. This city just keeps getting taller, refusing to let anything stunt its growth – much like the people who live in its turrets.

My phone lights up and buzzes angrily in my hand.

Dee: HELP ME HE IS A CRAZY PERSON

I smile as the taxi passes the looming ostentatiousness of Big Ben and we drive over the black currents of the Thames. There will never be a time when I don't want a mid-date message from Dee.

Tori: He can't be as bad as last week's surely?
Dee: He's married, Tor. HE'S MARRIED!!
Tori: Then why is he on a date with you?!
Dee: He said he WOULD get a divorce but he CAN'T FIND HIS WIFE BECAUSE SHE VANISHED.

I tap out a few replies as the cab plunges through the murky depths of South London – where glittering lights are replaced by concrete slabs of sort-of-affordable housing as long as your parents can help you with the deposit to dodge inheritance tax. I try to find the right mix of sympathetic, concerned, and taking the piss.

Tori: Seriously, are you OK though? It would only happen to YOU. X

Dee: I'm safe! I'm home. I really want to drink Merlot with my spritely young housemates but we've got the wedding of doom tomorrow.

Tori: Don't remind me. I'm still picking you up at 9, right? X

Dee: 9 it is.

Then five minutes later:

Dee: And, it's not me. This is just what dating is, Tor. Everyone apart from me is either boring or totally insane.

I put my phone away as we slow down around the park. The pavements are clogged with smokers and drunk people spilling out of bars, ripping into boxes of fried chicken, laughing loud and shrill and leaning into each other, and putting their hands on each other's chests. We pull up at a red light and the taxi throbs softly from the music blasting out of a flat above. London never rests. It doesn't do bedtime or catnaps or even dozing. It's so exhausting living somewhere this constantly awake.

The thought of coming home to Tom makes me feel safe. The thought that he will be there, and that he says he loves me; the thought that I don't have to go back out there into a world of ghosting and dick pics and messages with two ticks but no replies. But the thought of no Tom . . . I shiver. The thought of the alternative. The thought of starting again. Thirty-one and alone. Thirty-one and putting that number on an online-dating profile. Knowing the assumptions people make about that number. The wilting pair of ovaries they see. The desperation they smell. The sand you leave behind on the chair as the hourglass pours from top to bottom . . .

Tom loves me and I love Tom. That is special. That is rarer than you think. That is all you need.

By the time the driver has halted and pulled up his handbrake, I adore Tom. I feel blessed to have Tom. I'm even impatient to see him, snuggle into him and show him my love and my relief. I fiddle with the keys to our block of sterile, modern flats. Tom said it was better to get a new-build rather than a Victorian conversion. I agreed because it was easier, even though it was mostly my money paying for it. But I don't want to have bad thoughts about Tom. Not after tonight. Not when I know just how many people are rooting for us. He is my happily-ever-after and I love him and I don't want to be alone.

Cat greets me at the door, launching herself at my leg and twirling around it like a maypole, purring before I've even put my stuff down.

'I'm back!' I call out needlessly.

There is no response.

I can sense his presence here – the lights are on, his coat

is up on the hook, I can just *feel* him in the flat – yet he doesn't reply. I dump my stuff and pick up Cat. She resists, twisting in my arms and trying to bite me, so I relent and put her down. She scurries off into the bedroom and I follow her, shedding my coat on the way.

'Hey,' Tom says from the bed. His face glows blue from his iPad, his shoulders hunched over it. He does not even look up when he says it. 'How did it go?' he asks the screen.

'Yeah, really good.'

'That's great,' he tells the screen.

And, just like that, the love drains out of me. Like someone has pulled the plug on a cold bath.

Cat jumps up onto the bed and onto the lump of Tom's body. She thrusts her head into his iPad, doing an exotic cat-version of the Dance of the Seven Veils. Her assertiveness works when it never works for me.

Tom's face cracks into a smile. 'Hello Trouble.' He puts his iPad fully down and rubs Cat under her chin. I see the love pour out of him as I stand there in the doorway, hardly acknowledged, jealousy pumping through my body. This is a new thing. A new thing that I hardly dare admit to myself because of how truly pathetic it is.

I am jealous of my cat.

My boyfriend loves my cat more than he loves me.

He certainly touches her more . . .

I ask Tom about his day and he says it was OK. I ask how work was and he says that it was OK. I ask what he had for dinner and he tells me what it was and that there are leftovers in the fridge if I'm hungry. Then he's distracted by Cat rolling onto her back and kicking his hand away.

'What are you doing? Silly thing. *Oww, oww!* That hurts!'

My cat and my boyfriend are having a moment and I am not part of it. So I wilt out of my dress, peel off my matching underwear and clamber into my pyjamas. He's still playing with Cat when I go to the bathroom to brush my teeth and get ready for bed. I first take off my make-up using cotton pads soaked in micellar water, then I rub an organic cream cleanser into my face for two minutes before scrubbing it off with a flannel. I splash my face with cold water to act as a toner and dab it dry with my towel. I spill out some anti-ageing serum with retinoid onto my fingertips, dot it around my face and then rub it in gently. I go through the same process using my tiny pot of eye cream. I sit on the loo and pee while I wait for it all to sink in. Then, after washing my hands and brushing my teeth with my sonic toothbrush, I finish with a thick night-cream. Pulling the mirror out on its extendable arm and flipping it to the magnifying side, I examine my face. I turn this way and that, raising my eyebrows and lowering them at least ten times. Still surprised at the lines that are there. Already. But I've been told it would be worse if I didn't use the creams.

Tom's light is off when I return. He's curled up on one side, Cat twirled up on his feet like a fresh bagel. I feel so disappointed at such a simple act. But it's late and I have the wedding tomorrow and I'm lucky to not be out there alone, dating men with vanishing wives, and I don't want to get myself all wound up just before sleeping. So I get into bed and say, 'Night then.'

Tom's already half-asleep. He's always been able to find sleep easily. I joke that he's like one of those dolls you lay down and their eyes close. But he lets out a small grunt of happiness and reaches out to pull me into him. His body is safe and strong and warm. I envelop myself in his smell, closing my eyes, feeling loved and safe – so different from only moments ago. He wiggles and nudges his arse into my thighs and I laugh quietly in my mouth and obligingly take up position of big spoon. My boyfriend. All six foot of him. Yet always demanding to be the small spoon. I breathe in the smell of his back and let the heat of his body warm mine. I wrap my top arm over his stomach and lightly graze my hand over his naked body, brushing his unresponsive penis. Maybe just to check it's still there. It's warmer than the rest of him. I don't know what to do with my other arm, trapped beneath my body and folded at an awkward angle.

This is the first time we've touched all day. And, yes, he's only half-conscious, but still . . .

. . . oh hang on. He's snoring already. He is not conscious.

This is the first time we've touched all day and he is not conscious.

I lie there for a while, not even trying to sleep. Just enjoying the closeness. But, as if he can sense my neediness, he rolls onto his front. There is yet again a gap between us where the cold air rushes in. I chew on my lip. We've argued before about this. How it's 'unreasonable' for me to analyse his body language while he sleeps.

I wait a further ten minutes before shuffling up to a seated position and getting my phone out.

My feed is chock-a-block from tonight's event.

@rosianna_90 OMG. Still crying from earlier. Can't BELIEVE I got to meet @TheRealTori. I now know who the fuck I am and I'm proud xxx

@WhoTheFuckFanGirl THANK YOU SO MUCH FOR TONIGHT. I am so pleased you exist. I wrote a blog about tonight. Pls read it xx

I reply to as many as I can saying thank you. Lots have uploaded their selfies and I click on every single photo – looking only at my own face and trying to figure out if my forehead looks too big without a fringe. Oh, it looks really big in this one. I zoom in so that my face fills the whole screen of my phone and I tick off every single imperfection. I don't once look at the other faces of the other people in the photos. Just my own. At one point I zoom in so much that my entire screen is just my forehead. Then I Google 'haircuts to hide a big forehead' and scroll through them aimlessly, thinking they're awfully similar to the haircut I've just spent two years growing out.

@TheRealTori Oh my, my f*ckers. Thank YOU for tonight. I had the most amazing time meeting you all and hearing about your own journeys xx

The moment I hit 'send' my phone lights up with further notifications as it's liked and shared over and over. I swipe off and, stupidly, find myself on The Bad Website for some reason.

'You've got to stop going on it,' Dee keeps telling me. 'It's like self-harming for childless thirty-somethings.'

'I'm only on it to run my fan page.'

'Yeah? So why do you keep complaining to me about everyone posting photos of the inside of their wombs?'

'I can't help it! And what is *with* all the baby-scan photos? When did *that* become a thing?' I ask for a millionth time.

'I don't know, but there are now so many monochrome scans I feel like I've woken up in *Pleasantville*.'

'Dee?' I always ask. 'Why is everyone suddenly having babies and we're not?'

'Any idiot with a functional vagina and access to sperm can pop out a fucking baby, Tor,' she always replies. 'It's not exactly an achievement.'

'How are you allowed to be a primary school teacher again?'

Dee isn't here to stop me though, so I scroll past all the inevitables. Scroll scroll scroll. Judge judge judge. Feel empty feel empty feel empty. Smug couple pictures of smug couples going somewhere smug on a smug date and then taking a smug photo of themselves being there. The endless, *endless* baby photos and updates about all the major milestones said baby has got to. ('LOOK, SHE SMILES.' 'SOMEONE IS ALMOST WALKING.' Even: 'SOMEONE TRIED EGG FOR THE VERY FIRST TIME TODAY.')

There are endless likes and endless comments as everyone dutifully validates people making socially-acceptable decisions at the socially-acceptable age to make them. Well done, well done. Go you, go you. Congratulations. Go you for finding the person and doing the engagement photoshoot and buying the flat and having the baby in it. Well done, well done. That is what you are supposed to do, so well done, well done.

There's a photo of Jessica and her bridesmaids preparing for tomorrow. They all wear personalised matching dressing gowns and drink from champagne flutes. They are in a line with one hand on one hip and all their front legs bent to make them look thinner. I feel a stab of anger that Jess didn't ask me to be a bridesmaid, combined with relief that I'll never have to wear a personalised dressing gown.

Jessica Headly

Toasting my last night as a single gal. Can't believe tomorrow I get to marry my best friend and become MRS Jessica THORNTON.

Here are some of the thoughts I have:

You are a traitor for changing your surname.

You have lost lots of weight for your wedding and are now either as skinny, or skinnier, than me and now I need to set my alarm early so I can work out tomorrow.

If one more person tells me they're marrying their best friend I will run out of vomit.

Who is that girl two in from the left? She is prettier and thinner than me and I hate her. Maybe I should click on her profile and look at every single photo her privacy settings allow and torture myself with how she is prettier and thinner than me?

Who would I pick as my bridesmaid? No Tori. You don't believe in marriage, remember? Well, that's not quite true, is it Tori? It's Tom who doesn't believe in marriage. Well, it's not like he's said that exactly, just more that he seems very adamant that marrying you isn't a good idea at all. But that's fine, you don't want any of that archaic shit anyway.

I press 'like' and turn off my phone.

★

My alarm goes off at the rather painful time of six and I smack it off before it wakes Tom. Cat winds herself around my legs as I stumble to the toilet and doesn't stop figure-of-eighting until I've poured a generous amount of stinky food into her bowl. I change into my expensive workout gear in the spare bedroom, even though I have no plans to leave the flat. Then I tiptoe to the living room, close the door, and sync up my phone to the TV, turning the volume down low. I then pick a 'fat burning' HIIT workout from my subscription package.

I hit play.

I lunge and lunge and lunge. I squat and squat and squat. 'Deep squat now – deeper, deeper.' I keep my back straight when the instructor reminds me to. 'Tummy tight.' I suck in. 'Now really work those abs.' Crunch, crunch. 'Don't pull on your neck when you come up.' 'Now back for some final lunging.' Every time I deep-lunge I imagine what it will do to my legs. How it will make them look. Tight and toned and bump-free and how I'm told they should be. I will be able to wear short skirts in summer and people will look at my legs and know that I am in control of my body. 'Lunge lunge lunge, really bend your knee at the back. Go down, not forward.' The overexcited instructor yelps at me with enthusiasm, hardly breaking a sweat. She takes the word 'perky' to whole new Dante's-*Inferno* levels.

Afterwards, I try to take a post-workout selfie in my giant bathroom mirror. But I'm too red and too sweaty and I forget how mad I look without my eyebrows drawn in – like an egg balanced on a pair of shoulders. I reach for my make-up bag and pencil them in. Then I add a tiny bit of mascara, some under-eye concealer and lip tint. I take another photo. *Much better.* Though it still takes me twenty shots to get the exact combination of laissez-faire, empowered, and naturally-pretty-but-not-like-I-know-it. I brighten the photo up on my phone while my sweat dries and hardens into my clothes. Then I pick a good filter that makes me look even better, but not like I've obviously used a filter.

I post it.

Annoyingly True Things That Are Annoyingly True no. 256
Exercise really does help your motherf*cking mental health.
I cannot tell you how much I hate cardio. How much I dread
it. I will never, ever, be the sort of person who looks forward
to a run. But working out does keep my head in check, and

that's the only reason I do it. Not to look good, but to feel good. If any of you figure out a way to get healthy endorphins WITHOUT having to sweat them out – please DEAR GOD – let me know . . . #PostWorkoutSelfie #MentalHealth

It has over six hundred likes by the time I'm out of the shower – freshly shaved and my hair washed with thickening shampoo. I scroll through the praise as I dry my hair upside down for added volume. The comments are all lovely, as they always are. Most of them congratulate me for taking such a positive stance towards mental health. That is good. That is what I wanted. But I cannot ignore the spike I get in my endorphin levels when some of them miss the point and tell me how hot my body is:

'Wow – you are so beautiful.'

'Looking goooooooood Tori #WhoTheF*ckIsYourTrainer?'

'How do you get your thighs to look like that?'

And that's what I secretly hoped would happen and I'm glad it's happening because no one needs to know and it really has helped me feel better.

My body is not enticing to Tom, however, who is drinking coffee in bed when I return. Today's pathetic attempt to get him to find me sexually attractive is the most pathetic of pathetic attempts. I wander deliberately into our bedroom wearing amazing lingerie for today's wedding. The lingerie is red and lacy and slutty but in a sophisticated way. It

22

makes my breasts look like red velvet cupcakes – the sort you take a photo of before you eat them because they came from a trendy bakery. The bra just grazes my nipples; the pants are so see-through they may as well not exist. If I sneeze, it could rip the fabric.

'Morning,' Tom says, slurping from his coffee mug. He's on the iPad again, catching up on all the noise he missed while he slept. 'Did you sleep OK?'

I will try one more time. I stand with a hand on my hip, displaying my body at the end of the bed. 'I slept fine,' I reply, striking another unnatural pose. 'Have you seen the phone charger?'

He points to where it's plugged in on his side of the bed. I do not walk around to get it. Instead, I get on my hands and knees and lean over Tom to reach it. My red velvet nipples practically dunk themselves in his coffee.

'Careful, Tor. I almost spilled my drink.'

I grab the charger and lean back. *Do not cry, do not cry. You only have an hour to do your hair and make-up, you do not have time to cry.* I plug my phone in, and give up all hope of ever feeling good about this relationship again. And then . . . then Tom playfully slaps my bum.

'Good undies, Tor. You know I've always loved that arse.'

I beam back – instantly cured of sadness – and he's giving me That Grin. That Grin that I've missed so much. Like a schoolboy who's just dipped my pigtail in an inkpot. I launch myself at him. I may not have time to cry but I do have time to have sex. Sex is less messy than crying. I climb back onto Tom's body and kiss him aggressively. He kisses me back for ten whole seconds before he pushes me away by my shoulders.

'I don't want you to be late for this wedding.'

Years ago, at the beginning, Tom wouldn't have cared at all about being late for a wedding – not that we had many weddings to go to back then. Sex with me always came first. Sex with me even though we were late. Sex with me even though we'd had sex twice that day already. Sex with me because he found the TV show we were watching boring. Once, sex with me in the toilets *at* a wedding.

Now: no sex because you will be late for the wedding that I'm not even coming to.

I smile and draw the shutters on my humiliation. I climb off him and chastise myself for playing it wrong. Being sexually needy isn't sexy. I messed it up. He saw through the red velvet nipples. I'm too sexually available. Maybe I should try to withdraw again. Remove the interest, the pressure. Make him wonder where it's gone. Make him work for it. That's sexy, right? I did try playing sexually hard-to-get last year and all that happened was Tom and I didn't touch each other for a month. (He hardly noticed. If he did, he only seemed relieved I was leaving him alone.) But maybe I wasn't doing it *right*.

'No,' I say. I pull my dress off the hanger and cascade it over my head. I get out some body lotion to rub into my freshly-shaved legs. 'Can't be late. Jess would kill me.'

★

I pull up outside Dee's flat and fire off a message.

Tori: I'm outside. You better have the Moulin Rouge soundtrack with you x

I see one tick become two ticks but still turn off my engine. Dee is a minimum of ten minutes late for everything, to the point where she doesn't even say sorry any more. I'm on a yellow line but the road is as dead as the opening scene of a post-apocalypse film. Brixton is only quiet in the early hours of weekend mornings. The rows of converted Victorian terraces show no sign of life. Every curtain is pulled shut against the bay windows. Everyone sleeps. Evidence of the night before is everywhere. Takeaway packages spew up leftover chips and chicken wings across the pavement. A small puddle of lumpy vomit dries in the spring sunshine. This is London so no one will wash it away. It will stay there until it rains, or some desperate pigeons eat it. I grin at an empty bottle of Cherry Lambrini left upright on someone's front steps. But the grin quickly morphs into a pang. A pang for being younger. The sort of younger where you drink Cherry Lambrini on your front steps, sucking hard on a fag and talking with wild gesticulations at all the friends around you who are also drunk, smoking and talking animatedly about the state of their constantly dramatic lives. I know it isn't as fun as it looks – I wrote a whole book about how it isn't as fun as it looks – but it's not the fun that I miss, it's the fluidity. Where a chance encounter, or an impromptu night out, or a wrong turn, or a last-minute trip could suddenly somehow change everything, alter your direction so utterly – without it ever being too late to change course again if you didn't like the latest view. Yes, back then I felt lost, but now I feel so stuck.

Lost is easier than stuck . . .

The slam of a door and Dee wobbles towards the car under a teetering tower of luggage. She stumbles and a bag drops to the ground. She drops another as she bends down to pick up the first. She swears profusely.

I put the window down. 'We're only staying one night, you know that, right?'

'Yes,' she glares at me. 'But I'm having a wardrobe crisis and you need to help me decide what to wear.'

I release the boot and she chucks her stuff in with such abandon that my whole car shakes. Then she throws herself into the passenger seat, puts down the window and launches straight into a massive debrief of last night.

'So, this guy, right? Last night. Oh my *God*, Tor. It was the best date I've had in ages. He didn't send me a photo of his flaccid penis. Nor his erect penis for that matter – which is slightly better, but still a red flag. Then he actually took me to a half-decent place. Not Gordon's Wine Bar. I swear to *God* if one more fucking guy thinks it's "cute" to take me to Gordon's – where we just stand there awkwardly, watching everyone else around us on bad dates *also* standing there awkwardly – I may give up wine for *ever*. But *no*. He took me to this nice restaurant, with proper napkins . . .'

I just about manage to keep up as I wind us around hissing, lurching buses, and determined joggers who run out in front of me. By the end of the date, we're on the South Circular, which is surprisingly traffic free. I stream along it and Dee's hair blows all around her face as the breeze blasts through the window.

'Right, so *then* it's time to say goodbye,' she continues. 'And, for the first time in ages, I actually want someone to kiss me. I want *him* to kiss me. And we're all building up to it. There's leaning and positioning and chin tilts – the whole shindig. But, just before the lunge, he stops and says: "There's something I need to tell you."'

'Oh God.' I indicate to get into the left lane and swear at a bus that won't let me in. 'That is never good.'

'I know, right? But I thought maybe he was just about to go off to war or something.'

'We're not at war, Dee honey.'

'You're always ruining my fantasies.' She throws her head back and laughs. 'Right, so I'm there thinking the whole war thing might be quite sexy. That maybe being a military wife would suit me. I'd get months to myself, a nice army house to live in . . .'

'I love how you were married already.'

'IT WAS A GOOD FIRST DATE. You don't understand what that means, Tor. Aaaaanyway, I'm all ready to forgive him and tell him I'll wait while he's away on service or whatever it is. Until he says: "So, yeah, there's no easy way to tell you this but I'm married."'

I shake my head and check my rear-view mirror. Wishing I was more surprised. But, after hearing Dee's many, many dating stories, I am no longer surprise-able.

'And I said, "rii-iiight", and then he totally panicked and said, "It's not like that, I promise. I'm not looking to have an affair." So I ask him why he's not divorced yet and he says, "Well, I want to get a divorce obviously, but I can't find her."'

'He can't *find* her?'

'Yes.'

'Like she's a pair of car keys?'

'Like she's run away from him and vanished into the night. That's what he told me.'

I tune her out for a moment as I have to merge onto the M4. A looming deathtrap of a lorry won't let me in and I have to speed up to about 90 mph on the slip road to just about get in front of him. I join the clug of cars roaring away from London on their way to perfunctory Saturday activities and it takes several moments for my heart to recover from our almost collision.

'So, yeah,' Dee continues, oblivious to the near-death situation. 'What has he *done* to her to make her vanish into the night? But then he tried to claim *she* was the crazy one. Totally crazy. He went on and on about what a psycho she was and how running away was "so like her".'

'I bet she wasn't crazy until she met *him*,' I point out.

'Exactly!' She waves her hands as she speaks and her gold nail polish glints in the sunshine. It sets off her auburn hair just perfectly and I get the stab of jealousy I always get whenever I think about Dee and her hair. 'The last six guys I've dated have fed me the "all my ex-girlfriends were crazy" line. And I'm like, "Dude – who is the common denominator in this pattern? *You!*" Anyway, fuck this. Can we sing "Elephant Love Medley" now?'

'Only if I can be Nicole.'

'You always get to be Nicole!'

'Yeah, well, I'm driving us all the way there.'

'And I'm doing you a favour by being your plus one.'

In the end we decide to take it in turns. Four replays of 'Elephant Love Medley' and three of 'Come What May' get us onto the M40 where city life and urbanisation give way to trees and sheep and space. Hawks swoop and cartwheel overhead, floating on invisible air currents. Valleys of green lines stretch out for miles on either side of the car, and I get that gasp of . . . something I always get when I leave London. The feeling that there is more, that I deserve more space than the city gives me. But mixed with a pang of superiority that tells my gut, 'Yeah, but what do people out here *do* with their lives?'

We stop for coffee at a service station and I take various photographs of it to show off my painted nails.

'I'm going to pretend you're not doing that,' Dee says, tipping two sugars into her flat white.

'Oh shut up. I saw your post about the "beautiful sunset" last week.'

She holds her hands up. 'Guilty as charged.'

We fold ourselves back into the car, which has already become an oven in the short time we've left it parked. It's a gorgeous day and forecast to get even nicer. Jess is so lucky. Now, not only will the photos look great, but the unexpected sunshine will give everyone a great conversation opener for the pass-the-time-before-the-food-comes section of the day. I merge us back onto the M40, clutching my coffee in one hand and steering with my spare.

'So remind me whose wedding this is again?' Dee asks, with a croissant hanging out of her mouth.

'Jessica. She's a friend from home.'

'And who's she marrying? Do you know him?'

I bite my lip before replying. 'Tim. He's an accountant.' I add.

'Poor Jess,' Dee says sympathetically.

'Don't judge him too quickly,' I say, smiling. 'I mean, he has told me, at least twice, that "he's not like regular accountants".'

Dee tries to grab the wheel. 'Turn the car around, Tor. I am not going to this wedding.'

'Stop it!' I yell, laughing and slapping her hand away.

'There's going to be more than one accountant at this wedding, isn't there?'

'Probably.' Dee's hilarious wheel-grab means I've strayed into the fast lane. I smile and flirt with the male driver of the car that honked me, mouthing 'sorry'. He still shakes his fist as he speeds past.

'No wonder Tom bailed.'

'He didn't bail because of the accountants. He has this podcast thing.'

'Yeah yeah, I know. Convenient though, isn't it?' My fingers tighten on the steering wheel. Dee finishes her pastry and brushes the leftover flakes onto my car floor like buttery dandruff. 'Can we start a drinking game where we have to do a shot every time someone says, "I'm not like regular accountants"?'

'We won't be able to see by the time the speeches start.'

'*Precisely!* Can we just make the whole *day* a drinking game?'

'I don't know. Livers are apparently quite essential organs. How is this game going to work?'

'Simple!' Dee digs in her black leather handbag and pulls out a biro and a receipt. 'We have to drink whenever a wedding cliché happens. Like, umm, we have to drink if the bride stays silent throughout all the speeches.' She starts writing it down in her loopy, cursive writing.

I grin and start thinking. 'And if there's a photo booth with hilarious props for everyone to use?'

'Yes!' Dee punches the air and starts writing that down too, using her croissant-littered leg as a desk. 'And if someone makes a shit joke during the "if there's any reason you shouldn't get married, speak now" part of the ceremony.'

'Brilliant. And if someone does that reading from *Captain Corelli's Mandolin*.'

'If the best man makes a *hilarious* joke about the *hilarious* objectification of strippers during the stag do.'

'If they've "done something a little bit different" with their wedding cake – like cupcakes!' I put forward.

'Oooh, yes! With novelty iced figures on top. This is great, all great.' She runs out of room on the receipt and digs about for a new one. 'Right, it's on the list. Oooh, how about if the photographer takes photos of a) All the bridal party jumping into the air, and/or b) All the groomsmen holding this Jess girl up horizontally.'

I remember Jessica's group shot from last night and know, without a doubt, that there will be a photo of the bridal party all jumping in the air. I nod in agreement. 'If the groom says, "and you look so beautiful today", or, "I knew from the moment I met her" during his speech.' I point out my finger so she writes it down.

'BONUS POINTS FOR CRYING,' Dee shouts. 'And, Tor, I'm telling you, if there's a choreographed first dance, I will make both of us down an entire bottle of vodka through our eyeballs.'

I'm laughing so hard I almost veer into the next lane again. And I think, *thank God Dee is here and not Tom.* I don't know what that means and I don't have the emotional energy to even think about what that means right now. I take one hand off the steering wheel and pat her shoulder to let her know she is brilliant and amazing.

'Are we terrible awful people?' I ask her, still laughing too hard to sound like I care.

She shakes her head, her face suddenly serious. 'No Tor, we're not.' She sighs and puts down her littered receipt.

'I just find it weird that no one can see how lemming-like it is.'

★

I wind my car along the twisted driveway and pull up to the country hotel that has everything you'd want in a wedding venue. A lake with bowed willow trees grazing the water. Stone, weathered statues collecting just enough moss to look pretty. A view. A neatly trimmed expanse of lawn.

I check us into our room that, even with Jessica's 'brilliant guest discount', costs £215. I help Dee carry everything in and she lumps her stuff down on the best bed, silently claiming it as her own. The room heaves with tired grandiose. It still looks good enough that you want to take a photo to post on the Internet, but yawns with the need for refurbishment. The four-poster bed with draped, white silk curtains just about distracts from the scattering of damp spots Dalmatianing the ceiling, or the chipped paint flecking off the bay windows.

'Right. Help me decide what to wear,' Dee says. She parades a cornucopia of possible outfits while I curl my hair and offer feedback, and check my phone, and check my phone, and check my phone. My post from this morning is doing really well. I spray heat-protective spray on small sections of my thin hair, comb it through, and then use a gentle flick of my wrist to curl the sections with my GHDs. I then twirl each curl with my finger while it sets before letting them cool and separating them. I finish by gently coating my head with L'Oréal Elnett hairspray because everyone says that's the best.

Dee eventually decides on a black-and-white spotted wrap-dress that she twins with red lipstick and eyeliner flicks. She looks like she's just walked out of a Fifties film.

'I'm so fucking fat,' she moans, as we fight for mirror space with good lighting.

'Don't be ridiculous, you're not fat.'

I mean, she is a little bit fat. She has been since she started working at the school, where she says the teachers passive-aggressively force-feed one another biscuits. But you can't ever say that.

'It's OK for you,' she complains, tracing the outline of her lip in red pencil. 'You're so skinny.'

'No I'm not,' I protest. Even though I wiggle into the compliment and bathe in its warmth. Thinking, *it's OK because you're thin; everything is OK because someone just told you you are thin.* 'Anyway, if I *am* thin, it's only because I'm legitimately miserable,' I say. 'I'd rather be happy.'

Dee laughs and almost smudges her lip liner.

'It's nice to know my unhappiness is so hilarious,' I deadpan.

'Oh, but it is. Self-help guru . . .'

'Shut up.'

We smile at one another's reflections and my love for her bubbles up like hiccups.

'Do you really think everyone else is happier?' she asks, returning her attention to her outlined lip.

I think about it as I try and figure out which particular

curl to pin back to add volume without squaring my jawline. 'They *seem* happier,' I say. 'I mean, Jessica is bound to be happy today, isn't she? It's her wedding day.'

'Yeah, but would she have married this guy if she wasn't thirty-one?'

I open my mouth to lie.

'Honestly?' Dee warns.

I think about it and shake my head. The Jessica I grew up with would never have dated an accountant. I always worried that Tim was an overcorrection from her terrible break-up. But now she's marrying her overcorrection . . .

'I knew it.' Dee nods, her hair cascading down her back and making me jealous. 'Tor, be grateful that you're not trapped with Tom. Honestly. Getting married doesn't mean you're happy. Especially if you're suddenly getting married to whoever you're with at thirty because everyone else is doing it.'

'That does seem to be what's happening . . .' My phone vibrates and I check it again. It's full of more validations and likes and favourites. It's running out of battery already so I turn and rummage in my suitcase for my travel charger. The thought of it running out makes me feel mildly panicked.

'Of course that's what's happening,' Dee says. 'Turning thirty is like playing musical chairs. The music stops and everyone just fucking marries whoever they happen to be sitting on. Now, Tor?' She turns around and pouts. 'Does this colour lipstick clash with my hair?'

★

Soon we are preened and perfect and ready to have our photographs taken by the two roaming professional photographers who will have cost over a thousand pounds. One photographer is in charge of collecting 'official shots' to display on Jessica and Tim's mantelpiece, or to sit within the tissue-papered pages of their official wedding album (an extra £700). The second photographer is there for the 'natural shots'. The shots that show just how *fun* the couple is, and how *fun* their friends are. Look how we talk and laugh in groups and how *fun* we look as we do so.

Dee and I mill around outside the hotel's chapel, making pre-ceremony talk with people we don't know very well. I cannot concentrate as the photographer crouches around us. I'm trying to be interested in some random guy's job and what a nice day it is and how lucky they are with the weather, but I'm highly aware that the 'natural shot' photographer is getting my bad angle. The angle where my chin looks weird. I'm conscious of laughing attractively, so when the photo goes up on the website in two months' time, people will think I look pretty. Even though they'll probably only scroll past to see what *they* look like, I must still look pretty.

We eventually trickle into the chapel and I manage to locate the friends who also weren't picked as bridesmaids. Andrea calls my name and beckons us over to the seats she's saved for us. I hug her hello, and Olivia, whose pregnant stomach blooms out from under her tasteful maternity dress.

'Oh my God! Look at your stomach!' I say. I make my voice high-pitched and enthusiastic and tell her she's glowing and congratulate Steven. 'This is my friend, Dee, from uni. She's my plus one for today.' I introduce them to Dee who shakes their hands and dazzles them with her primary-school teacher charm.

'I love your dress,' she tells Andrea. 'Where did you get it from?' And, just like that, they slot in together, discussing how Marks and Spencer's really going through a surprisingly good patch then laughing that maybe that's because we're all just old now.

'Where's Tom?' Steven asks, realising he's the only man on our aisle and looking panicked. Also, everyone always wants Tom to come to everything. He's such very good company. I spend my whole life watching people be disappointed when it's just me attending.

'Oh, he's got a podcast thing he can't get out of,' I say. I take care to mention which newspaper it's with because it's impressive and I want Steven to know that Tom is only missing this wedding because of his huge career success as a travel journalist.

Steven takes the bait. 'You two really are a little power couple, aren't you?'

I laugh and deny it but bathe in the glow of how we must look from the outside.

The mood of the conversation next to me has turned bitchy and I tune into their frequency.

Andrea is whispering under her breath, complaining about

Jessica banning children for the day. 'Well, I had to leave Dylan at home with Sam,' she sighs. 'I know it's her day and all, but we couldn't afford a babysitter and . . . I was just really shocked, you know? It's typical I guess. You just don't understand what it's like until you have children . . .'

Olivia nods along, stroking her stomach like her bump is personally offended. She mutters 'of course', and 'I can see why it's difficult', and 'people don't understand how expensive babysitters are'. She turns to Steven and asks him what he thinks and Steven is smart enough to say how unfortunate it is. I try to nod noncommittally in the right places but Andrea's really worked herself up into a state now. She's been boiling since the cream invitation dropped onto her doormat, politely requesting she leave her baby at home for six hours until the evening.

Bored – and secretly, selfishly, glad there are no bratty children running about – I look around the ornate hall they've tried to make as churchy as possible. Daffodils drape every available surface and I feel a tug of annoyance because I always wanted to have daffodils at *my* wedding and now Jessica will think I'm copying.

'Is that the accountant?' Dee whispers, pointing towards the front of the hall with her head.

I nod. Tim the accountant sits on the edge of the front bench, looking like a cute child playing dress-up in his baggy, powder-blue morning suit. I would put all my life savings on it being Jessica's idea that he wear a pink cummerbund. Aware he's the centre of attention, he catches many people's eyes and pulls a hilarious freaked-out face – all over the top, chewing on his fingernails. Laughter ripples around us. I hear the click of the 'natural shot' photographer. Tim's asked to do it again by the 'official shot' photographer. And we all watch as both cameramen crouch in the aisle and make Tim hold the pose for half a minute.

'He really isn't like other accountants, is he?' Dee muses and I giggle.

'I told you. Just wait until the dancing later. Then you'll—'

The room quietens all at the same time. Someone at the back must've given the signal. Without being told, we all stand up. Jessica is about to arrive and walk in a straight line and we need to stand to witness this miraculous event. A violinist pops up from nowhere and stands alongside some guy on an electronic keyboard. They obligingly start playing James Blunt. We turn towards the daffodil-lined aisle and watch the bridesmaids shuffle up it self-consciously. Their faces are frozen into demure smiles. Their bodies are stuffed into clingy, pink dresses which I'm sure Jessica is pretending, even to herself, are tasteful and flattering. Their hair is plaited down over one ear. Their cheeks are rosy, their lips are pink and glossy. It's time for the big moment and the air in the room fills with anticipation, like someone famous is about to come in. And I guess Jessica is famous – for today at least. She is getting married and therefore this little microcosm will orbit around her all day, making her feel the most special and totally worth blowing twenty grand on. Here she comes.

She steps forwards and we twist and crane to get a look of her. I am immediately analysing her for how pretty she looks. For what the dress is like, what her body looks like in it. How her hair is done and if her make-up is enough but not too much. It is what we are conditioned to do. *How pretty do you look? Have you managed it? Have you made all the right style choices? Oh, how we will notice if you haven't and discuss it privately, bitchily, at the end of the day.*

Jessica does look pretty as she walks past our row. Gorgeous. Demure. Her arms thin enough at the top to wear that strapless dress. She grins inanely like she's in a dream. She clutches her daffodils to her chest and smiles some more as she ends a decade of worrying that this moment would never happen to her. I smile as widely as I can as she passes, but she doesn't notice me, and I feel a small twinge at not being important today. Her wedding gown is tasteful and expensive and pure, pure white. When she reaches the front and Tim admires her in all his I-can't-believe-how-lucky-I-am glory, I get a sudden flash. Of Jessica when she was twenty-seven – after Jamie broke up with her and she self-medicated with gin and casual sex for over a year. But still she wears white. Who needs a hymen when you can spend £2,000 on white lace? Jenny Packham can metaphorically sew you back up again.

Oh, I am a cynic. I know I am a cynic. But it never lasts.

Yet again, the ceremony starts and I buy into each and every beautiful moment. I find myself almost crying. God, the way Tim looks at Jessica. Like she's a shiny penny, like she's the answer to everything, like she's a goddess. His eyes moisten with tears as he stumbles over his vows. Jessica is equally smitten, clutching at his hand like he's holding the necklace from *Titanic* or something. When it's time for the reading, a friend of Tim's stands up and nervously makes his way to the microphone.

'I'd like to read a piece from *Captain Corelli's Mandolin,*' he says, before coughing and starting.

Dee kicks me under the chair. 'Shot!' she whispers.

I'm about to roll my eyes when it starts. Tim's friend tells us how love is a temporary madness. By the time it ends – with the part about a couple becoming one tree, not two – I'm almost crying again.

It is a really annoyingly good reading.

My thoughts are with Tom for the rest of the ceremony. Thinking of him, imagining him at our wedding. What his face would look like standing at the end of an aisle. He'd wear green because it would bring out the colour in his eyes and I wouldn't wear white to make a statement. I pick which nice memories he'd use in his speech about me. Captain Corelli has made me feel better about us. I realise I am silly to think love can stay like it is in the beginning. Yes, some of our leaves have fallen but they fall for everyone. We're not broken, we've just been together for six years. This is what everyone is like after six years, right? Less sex and more box sets. Simmering resentments replacing surprise mini-breaks. The registrar lady announces Jessica and Tim husband and wife and we all cheer and clap as they kiss in a way that will look good in photographs. And I really can't cry. Not here. Especially not with Dee next to me.

We get to the boring bit where the couple have to sign all the paperwork. We turn and talk amongst ourselves while the violinist screeches out some sophisticated tune. Feeling less shy with one another than we did before the service. Jessica and Tim and the public declaration of their love has united us, has melted the ice. We now also have the extra conversational prompt of agreeing on how lovely the ceremony was.

Dee turns and says, 'Well that was relatively painless, though we now have to drink at least two shots.'

Eventually the happy couple emerge. The photographers go berserk as they scramble to get the best snaps of the couple walking down the aisle: the money-shot moment. We all stand and jostle with our phones to also try to get a good photo to post online. Jessica and Tim walk very slowly, aware of all the phones and how they only have one chance to get this moment documented. The photographer even asks them to stop in the aisle, and they comply and smile and look at one another with so much love in their eyes. Then Jessica turns to the photographer and asks, 'Did you get that? Or do you want us to do it again?'

*

We mill around for ages while tux-decked waiters constantly ply our glasses with champagne. We are led to a gorgeous conservatory and we twirl and mingle and ask the waiting staff what is on the silver plates they offer to us.

'A poached quail's egg with Scottish smoked salmon on brioche.'

'Prosciutto and celeriac twists.'

'Roast beef blinis with crème fraiche.'

Dee has one of each spread out on her hand like it's a serving platter. 'You never see a bowl of Twiglets, do you?' she asks. 'And I think I speak for everyone here when I say a bowl of Twiglets would be pretty welcome right now.'

There's only one vegetarian canapé – a 'kebab' of a baby tomato, buffalo mozzarella and a single basil leaf. I hunt them down like a determined spinster at the countdown to midnight. I manage to find three, which isn't enough to absorb the huge quantities of champagne Dee tips down my throat.

'This glass is for Captain Corelli, this glass is for the *hilarious* James-Bond-themed seating plan I've just spotted. We're sat next to someone called Nigel by the way. Who the holy fuck is called Nigel in this day and age? Imagine calling a tiny little baby *"Nigel"*?'

We speak only once to Jessica, as she comes in to frantically thank everybody for coming between her epic photoshoots on the lawn. I introduce her to Dee, though they've met before at my thirtieth birthday. We chorus that she looks so beautiful and compliment her on her dress. She says thank you while her eyes scan the room over our shoulders, looking for other people she needs to speak to.

Lots of people come up and congratulate me on my success. 'You're the writer, aren't you?' 'My niece loves your book.' 'Have you thought about turning it into a film?' I blush and say, 'Oh no, it's nothing really.' Playing humble, but feeling so much better that they've said it.

A Thai-style chicken kebab platter does the rounds so everyone has bad breath for the next hour until we're called in for dinner. I make my excuses and go to the bathroom to run my hands under cold water.

I send a message to Tom.

Tori: Wedding lovely. How was the podcast? Love you xx

Countless glasses of champagne later and I'm sitting at a table called 'Octopussy'. Dee and Nigel get on surprisingly well and I'm looking desperately at the teeny-tiny square of puff pastry that is my vegetarian option.

'Oh yes, being a primary school teacher is *great*,' Dee enthuses, tossing back her cascade of auburn hair. 'I only do the younger years. No SATs or premature puberty thank you very much. I just like getting paid to play in a sandpit.'

'Dee?' I ask her back. My voice is more slurred than I thought it would be. 'Can I have your bread roll?'

She nods without turning and I pounce on it, rip it to shreds and stuff it into my mouth. I tune out for a while, the wine making my mouth dry and my head fuggy. I stare at Andrea and Olivia sat on the other side of the table, telling Steven hilarious stories from secondary school that

I'm sure he's already heard. Andrea's recovered from the slight of her child not being welcome and looks ten times drunker than I am. She pours wine like it's the elixir of life, spilling half a bottle of white onto the pressed cream tablecloth then howling with laughter.

'So, what do you do?' Nigel's friend asks me, because what else can you talk about after you've exhausted how you both know the couple (he's Tim's mate from uni).

I tip some sharp white wine down my throat. 'I'm an author. Hey, are you going to eat your bread roll?'

'Oh wow, an author,' he says, like they always say. I can't remember his name already. 'Anything I've heard of?' he asks, like they always ask.

'It's a self-help memoir called *Who The Fuck Am I?*'

I wait for the look of disbelief that he's actually heard of it.

Oh yep. There. There it is.

'Oh, I've even heard of that.'

My grin could turn Medusa to stone. 'Crazy world, isn't it?'

He's now talking about how he has always wanted to write a book, and you know what I really need to do is sell the movie rights, that's where the money is, and he wishes he had time to write a book, and then time passes and the speeches have started.

I will Jessica to speak. *Please speak please speak please speak. Please get out of your fucking chair and fucking say something. You have a Master's degree. Please speak please speak please speak.* But she doesn't. She sits there in her Jenny Packham and wipes her eyes delicately when her dad tells her how proud he is and she smiles demurely when Tim drops the big, 'And I cannot tell you how beautiful you look today.' Dee extracts herself from Nigel long enough to turn and tap my glass. I sigh and tip yet more acrid wine into my hungry body. The best man does the joke about the prostitutes in Amsterdam and all the men from the stag cheer *'whey'* and I think about how many prostitutes in Amsterdam are actually illegally trafficked and repeatedly raped by their pimps but I don't think you're allowed to bring that up at weddings. Then it's all over and the bad dancing has started.

And I am alone.

And I am drunker than I should be.

And I am starving. So starving.

There must've been a first dance but I can't really remember it. Dee and I spent fifteen minutes in the loos together, giggling as we took selfie after selfie. She grabbed at my shoulder and her eyes hardly focused and she asked, 'So, is Nigel cute or am I just drunk?'

'It's a little bit of both.'

That was enough of a green light. They've been sprawled over each other since, leaning their heads close to be heard over the music. I've had to join in this little circle of naff dancing with Andrea and Olivia. It's dark and the children have been allowed to arrive. They're skidding all over the dance floor in their mini tuxes from Next and everyone is saying 'Oh, aren't they sweet?' Andrea has her baby on her hip as we *step-tap-step-tap* to 'High Ho Silver Lining'. At some point, a red-faced Jessica storms past us towards the DJ booth, muttering, 'He's not keeping to the agreed playlist!'

I'm outside and it's freezing and there is a message back from Tom.

Tom: Glad the wedding is going well. Podcast good. Love you too. X

I find myself scrabbling with my keys, punching out a reply.

Tori: It's not 'Agadoo' without you. Love you so so much. Love you xxxx x xxx See you tomorrow love you xx x x

My stomach is gnawing itself and my mouth is watering to the point that I really think I might actually be sick. A brainwave! I find a delivery app and order a pizza to be delivered to the front gate of the hotel. A vegetarian supreme. A large. Oh, yes, go on, a bottle of coke too. No one need ever know. I pull myself back to the dance floor in search of Dee, to tell her where I'm off to. I only see the back of her head. Her head that is kissing Nigel's head. Right there in the middle of the dance floor. With disco lights flashing off them and children pushing past them so they can stand right in front of the exciting smoke machine.

I feel a melancholic pang. Because even though she will wake up and regret this in the morning it certainly looks like fun just for now. I can't remember the last time I kissed Tom. Proper kissed Tom. With tongues and heady abandon, like teenagers who aren't ready to have sex yet. I'm outside in the cold again and my heels plunge into the grass as I stumble towards the gate. I'm so glad I've ordered pizza. A hog roast has just been rolled out – the guests drunkenly flocking to the speared pig. An upgrade from the kebabs of only ten years ago – but at such a cost. I twist my ankle and swear under my breath. I stop under a tree and pull out my phone to see if Tom has replied. He hasn't. I re-read his other message and he did say 'I love you too'. Yes, it was perfunctory, but some people go their entire lives without anyone saying that to them, even once.

I am lucky.

I am so, so lucky.

God, I'm lonely. So lonely.

I sit down in the grass. My dress sucks up the dew, turning the red chiffon to damp clumps, but I don't even care. I scroll through the photos of Dee and me, looking for the best one. The photo that can encapsulate everything I want the world to think I am. Funny and pretty and carefree-but-sophisticated, but not taking myself too seriously. I stumble on one where I'm pouting in just the right amount of piss-taking and actual attractiveness. Dee could look better. She's squinting slightly and there are other photos from this sequence where she is the one who looks better. But she looks nice enough that she can't tell me to pick a different one. I scroll through filters and add a vignette to hide the fact we're just in some toilets.

I caption it: Oh my F*ckers, with friends like these there ain't nothing, NOTHING, you can't do. #FemaleFriendships Forever #MyBestFriendIsMyPlusOneTonight #YesIDidA ShotThroughMyF*ckingEyeball

I hit publish and slump back in this wet grass, waiting for the likes to come in. For my phone to come alive. I like how I look in this photo. I like the person this Tori is. This Tori has friends and a life and she doesn't care and she has fun and don't you wish you could be her?

I wish I could be her.

Through the haze of champagne and through my dry mouth that is only getting dryer, I'm able to comprehend that I *am* her. I am that person, and I do have friends, and I do have a life, and I do have fun. That is not a lie.

It is the truth.

But if it's really true, then why am I so desperate to share it?

I blink into the arriving headlights and wobble up towards the front gate – wanting to apprehend the delivery guy before he reaches the venue. I try to brush the mud off my dress but know it is probably ruined. Which isn't the end of the world, because you never wear the same dress to a wedding anyway, do you? I rummage in my clutch bag for some cash and stagger towards the source of the light. I wave to stop the car.

The pizza guy gets out with his hot bag. 'Delivery for Victoria?'

The smell hits me and brings back a thousand memories. Of my first boyfriend, Johnnie, who used to deliver pizzas around our town. Who used to pick me up after his late shift and drive me to a car park somewhere and go down on me in the backseat and I had to pretend he was good at it.

'That's me,' I tell the teenager, reaching out for the warm box that smells of my youth. I hand him the money and he doesn't make any comment about the weird location of this delivery. God, this boy even *looks* like Johnnie did. They've got the same hair, the same way of slouching as they walk. I suddenly want to tell this seventeen-year-old pizza boy that he reminds me of my first boyfriend. But I am thirty-one and that would be pathetic. So I say thank you and tip him and watch him climb back into his car.

I wait for him to reverse out of the ornate gateway, the thud of music throbbing from his crap Peugeot. Then I cross my legs under me, balance the pizza box on my lap and eat the entire fucking thing in the dark.

Month Two

Review of **Who The F*ck Am I? Summer Edition Tour**

★ ★ ★ ★

The Queen of the quarter-life crisis, Tori Bailey is not afraid to tell people the truth. The gritty, expletive truth about the pressures on young women and the *must-must-must* narratives thrust upon them. This tour will not disappoint fans looking for a hilariously brutal account of Tori's early twenties and how they led her to write the bestselling *Who The F*ck Am I?* There's nowhere she won't go. Whether it's ripping the merciless piss out of unpaid internships, inadequate cunnilingus, or the time she verbally assaulted a smug yogi, Tori does not bend to what society expects of her. This tour is a giddy empowering reminder that you shouldn't either. However, as Tori's readers grow older, it'll be interesting to see what she has to say about the next chapter in their lives. I'm sure I'm not the only fan who was disappointed that her 'new book' was just a re-jacketed edition of her original with an added foreword. Take it as a compliment Tori when I say, 'we want f*cking more!'

Tori: *Has sent a link* http://guardian.co.uk/who-the-fuck-am-i-tour-review

Who is this fucking bitch?

Dee: Oh my GOD. How DARE she give you a glowing review in the *Guardian*? LET'S BURN DOWN HER HOUSE.

Tori: 'I'm sure I'm not the only fan who was disappointed that her "new book" was just a summer edition.'

Tori: IT WAS THE SAME BOOK TITLE WITH THE WORDS 'ADDED FOREWORD' ON THE COVER. IT WASN'T EXACTLY MISLEADING!

Dee: I refuse to offer you emotional support for this.

Tori: Can you offer me wine? Tonight?

Dee: I'm not drinking! The brats at school have given me horrid lurgy bug of HELL. But coffee? I can certainly do coffee? Tomorrow morning?

Tori: Yes to coffee! You can tell me all about your latest date with Nigel.

Tori: I will never get bored of the fact you're dating someone called Nigel.

Tori: Nigel

Tori: NIGEL

Tori: Nigel Nigel Nigel Nigel Nigel

Dee: Meet you at the Lido cafe at eleven? I hear the coffee there is very photogenic.

Tori: OK Nigel.

Dee: I hate you by the way.

Tori: Sorry Nigel.

★

We have to wait for a table. Of course we do. The coffee here looks good when you take a photograph of it from above. People queue for that kind of thing now. It's a good way of filling their feed with proof they are an interesting person who drinks grown-up artisan coffee. But it's a pretty enough place to wait, watching the swimmers flop up and down the lido in their wetsuits. Enjoying the pool being mostly empty as May shows no sign of getting warmer anytime soon. Dee and I both take photos of the pool, even though we've been here a gazillion times before and took photos of it all those times too. Eventually a flustered waitress shows us to a tiny table near the giant windows. We order overpriced coffee and a stack of pancakes to share.

'Christ my boobs hurt today,' Dee moans, clutching at them. 'I can hardly wear a bra.'

'Period due?'

'Yes, tomorrow. It's bollocks. It means Nigel and I won't be able to have sex for five whole days. We'll break our rhythm.'

The coffee arrives and it does, indeed, look marvellous. I hate myself as I take out my phone and take a quick photo of it. And yet I do it anyway. And it's not like everyone around me isn't doing exactly the same thing.

'You can have sex on your period, you know?' I tell her, picking up a small spoon and stirring the foam in.

She shakes her head. 'Not on my periods. It would be like that scene from *The Shining* where that tidal wave of blood cascades all down the hallway.' I put down my drink and Dee notices and starts laughing.

I am so jealous of Dee and all the sex that she's having that I almost can't bear to look at her. I stir my coffee more vigorously and can hardly bring myself to ask about him.

I did not see this coming.

I did not invite her to the wedding as my plus one only for her to never come back to the room because she was having ridiculous sex with Nigel. We were supposed to stay up all night laughing and watching the film channel. Instead I lay on my four-poster bed, cradling my swollen pizza-stomach and listened to someone have sex through the wall. It might've even been her. But I am a friend and I am happy for her and she deserves to be happy, so I say, 'Things still going well between you?'

Dee's face softens and she smiles shyly. The sun hits her hair from behind and she looks so beautiful I could spew. 'They seem to be,' she says. 'I don't know. It's early days, isn't it?'

We discuss all the ways in which it could go wrong from here. We pore over every bit of evidence we've gleaned so far about Nigel, and Nigel's life, and Nigel's ex-girlfriends, and Nigel's pension plan, and the fact that Nigel owns his own place in Clapham. But I can see from the way her eyes are dewy, and from the way she smiles whenever I say his name, that my friend is falling for this man. This man is going to be on the agenda. Whether they end up married and growing old together, or in a future break-up where we'll pore again over all the aforementioned evidence in the stark light of hindsight, whichever way it goes, Nigel is going to be A Significant.

Swimmers butterfly through the turquoise water, circles of trendy mothers jiggle babies on their laps and attempt to catch up through them, and I try to smile for Dee. Try to smile and be a good friend and be happy for her while her glow only reminds me of my lack of glow.

The pancakes arrive and we laugh at how small they are and order another stack. I eat them greedily and then hate myself straight afterwards and work out how many extra steps I need to do to alleviate the guilt. I suggest a walk around the park and we push back our chairs and join the throngs of people circling the enclosed green square.

'What's Tom up to today?' Dee asks, as we stand to one side so we're not mown down by children on scooters. The parents run after them and apologise with that 'I think they're cute so this isn't a real apology' arrogance. Dee and I smile through gritted teeth and say it's OK when it isn't.

'Working. He's on deadline. But we're having a night in together. They've just released series two of *The Reckoning.*'

'Oh, I've not started that yet. But everyone's raving about it.'

'It's shit,' I inform her. 'And everyone's lying so they sound smart and sophisticated. But it's the only thing Tom will agree to watch with me at the moment.' I sigh, not wanting to go there. I feel like whenever I talk to anyone about him I spit out poison. Like bitterness hiccups.

'Anyway, what you up to tonight? You going out with Nigel?'

Dee's smitten smile appears again and she plays with her silver necklace. 'Yeah. He's booked a table up the Shard. I've never been up there actually.'

'Oh real dates! I miss real dates,' I complain. 'I miss doing exciting things in those beginning days.'

Dee doesn't even deny that it's good. That it's better than what I have. All she says is, 'At least you don't have the stress about needing a poo in his house though.'

'I mean there's always, always a silver lining to everything, isn't there?' I laugh.

The park is filled with late daffodils and the hopeful promise of a good summer. We stroll around the park three times, always keeping our heads turned away from the trafficky road that circles us. I smile as I remember the poo obstacle-courses I went through at the start with Tom. Like on our road trip around America, where I kept coming up with excuses to 'go to the hotel lobby' so I could use the loo next to reception. And the first evenings at his flat, where my stomach became bloated and sore from holding in wind.

Dee gets out her phone and I know it's Nigel from the way she smiles. *I am happy for her, I am happy for her, I am happy for her.* I check mine, almost out of instinct. There's no message from Tom because he knows where I am and all our messages are totally mechanical these days. 'My train is delayed, won't be home until ten.' 'Do you mind getting some milk on the way back from work?' 'Out of cat food.' Sometimes we really go for it and send each other photos of Cat sitting in a funny position. But only rarely. My phone is clogged with notifications though. I put up an old photo this morning of me wearing 'ice-cream-leg jeans' when I was twenty-seven. 'Remember these, f*ckers?' I'd asked.

A thousand likes suggest they remember.

'So, you still upset about that review?' Dee asks me, putting her phone back into the pocket of her yellow mac.

'Yes. She only gave me *four* stars, not five.'

Dee navigates the next question expertly. 'I mean, she's clearly a heinous bitch but, Tor, do you have any idea – any – about what to write next?'

I dodge another scooter and glare at the offending child. 'I've not got time to write,' I snap. 'They're flying me all over the freaking world to promote this new book.'

'Yes, I know that but . . . well . . . it's not a *new* book, is it?' Dee says delicately. 'It's your old one with an added foreword and a summery jacket? You've not written anything new in years. Is there not another topic you want to explore or something?'

I am not happy she is bringing this up. Especially as she knows all this. She knows about my clichéd second-book-syndrome and adjoining writer's block. Since *Who The F*ck Am I?* came out, it's been so nuts I've not had a chance to think. That's why we've re-released it as a summer edition – to give me time to come up with something else to say.

'What's your point?' I ask her.

'I don't know,' she admits. 'It's just you were so happy when you were writing your book. And I want you to be happy again. I think it would help things with Tom if you had a new project to focus on.'

I shake my head. 'Tom and I are fine. *Really*,' I protest as she pulls a face. 'This is just what relationships are like after six years. No matter how in love you are at the start, it's always stale and hard work after six years. Love changes over time.'

Dee looks unconvinced and I feel a stab of anger. I mean, it's not like she would know. She's never been in a relationship that lasted more than two years. And yeah, Nigel probably seems like Prince fucking Charming right now, but everyone does at the beginning. There is so much you can project onto a new person before you know what their poo smells like and at what time of day they tend to do one.

I do not like the atmosphere crackling between us as we take in the spring blossom and laugh at the family of baby ducks on the pond. There's a tiny sliver of judgement oozing from both sides and I hate how this happens. How friendship is a constant acclimatisation to your ever-changing life circumstances. Dee and I were fine when we were both cynical and unhappy. But now Nigel's turned up and is taking her up the Shard and she's temporarily happy and I'm permanently not and we have to adjust again.

It won't last, I think.

I'm not proud of myself for thinking it.

But it won't.

It never does with Dee. The reasons why it won't last are already laid out like a trail of coins to be collected by Sonic the Hedgehog. He works in finance and she will get bored of him. Her whimsical nature will become jarring after a while, when he stops finding how often she leaves her phone on the bus cute. Nigel will, at some point, struggle with how many men she's slept with. Her totally messed-up relationship with her parents will start seeping into them. He will secretly worry that she's damaged. He will start looking for signs of damage to prove his hypothesis and then wilfully misinterpret her behaviour. He's probably even shit in bed, but she'll only admit this a month after the break-up after three bottles of wine. 'I know we had sex all the time, but I never came,' she'll say and I'll gasp in horror and say, 'Oh my God, really? Back then I was so jealous of you.' She'll laugh and say, 'Well I didn't want to admit it to myself, did I? I thought he was The One, Tori, I really did.' And I will say 'I know you did.' And I'll put my arm around her and let her cry on my shoulder. Because this is what always happens and I can't see why Nigel will be any different.

★

Oh, this is better.

My head lies cradled in Tom's lap and his fingers run through the lengths of my hair. We've pulled the curtains on the glinting London skyline and we're curled around each other, watching TV with Cat asleep on the armrest. This feels good. We've had a Marks and Spencer's 'Dine in for Two' deal and didn't even argue about which main to pick. Tom told me all about the upcoming article he's writing about Las Vegas tourism and it was actually pretty interesting. We've got ten whole days before either of us have to go away on business and we chatted through our calendars, working out when we can spend quality time together. Acknowledging we will miss one another, that the bond will be strained – and the thought makes both of us sad and uncomfortable. It's such a relief when you realise you will still miss them when they go away.

'We could even get cocktails up the Shard next weekend,' I say hopefully.

'That's a great idea.'

See! We can do it too. You just need to make the effort sometimes. That's what everybody says anyway. And, yes, Dee may be having heady depraved sex in all sorts of positions right now but I wouldn't swap that for this. This feeling of comfort and security. The fact that I know everything there is to know about this man running his fingers through my hair. Intimacy. That is what this moment is. Intimacy. It cannot be rushed or forced. It can only be grown delicately over years of learning, sharing and negotiation, and even then it's a fair-weather crop. Like asparagus. Intimacy is like asparagus. *That's quite good actually, I should use it in one of my posts.*

We watch *The Reckoning* and you know what? It's OK really. I can see what all of the fuss is about. It's really well shot and well acted and there is a strong female lead that's problematic enough to keep newspaper columnists busy discussing whether she's a good feminist or not. Tom really likes it. I bliss out, my eyes heavy with contentment as we watch the first half. Tom even bends down and kisses me on the cheek. The gentleness of it. *Oh, I love him. I love him I love him I love him.* I know I complain about him constantly but I do love him. I just forget sometimes that it can be like this. So safe, so secure, so snugly. Totally in tune with one another, focused on one another.

The adverts come on. All three minutes and twenty-nine seconds of them.

Both of us get out our phones.

Scroll refresh. Scroll refresh. What have I missed since last time?

@TheRealTori Watching #TheReckoning. If last series is anything to go by, whoever I fancy will end up being the one who did it.

Tom sits up alertly, tipping me off his lap so he can check up on numerous sporting achievements.

'For fuck's sake,' he mutters, and I know his football team must've done something wrong. I also know better than to ask him about it. The news is like a bad smell, seeping into the air around us. He's going to be twitchy and irritable now, unless they pull it back. This is something I've never been able to adjust to. My relationship and my own mood and how nice my evening is depending on whether a bunch of overpaid eighteen-year-olds kick a ball in the right way. But I know better than to argue. I just tune it out. Turn down the dimmer switch, pretend it's not happening. They may score by the next ad break and then Tom will smile again and clap and beam at me and reward me with a big hug that I know has nothing to do with me but makes me feel happy anyway. And it's not like I'm not distracted by my own phone and the things it tells me. Counting notifications, frowning at a post from a rival author thanking the *Telegraph* for picking her book as a 'top summer read' and not mine. The adverts finish and Tom puts his phone back but he doesn't return my head to his lap. I can almost taste his sourness on my tongue. Why can't he support a better football team? One that actually wins? If you're going to chain your emotional well-being to the outcome of a football team, why pick *Aston Villa?*

We are jolted back into the programme, however, when someone is shot in the face. They zoom in on the exploded skull and the violence is unnecessary and awful, but Tom doesn't seem to mind as much as I do. I bury my face into his shirt as a joke, but also to try and revive the physical closeness. He laughs, but gently pushes me off him. The rejection stings yet I stuff the feeling down into my guts because we are having a nice evening and it wasn't a big deal anyway. The programme goes on. The strong female lead finds the dead body with the exploded skull and has a theory about what happened that none of the male characters agree with. Tom's distracted. He keeps checking his phone, making exasperated gasps each time. There's yet another ad break and I retrieve my own phone to see if anything interesting has happened in the ten minutes since I last checked.

Bingo. Jessica has uploaded her honeymoon album.

I double-tap eagerly, turning my screen sideways so it takes up the entirety of my phone. Jesus Christ, she's published over *four hundred* photos. Every single second of their Caribbean trip has been documented. Every single outfit she's worn has been photographically noted, full-length, before going out to a place where she has taken a photo of every single meal before eating it. They have cheersed themselves with cocktails and taken a photo of the cocktails and the cheersing. There are photos of them at the airport and on the aeroplane, and of every towel-arrangement the hotel staff left for them on the end of their bed. Jessica's painted toenails appear at least five times against the backdrop of a beautiful beach. There are dozens of stealthy photos of Jessica, taken as though she's just naturally rollicking around on the beach and just *happens* to be in her bikini – all for the sole purpose of us seeing the lasting effects of her wedding diet. She cartwheels on a plain of white sand, oh, so carefree is she – her legs open to better show off the un-bulginess at the tops of her thighs.

I shove my phone at Tom in disbelief. 'Look at this!' I say to him. 'Jessica's uploaded over four hundred photos!'

Tom pulls a face, but it's not at what I'm showing him

on my phone. He's pulling a face because he's annoyed I'm trying to talk to him when he is still preoccupied with the football.

'That's just Jessica,' he says, dismissing it as nothing before jabbing his thumb on his own phone to refresh, to refresh, to refresh.

I ignore his lack of interest because I need someone to vent to. 'I mean, it's like they've spent every second of this honeymoon taking photos!' I cry, waving my phone closer. 'Aren't they supposed to be banging each other's brains out? I mean, if they were really *that* happy, why are they spending so much time trying to convince us of that?'

'Hmm.' Tom looks down at his phone. He hits refresh again.

'I mean, it's madness, right?'

'YES!' Tom leaps in the air. The smile on his face is so huge, so much bigger than one I am ever able to give him. 'GOAAAAL,' he yells. 'GOAAAAL.' He reaches out and pulls me up to celebrate. Cat is so startled she runs out of the room. Tom spins me around on his arm, then dips me backwards to give me a Hollywood kiss. I laugh and pretend I'm dazzled by it.

'You scored?' I ask, like he had anything – *anything* – to do with it.

'We scored! Last minute of the game and we only needed to equalise. Get in. *Get in.*' He dances out of the room and comes back cradling Cat like she's the FA cup. She squirms in his arms as he ballroom dances with her regardless.

I suppose he thinks I find this attractive.

I don't.

And I try not to think about why it's OK for him to care so much about this pointless game when he cares so little about other things. Like cancer going uncured and children starving in Africa and one in four women being a victim of rape, and his girlfriend needing him, really needing him to act this happy about her. But we're having a nice evening and this is so preferable to how he'd behave if they'd lost, so I dance with him and Cat and let him spin me.

The programme starts again. It takes a while for Tom to get back into it. He's scrolling through his phone – checking to see what people online are saying about this particular game of football. I take a bitchy screen-grab of Jessica's honeymoon album and fire it off to Dee for re-assurance. It takes a further fifteen minutes for Tom to settle but he's so happy that he puts my head into his lap again. I can feel him smiling. We drift back into the show and lose ourselves in the strong female character proving everyone wrong yet again. Tom rubs my back and strokes my face with his finger and it feels amazing.

In the last ad break, I roll over so I'm looking right up at him. 'Your face looks weird from this angle,' I tell him. 'It's like an alien's.'

'Yours does too.'

We both start pulling faces, grimacing, poking our tongues out, raising our eyebrows, making our faces weirder. 'Stop it! You're freaking me out!' I tell him.

'You are too.'

I lean up and kiss him. He makes a noise like '*Mwha!*' and raises his eyebrows – stopping the kiss from progressing before it's even begun. But we still kissed. We still did the kissing that couples do.

In the final quarter, the strong female lead is kidnapped by her crazy ex-boyfriend who she still has a thing for. He's only kidnapping her for her own safety, he tells her. Because she's got too close to the wrong people. She kicks herself around in the chair she's tied to and shakes her head angrily at him. He leans down to remove her gag and, the moment he does, they are kissing. Hungrily. Angrily. The sort of kiss that is so damn sexy and yet you don't dare admit it for fear of what that means about your feminist sensibilities. Soon the crazy ex-boyfriend has pulled down her top. He's kissing her breasts and she's groaning loudly and you know they're about to have incredible sex. And even though everything about this scene is completely messed up, and problematic, and even though it's just two actors simulating something, and even though the newspaper columnists are going to have a field day with this tomorrow . . .

It's making me horny as hell.

Tom and I watch in silence as the ex-boyfriend grabs her out of the chair and starts having sex with her against the wall. Her hands are still tied behind her back. I feel my body stirring. Pinpricks of arousal pulsate up my legs. My vagina involuntarily throbs. Just once. Like it's a smooth lake and someone has chucked a giant pebble in.

'*Oo-err*,' Tom jokes, trying to diffuse the sexual tension radiating out of our widescreen television. But I can tell it's stirring something in him too. His hand tightens on my back, his breath is suddenly more ragged. The frustration that's been building inside me for six months wells up and swirls over like water bursting through a dam.

I want to have sex.

I want to have sex like the sex the woman is having on the TV. Angry and hard and so full of lust you can taste it in the air.

I want to have sex with Tom.

Do I make a move?

I'm not sure I'll be able to stand it if he rejects me. Not when I'm this desperate to be touched. *This is ridiculous! He's your boyfriend, Tori. You can have sex with him. That is the general point of boyfriends.*

Tom's grip is still tight on my back. He *must* be horny too. The actor has now bent the strong female lead over a desk and slams into her as she grunts in appreciation.

I twist in his arms and smile at Tom. 'Hey Tor,' he says with a playful smile.

I cover his smile with my mouth. I turn completely, placing a bent knee either side of his pelvis, straddling him. Pushing my body against him. I kiss him hard with anger and lust. *Please don't end this kiss, please don't break off this kiss.*

He doesn't.

Tom's hands wrap around my back and pull me closer.

Our faces mash into each other and his tongue plunges into my mouth. We're half biting each other and oh God, we've not kissed like this in years. Why did we ever stop kissing like this? I forgot how good he is at kissing. I forgot what his mouth even tastes like. His hands stroke up and down my back, getting quicker and more frantic. It feels so good to finally be touched, I cannot even tell you. The relief. The relief at finally being touched. It releases another grenade of lust. I feel my nipples harden through my bra. My body throbbing in desperate desire. I unbutton Tom's shirt and he clumsily pulls my top over my head. His bare skin sends another wave of arousal crashing through me. I start kissing his chest. Licking it. Biting it. I want my mouth on his skin. All of his skin. I kiss down and down, showering his pot belly with my kisses. But I don't even care that it's there right now – even though it shouldn't be (and it's only there because he *keeps* ordering takeaway). I just care that he's letting me do this to him and we're *finally* going to have sex. Hot sex! Right here on the sofa! Like happy, healthy couples do.

I bring my face up to his and kiss him again. His tongue lunges out of his mouth, missing mine. He licks my cheek, dousing it with the tang of his saliva. His eyes are closed. His hands paw at my skirt, pull it up, tug my knickers down. I kiss his chest again while unbuckling his belt and undoing his jeans. I tease him with kisses as I pull down his boxers and unleash his erection. It springs out into my face, almost poking me in the eye. It stands straight, pointing to the ceiling in proof that I am still attractive to Tom. I cannot even tell you how validating an erection can be sometimes. I look up playfully as I kiss down the trail of pubic hair leading to his penis. Tom's eyes are closed, his head thrown back. *Oh, I was hoping for sexy eye-contact.* And I'm just recovering from that disappointment when he quietly, assertively, forces my mouth down onto his penis . . .

OK then, I can give him a blow job. I mean, I'm his girlfriend. That's what girlfriends do. I'll give him head for a while to make sure he's hard enough for sex, because we've had trouble sometimes when it comes to keeping him hard. Then I can climb on top and finally feel my boyfriend's body inside mine, finally feel like we're lovers again and not just stale housemates. *Oh God, I'm so frustrated. I don't know how long I can do this for.* But I suck obligingly and do that thing with his balls that Cosmo told me to do when I was seventeen. I try to go as deep as I can without gagging, twisting my head so his penis lands in the pouch of my cheek rather than hitting my tonsils. I forgot how exhausting these things are. I bob up and down and try not to roll my eyes now. I'm wondering how many minutes I can get away with before turning this into actual sex rather than just oral sex. I can feel he's close. Six years and I know all his tells – Tom's orgasms are like a paint-by-numbers. And I'm just about to stop when Tom, sensing it, puts his hand on the back of my head. He wraps my hair around his hand, tugging it hard like a crazed puppeteer, and now he's . . . he's . . . *forcing* my head up and down like I'm a porn star.

I can hardly breathe. He conducts my head urgently, pushing me so hard I have no time to recover from each thrust driven down my throat. *Ouch*. His penis hits my gag reflex and my body jolts accordingly. I convulse, but his hand is still tangled in my hair and he shoves me down for another go. I blink madly up at him to signal this is not OK. He doesn't see me. His eyes are still closed in bliss. He is chasing his orgasm and I am not, apparently, a part of that. Just my throat is. I don't know if I should hit him to make him stop. I'm not sure what's happening though. This has not happened before. I'm too shocked and confused so I just let him. Let him use me as his puppet and try to breathe through my nose. He's pushing and groaning and thrusting. His entire pelvis lifts up and he yanks my hair as he lets himself go into my mouth. I swallow half of it by accident. The other half dribbles down my chin, drips onto my chest.

This is when Tom releases my head.

He flops backwards, grinning like a stoned Cheshire Cat. Every limb of his body relaxes. I run to the bathroom and stumble on the way to the sink. I spit everything out and grip the sides of the basin for a moment, staring at my haunted reflection.

Did that just happen?

It did just happen. That wasn't OK. I know it wasn't OK. But . . . well . . . I don't know. Maybe he got carried away. I mean, he had his eyes closed, he couldn't see I was uncomfortable. And I didn't say stop. I never said stop . . .

I stare again at myself and take a long breath in and a long breath out. Then I inhale all the uncomfortable emotions and I push push push them down down down because we've had a nice evening and I'm sure he didn't mean it. That's just how sex is sometimes. Don't you dare pretend you've not been here too.

I bend over and wash my mouth out from the tap because otherwise Tom won't kiss me afterwards. He doesn't like to taste himself on me. He once called it *'gay'*.

When I get back to the living room, the programme has finished and the TV screen glows blue. Tom has pulled on his trousers and buttoned up his shirt. He doesn't look at me while I make my way back to him, my bottom half totally naked. He offers up one arm though, with his eyes still closed, and I snuggle into him. He doesn't say anything. He doesn't comment on what happened at all. I mean, he's put his trousers back on so I guess that means we're not going to have sex any more.

'Was that . . . was it . . . OK?' I find myself asking. I want him to be pleased. I want him to have enjoyed himself. I feel insecure that maybe it wasn't good enough.

He lets out a low purr and pats my head like I'm a dog who has fetched him his slippers. I assume that means yes. I do not think it fair that I needed to ask. He could have said 'thank you'. I put my knickers back on and nestle further into the crook of his arm.

I don't know how I feel: horny, sexually frustrated, used and violated, angry and resentful, worried that the blow job wasn't good enough? I know not to talk about it though. That is what Google has told me, over and over, while I've lain next to his sleeping body after yet another night of sexual rejection, desperately searching the internet for answers.

'My boyfriend doesn't want to have sex with me.'

'We never have sex.'

'We've not had sex in six months.'

'Is it normal to stop having sex?'

'How often should you have sex?'

'Does my boyfriend have clinical depression or is he just not that into me?'

You never hear about it this way round. Men are the sexual ones. Women are the ones who need to sometimes lie back and think of England. My friends in long-term relationships drink too much wine and whinge to me about how their husbands always 'pester' them. I nod and smile and drink my wine and say, 'Oh yes, men!' and roll my eyes. But really I'm thinking, *Why does my boyfriend not want to have sex with me? Don't you realise how lucky you are? I'd give anything to be 'pestered'.*

Just as I'm on the cusp of crying – my throat catching, my eyes producing a thin veil of moisture to be released as tears – Tom opens his eyes. He turns towards me, reaches out, and gently cups my face. 'Hello gorgeous,' he murmurs, leaning down to kiss me on the lips. I dissolve into the kiss, pushing into it. I need this kiss. Oh how I need it. But then Tom makes that '*mwah*' noise again to signal that the kiss has ended. He leans back, smiling at me mischievously, like he didn't just do that. Then he holds up his hands and says, 'So, I guess you'll be wanting me to do something to *you* now, won't you?'

Before I can compute, he's shoved his hand between my legs and is half-heartedly tapping at my vagina. He's a full two centimetres away from my clitoris. I look up at him but he's not making eye contact any more. In fact he's . . . he's . . . he's sort of staring out of the window through the gap between the curtains. He looks *bored.*

Is it possible to give someone an orgasm *passive-aggressively?*

Because that is definitely what this feels like.

I close my eyes, so I can at least try to focus on the sensations. Google said you should 'build on small positive sexual experiences' and that is what I need to do. If I tell Tom I'm no longer in the mood, or even move his hand to the right place, then that might damage his confidence. So I wiggle into his hand and moan, and it feels good to be touched. Even passive-aggressively. Tom interprets my moan as a direction to get rougher. He inserts two fingers into my dry body. He jabs them back and forth with bored aggression. *Oww*, it's really quite hurting. What do I do? I can't tell him it's hurting. He'll never touch me again, but *oww*. I wince. Oh why can't sex be like it is on the TV? Where the men know how to touch you and you have one of those vaginas that's angled in a way that means you can orgasm through penetration? My whole body flinches and

I grab Tom's hand instinctively to stop him. Then I smile up at him, looking grateful. 'Thank you,' I murmur, kissing the offending hand.

He doesn't seem to be wondering why I stopped him. In fact, he looks proud of himself. He pulls me into his armpit again and kisses the top of my head. 'Horny thing, aren't you?' he comments. And now, on top of everything, I'm trying to figure out what the hell that's supposed to mean.

I can't cry though. Because if I cry that will make this a negative experience and you need to build on positive experiences. Maybe now we've had this positive encounter, Tom will make the next move? Maybe I'll come home from a talk and he'll surprise me by kissing me the moment I walk in the door and go down on me while I'm pushed against the wall. Maybe we'll have sex in the shower again. We've not done that for at least four years. I soothe myself with these fantasies as Tom strokes my hair again.

Some programme about gap years comes on and we watch it in a daze, making comments about how much we hate all the young people in it. Dee hasn't replied to my message about the honeymoon photos – probably too busy having sex with Nigel. Well, screw you, Dee. I've had sex too! Not actual, penetrative sex, but Google says we're too focused on penetrative sex. Just touching each other counts as sex, Google says. Try not to get het up about how many times you have sex and just enjoy exploring each other's bodies, Google says. And Tom and I did just that. I don't have to worry that we're one of those couples who never has sex. I've reset the worrying-about-it clock. I can relax for at least a month.

Cat jumps onto my lap, rotating a few times before she slumps herself down. I stroke her head and let her purrs quieten my mind. I try to bathe in the afterglow. Because there is an air of sex that hangs heavily around us.

Tom suddenly hugs me out of the blue. So tight I almost cannot breathe. I squeal in his arms, feeling the pressure of him pushing on my ribs. Then he lets go and looks right into my eyes.

'What was that for?' I ask, delighted.

'I love you Tor,' he replies, before returning his attention to the television.

And I've forgotten how messed up I feel about the blow job by the time the adverts roll around again.

Month Three

Amy Price has posted an image:

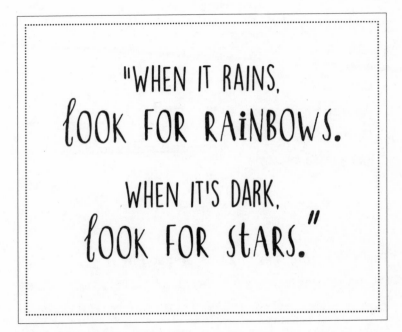

23 people like this

★

Olivia Jessen has posted an image:

F. E. A. R.

Fear has two meanings:

Forget. **E**verything. **A**nd. **R**un.

——————————— *or* ———————————

Face. **E**verything. **A**nd. **R**ise.

The choice is yours.

---

8 people like this

Comments:

Andrea Simmons: Everything OK, hon?

Olivia Jessen: Yeah, I guess. I don't know. Things are just a bit tough atm

⋆

Tori's *WhoTheF*ckAmI?* Official Fan Page:

OK, so I've got something to say about f*cking advice. Advice is good, advice is great, advice is well-meaning. But whoever takes it? Who has ever seen an inspirational quote posted on a beautiful background of Paris and suddenly been cured of all their problems?

Here's the thing: we all know when something is wrong. Your gut tells you. But sometimes you're not ready to listen to your gut. Or maybe life won't 'allow' you to listen to your gut? We have rent to pay and reality to face. If everyone spent every day following their gut and inspirational advice posted in pretty font, the world would cease to function. So, while you're waiting for your life to catch up with your gut, here is some *actual* life advice. Things you can actually do today to make life easier or better.

Ready for my #ActualF*ckingLifeAdvice?

- Do not try to drive anywhere on a Friday afternoon if you can possibly f*cking help it
- Wear a f*cking skirt when you go for your smear test
- Add some f*cking mustard to scrambled egg
- Own-brand painkillers work just as f*cking well as the expensive ones
- If you like drinking Merlot, always buy bottles from Chile or the f*cking South of France

What's *your* #ActualF*ckingLifeAdvice? Please do post below.
Love you,
Tori xx

★

My sister's house is only a five-minute walk from my parents' house where I'm staying over later. A nice quiet walk, with hardly any traffic, pavement on both sides of the road, and even punctuated with bird song. It's steaming hot and everyone is out in their gardens.

I ring the doorbell at Lizzie's semi-detached three-bed-with-two-bathrooms (and an adjoining garage you could build into an extension). I hear childish shrieks and her telling Georgia to 'calm down'. Then the door opens and Georgia shoots through the bottom like a greased pig.

'AUNTIE TORTOR, AUNTIE TORTOR!'

I bend down and she wraps her tiny arms around my neck. I smell her hair, and feel at peace. Love oozes out from every pore of my skin as this little person clings to me like a clam to a ship. Lizzie laughs behind her.

'She's been excited all morning. Georgie, darling, let Auntie TorTor breathe.'

Georgia reluctantly withdraws and I stand up and kiss Lizzie on the cheek hello. 'Hey you,' I say, then put my hands right on the convex curvature of her stomach. It's popped since the last time I saw her. 'How's the parasite?'

'Honestly! Tor!' But Lizzie's laughing and letting me in.

Georgia skids around our ankles, demanding I read her a book, demanding I come and see her new stickers, demanding I play with the ball. Lizzie makes us tea but Georgia doesn't let us drink it. The moment I even try to take a sip, she's shoving *That's Not My Badger* into my hand or lifting up her dress and showing me her tummy and insisting we show her ours.

'Mummy's tummy is the biggest,' she declares after we obligingly reveal our stomachs. I cannot look away from my sister's bump. It's weird and grotesque when it's not covered with floaty clothes – blue veins decorating it like piped icing, her belly button engorged like it's sniffed loads of poppers.

'That's because mummy is growing a baby,' I say. 'You're going to be a big sister, isn't that exciting?'

Georgia smiles but you can tell by the blank expression that she has no grasp of the concept. 'Can I watch *Peppa Pig*?'

'I thought you'd never ask.' Lizzie bends down and kisses her on both cheeks. Georgia giggles and blooms under the love. It takes a while to get the remote working and to get the TV onto the proper channel. 'Jake's always messing about with it so he can play his games' but eventually *Peppa Pig* squeals from the screen. The transformation in Georgia is instant. She sits as close as she can, her mouth hanging open. Lizzie shoots me a fake-guilty look and she refills the kettle for a second attempt at tea.

'I feel bad,' she says. 'They're not supposed to watch too much TV, it messes with their development or something.' She flicks the switch on and the water starts gurgling slowly. 'But I literally wouldn't have a chance to wash otherwise. You have no idea, Tor. No idea. I tried to have a shower the other day and Georgia screamed outside and tried to bang down the door. I eventually had to let her in.'

When the tea is made, we take it into the living room and ease ourselves into the leather sofa. Everywhere I look there are framed photographs of Lizzie and her picture perfect existence. There are the professional shots they got taken of Georgia when she was only two weeks old – put into a flowerpot like an Anne Geddes baby. There's a collage Lizzie's made of her and Jake in all their different incarnations –

different haircuts, different holidays, different fashions. They've been together since they were at school. And over these twenty years I don't think either of them has once wondered if there's anyone better out there.

'So, how's it going?' I ask, gesturing towards her bump and slurping from my tea. 'It all OK in there?'

Lizzie's hands massage her stomach absent-mindedly, and she smiles. 'Yes, it's all good. Though I can't believe how much I took the first pregnancy for granted. It's so much harder when you already have another child to look after.'

'Georgia seems excited though.' My mug feel greasy, like it's not been washed properly, but I keep sipping.

'Ha. We'll see. Some of her friends at nursery have had siblings and they turned into attention-seeking monsters overnight.'

We sip and enjoy the relative quiet. I can hear Peppa squeaking from the other room, keeping Georgia dormant.

'So, how's it all going with you?' Lizzie asks, stretching her legs up onto the table, her pink mumsy slippers hanging off her heels. 'Where you flying off to tomorrow? Haven't you got that big thing?'

I nod, feeling nervous just at the mention of it. 'Berlin, for this TED talk. I'm bricking it to be honest.'

My sister gives me a sympathetic smile. 'But you're so good at this sort of thing, Tor. And you're used to talking in front of crowds. You'll smash it.'

'God, I hope so.' I sip from my drink again. 'Mum and Dad don't understand what a TED talk is.' We both giggle guiltily. 'Plus,' I say, perking up and wiggling in my chair, 'You'll never guess who's doing a TED talk on the same day so I'll get to meet her? Only Taylor freaking Faithful!'

'Oh my God, Tor! You're obsessed with her. You must be so excited!'

I giddily take another glug of tea. 'I just hope she's nice, and that she likes me. It will ruin everything if she doesn't like me.'

'She'll love you. Just maybe don't bombard her with how crazy you are about her book . . . I still remember when you read it for the first time and kept sending me your favourite quotes. That's so cool. And how's things with Tom?'

I nod and look into the steam rising from my cup. 'Tom's good. He's in Las Vegas actually, for work.'

'Poor Tom.'

I shake my head. 'I know. We had a bit of a tiff before he left . . .' I tail off. It was more than a tiff; it had been a full-on fight that had come out of nowhere. I'd jokingly said, 'no strippers', which I thought went without saying. Thus the joke. But then Tom accused me of being abusive again for trying to 'control his behaviour'.

'What if all my colleagues go?' he'd yelled. 'What do you want me to do? Tell them they're sexist pigs and stand by myself outside?'

'Er, yes? Because they *are*?'

'You can't control people like this, Tor. What's happened to you? You used to be so laid back. What happened to that carefree girl I met in America?'

87

'SHE WAS *TWENTY-FUCKING-FIVE!*'

I watch all the unsaid responses cross Lizzie's face. 'Oh dear,' she says and drinks her tea.

'We made up though!' After hanging him out to dry, suddenly I'm rushing to his defence. I don't want her to dislike Tom. Because once we work through this bad patch maybe we'll get married one day, when he finally allows me to talk about it, and my sister can't hate my husband. 'Look,' I get out my phone and show her the message he sent.

Tom: I never want us to fight. I love you. We'll Skype when I land. Xx

Then he'd sent a photo of my book sitting at number thirty-five in a bookshop chart.

Tom: PS: Look what I found in the Heathrow departure lounge. Always so proud Xx

'See!' I push my phone to Lizzie's face.

She takes it, smiles, then returns it. 'Well then it's all sorted, isn't it? So, you just going to Berlin?'

'I've got to do a thing in Paris on my way back.' Two sold-out shows in two capital cities. Telling people how to live their best lives, when I no longer have a clue.

'You're so lucky!' Lizzie sighs and readjusts herself, curling her feet under her bump. 'Your life is so much more interesting than mine. Having kids is so dull. The most exciting thing I did this week was look down Georgia's bum hole with a torch to see if she has worms.'

My face screws up. 'I didn't know that was even a thing. Anyway, it will all be worth it when you're older and she comes to visit you in the old folk's home. Whereas my face will get eaten by cats. Did you know, if you die alone with a cat, they go straight for your face? Right away?'

'Tor, that's the most disgusting thing I've ever heard.'

I point to my face. 'Enjoy this while it lasts,' I tell her. 'It will end up in the colon of a cat. You won't be jealous of my Berlin trip then.'

She cackles and her entire belly rolls as she does. 'Oh bollocks, you've woken him up.' She hoicks up her top, revealing her veins again, and starts whispering calmly to her bump. 'There, there, did Auntie Tor upset you? It's OK. *Shh, shh.*' I watch as she settles her unborn child, as her stomach obeys her nurturing voice. When the squirming under her skin stops, she looks up. 'You're not going to die alone anyway, Tor. You and Tom will get around to having kids, won't you?'

I open my mouth to say something but I don't know what it is. I'm interrupted anyway by the closing music of *Peppa Pig* and the thundering sound of tiny feet.

Georgia appears at the door, grinning wildly. 'BABY-CHINO!' she shouts at us. 'I WANT A BABYCHINO!'

I shake my head at Lizzie. 'She can't pronounce my name properly and yet she can ask for a babyccino?'

'What can I say Auntie TorTor? She has her priorities right.'

★

I join Lizzie and Georgia on their excursion to the park-with-adjoining-café. Mum and Dad are out all day and spending time with a toddler is preferable to spending any time in my own company at the moment. When I'm alone, I just start randomly crying, and sometimes I scratch at the skin on the top of my thighs until it bleeds. So we smother Georgia with gloopy white sun-lotion, load her into the buggy, and push her through my hometown and into the local park I used to go to.

Things are still much the same. The play equipment is new, but all the trees are where the trees used to be; all the benches are where the benches used to be. I push Georgia on the swing, and I congratulate her for going down the slide, and I watch her carefully as she balances on the logs, and I tell her she isn't big enough yet for the zip wire. Lizzie sits on a bench with her eyes closed to the sun, stroking her tummy and shamelessly letting me babysit.

I am good at this, I decide.

I am looking after a small child and I am good at this.

I could be a good mum. A great mum. I'm so creative and caring. I don't get too flappy and look how much Georgia loves me. Imagine how much my own actual child would love me. A selfish part of me longs for that – the unconditional love a child would always bring. Oh, I *do* want children. I do I do. I want to grow one in my stomach and see what my body is capable of and feel so much love for something that it eclipses every other part of my life. I watch Georgia navigate the roundabout and I remember seeing her for the first time. I'd turned up with flowers, feeling weird that my sister was somehow now a mother. Lizzie had met me at the door and we'd hugged and I'd asked her how bad childbirth was, and she just shook her head. 'Where is she?' I'd asked, and Lizzie had pointed to a tiny cot in the corner. I'd walked over and peered in and there . . . there was Georgia. The love had arrived clear, unwavering, and instantaneous. I'd never felt love like it. Before then, love was something I'd only ever grown into with time – like with Tom. But, with Georgia, my heart immediately and instinctively grew more room for her. Just like that. And, if it was like that with just a niece, how much more powerful would it be with my own?

Georgia has left the roundabout for the slide now. She shuffles to the top and pushes herself over the edge. '*Weeeee,*' I coo, reaching out to catch her lumpy little body at the bottom. *Oh, I do want them. I need to talk about it with Tom. We need to finally bring this up in tangibles – when and how we want to go about doing this. We could be good parents. We don't even have to get married if that's what scares him. Oh I want a child, I want one, I want one . . .*

Georgia has to wait for her second turn on the slide and this is unacceptable. She pushes the boy blocking her path and he tumbles too quickly down the metal chute and bangs his head as he lands on the red tarmac. The boy erupts into tears, his mum rushing over and glaring at me. Georgia, unbothered, flies herself down the slide again, but I pull her off at the bottom. I make a big show of telling her off. 'You *cannot* push, YOU CANNOT, THAT IS NAUGHTY.'

Then it's her turn to erupt into tears. Not just tears –
hysteria. She throws herself onto the ground, limbs flailing,
her screeches turning the entire attention of everyone
towards her tantrum. Lizzie jogs over and tries to stem the
flow with Bessie the rabbit and a small box of raisins and
promises of a babyccino. Nothing will calm her. Georgia
screams and screams into the sky and everyone is looking
and Lizzie looks so stressed and exhausted and embarrassed
and she says sorry to all the other parents and I can feel
my stomach bubble with . . . *ergh* . . .

No, I don't want a child.

Not yet, anyway.

Maybe not ever.

★

I have a lovely, long-overdue, catch-up dinner with my
parents. It's tradition that I always stay the night before I
have to fly somewhere. Dad insists on lighting candles and
putting on Norah Jones and we have a quiet evening
discussing Georgia's various development milestones. I watch
my parents as they wash up together afterwards. There is
such intimacy in the way they hand soapy plates to one
another, Mum letting Dad do the stacking of the dishwasher
because he's better at arranging things. I ache for what they
have. I ache for the relaxed way in which they love each
other. That it's a given: them, together, forever. They don't
wonder or worry if there is someone else better, or, at least,

they don't *seem* to. I think of the mental energy this must free up. How much space you must have in your brain when it's cleared of thoughts like: *What are you thinking? What did you mean when you said that? Is this it? Is this the best love I can hope for? Is this what my life will be every day? Are you The One? Do you hate me as much as I hate you? Why are we doing this to each other?*

With the table cleared, and the dishwasher gurgling, they pour out another glass of red wine each and we settle by the candlelight. I'm filled in on the important developments in the neighbourhood. Rose-from-next-door's melanoma has been caught in time. Over-the-road have gone on their third holiday this year already because he's got such a good pension. Do I remember Natalie who I used to play with around the corner? Well, she has moved to Australia with her husband. After two glasses of Merlot, I am warm enough and secure enough to talk to them about it.

'Mum? Dad?' I begin, swirling my drink in my glass.

'What is it poppet?' Dad asks.

I pause and swill the crimson liquid around some more. 'How did you know you were each other's One?'

They both laugh at exactly the same time. Mum reaches over and puts her wrinkled hand on top of mine.

'What is it? What's so funny?' I say.

'It's just I don't think I ever thought about it,' Mum replies, before turning to Dad. 'Did you?'

'I knew I got on better with you than I did with anyone else.'

'Yes, me too. We just got on.' She turns back to me. 'Your

93

generation are way too preoccupied with this sort of thing. I think if I'd looked at your father thinking, "are you The One? Can I spend every moment of my life with you?" I would've freaked out and got on a train to Timbuktu.'

'Hey,' Dad protests. Smiling and soppy from wine.

Mum laughs again, but her grip tightens on my hand. 'Have you had another fight with Tom?' she asks softly, rubbing the top of my thumb.

I gulp down the last of my wine. I wish I hadn't brought it up. I have to ration how much I complain about Tom. 'Just a small one . . . he's in Vegas for work. I didn't want him to go to a strip club.'

Both of them pull a face. 'He's not going to one, is he?' Dad looks mortally offended by the idea, reassuring me that I am in the right about this. Dad is a man and doesn't go to them. It is not 'inevitable' that men will do this. Only some types of men . . . my long-term boyfriend, for example.

I shrug and my gut tightens. I picture Tom grinning as he tucks money into another woman's underwear. I picture him laughing with his disgusting work friends about which one is the prettiest. I picture him telling them I objected, but that he came anyway and them all cheering for him. 'I don't know,' I answer honestly. 'He said he didn't want to go, but everyone at work was going.'

My parents say nothing. They've learned not to. For I ring them so many times, telling them about something Tom has done and asking if it's OK that I feel this upset – saying enough is enough and I can't take it any more. Then they admit that They Think I Can Do Better, and that it's been clear for years that We Don't Make Each Other Happy, that I Need To Leave. Then Tom buys flowers and apologizes and becomes the man I know he can be. He regenerates into the emotionally-intelligent, kind, caring, soulmate that he was when we first met. He promises that things will be different, that he's never met anyone like me. That he can't believe he has such a beautiful, talented, successful, creative, kind woman as his partner. That he's never felt this way about anyone so that must mean we are supposed to be together. And over and over again I melt into his promises. Because it's so much less painful to believe him, than to leave. And I betray Mum and Dad and their support.

'I'm sure you'll sort it out,' Dad says. He will not meet my eye.

We share out the rest of the bottle and they ask me about my flight. They are excited about my trip, and my TED talk. Though they ask again for me to explain what it means.

'Hang on to all these things you are achieving,' Mum begs me, as I excuse myself to go to bed. 'Don't let your problems with Tom ruin how happy you are.'

I've gone to bed too early and can't get to sleep.

My alarm is set for 5a.m. and I'm annoyed I drank three glasses of wine as I'll need a wee in the night. After an hour of twisting my duvet into contortions, I give up. I turn on my reading light and look around my old room – more a shrine to my success now, than a childhood bedroom. The dusty, pink paint is littered with blobs of random discolouration from where I Blu-Tacked different posters to the wall. Mum and Dad have collected everything along the way – all my achievements. They've framed key newspaper articles and arranged all thirty-two foreign editions of my book on a specially made display shelf. Their pride leaks from the walls and I marvel for a moment at where life has taken me. The little girl who lay in this bed and kissed her Spike from *Buffy* poster every night before bed could never have imagined what this room would become.

I wonder if Tom went to a strip club . . .

No. My parents are right. I spend so long thinking about Tom and worrying about our relationship – and worrying about what Tom thinks about our relationship – that I miss so much. I will not let this argument stew in my head. I lean over and pick up my old Taylor Faithful book. I've been trying to re-read both of her books before I meet her in Berlin. This is her slightly newer one. It's called: *Love Me As I Am.*

Because even gurus need a guru, right? Taylor Faithful is mine. I stumbled across her first book, *Spiky Around The Edges*, when I was twenty-three and it became my life raft. My lighthouse beam to follow. She is uncompromisingly difficult. She refuses to mould herself to fit around the gaps in others. This book is all about looking for a man who loves her for exactly who she is. And she found him. And she got married in red and didn't change her surname and they've agreed they don't want a baby. I want all that. Maybe not exactly all of it, but I want the relationship she has. It sounds so perfect in this book, so easy.

I want any relationship that isn't mine.

Then why aren't you leaving, Tori?

It is the question that haunts me. The question I do not have an answer for, only a delay tactic. The thought of leaving Tom is as bad as the thought of staying with Tom. I never thought I'd be one of those women who stays in a relationship because she is scared, but maybe I am. Or maybe this is just a bad patch and we'll work through it. His lack of commitment and refusal to discuss the future has been poisoning us for years now although I'm sure, in his head, everything is somehow my fault. What's so hilarious is I'm not sure I even *want* commitment. I don't know if I *want* marriage and kids and till death us do part and watching the small amount of hair Tom has left disappearing entirely. Part of me wants it only because he's not willing to offer it. I feel I cannot know if I want Tom until he wants me. I know this makes me a total failure as a modern woman in every possible conceivable way – but that's the truth. *Who the hell is this woman I have become?*

I hear Mum and Dad's going-to-bed noises creak across the landing. They talk in hushed voices, thinking I'm already asleep for my early flight tomorrow. There is gargling and the turning on and off of the bathroom light, then the click of their bedroom door closing. I start reading my book again, running my finger over the sentence that I keep coming back to:

'You can be difficult, and yet someone will find it so easy to love you.'

I do not know what to do about this sentence. This sentence that I know tells me everything I need to hear. I am not ready to act on this sentence and make the decisions that need to be made because of it. But it dissolves in, like honey in hot water. And I know, one day, this sentence will change everything.

Just not today.

★

@TheRealTori Up at the sparrow's fart to fly to Berlin for TED talk prep. OMFG WHAT IS MY ACTUAL LIFE?

@TheRealTori How many Imodiums do you need to take for an eighteen-minute TED talk? I've gone with four.

@TheRealTori Panicking now. Am going to try to buy prunes.

@TheRealTori OK, so, like it's literally impossible to buy prunes in Berlin airport. Who knew?

@TheRealTori

Does my hotel room look big in this?

★

I see nothing of Berlin.

Travelling the world sounds so very glamorous but I've actually seen very little of it. I only see airport departure lounges and the inside of five-star hotels. But, before you even get jealous about those, I'm never actually inside them for very long. I never get any time to explore a city or figure out where the best places are to eat.

This trip is crazier than normal. I'm picked up at the airport by a friendly TED looker-afterer. They bleat enthusiasm at me. They ask me how my flight was. They ask me if I'm excited. They tell me it's going to be '*awesome*'. I'm driven straight to the university venue. The building's made of white stone that reflects the sun off it and stretches up into the piercingly blue sky. TED banners hang over the door. Important and busy people wander around with walkie-talkies and clipboards and shout instructions to one another.

I start to feel nervous.

'Victoria, welcome.' A man appears at reception after I've checked in my wheelie suitcase. He wears Converse but carries himself with importance. 'I'm Brian, Event Co-ordinator. We're so glad to have you here. Come, come. Meet the other speakers. We've got welcome drinks in the hall.'

I follow Brian nervously down corridors and around corners, trying to keep up with his pace in my heels. 'Is Taylor Faithful here yet?' I ask his back.

He turns and his smile shows he knows I'm a fan. 'She's

99

not flying in until tomorrow, I'm afraid. We're a bit worried about her doing it without a rehearsal, but she's such a professional it should be OK. I mean, the woman's a regular on *Oprah*.'

'Oh.' I continue to scurry after him and try to hide my disappointment. I did not want to meet her on the actual day of the talk. I'll be terrified as it is.

We push through some double doors and emerge onto a stage in a giant, ornate hall bedecked with TED branding. Chairs spread up and out around me until the ones at the back are like dots. This must be the place. *Oh God*. I can't even have a nervous breakdown because the other speakers are here already, milling around and chatting next to a table laden with flutes of orange juice, sandwiches and miniature German hot dogs.

I'm introduced to everyone. There's a brain cancer doctor, and a neuroscientist. They bond over brains and MRI scans. Then there are two women – older, holding themselves with the puff of academic achievement. One is an expert in body language. The other is a historian who specialises in how language evolves.

I am a huge fat fraud and none of them have heard of my book.

'What's your speech about?' The historian asks, after we're all introduced and are sipping orange juice and sharing how nervous we are.

'Umm, they're calling it, *Ripping Up the Rule Book*.' They all continue to peer at me, wanting more. I chug down my orange juice and wish it had vodka in it. 'Umm, it's about how, like, when I was twenty-five, I had, like, a nervous breakdown and went travelling for a year. But, like, umm, it was just a stereotypical gap year – you know? I did loads of chanting and yoga and it didn't help and so I decided to just *fuck everything*.' I throw my hands out and some orange juice slops over the rim of my glass. 'And, yeah, I wrote a book about living the life you need to live, rather, than, like, the life you *think* you need to live . . . Oh God, I hope I'm more eloquent tomorrow.'

They all laugh politely.

'What's your talk on?' I prompt.

The historian lady looks right at me. 'Mine's called, *Can Words Stop This?* It's about the etymology of language in social resistance and whether stories can contribute to positive social change.'

'Riiiight.'

I do not have time for a crisis of confidence though because the snacks are quickly taken away and Brian reappears to give us a long talk. I say 'talk' because he may as well be threatening to kill my family, he's being so scary about tomorrow. About how big a deal it is, and about how *famous* previous contributors have been, and how it's *live* and there is no room for fuck-ups. If I was nervous before, by the end of this pep talk I'm even more so. We're allowed a loo break and then the training and rehearsals begin. We only have eighteen minutes to tell our story. A big red clock starts to count down the moment we start speaking. We are encouraged not to move on the stage if we can possibly help it. 'Own your space, own your story.'

It's beyond dark when I'm finally driven, exhausted, to my hotel. They drilled us so hard that I'm feeling less stressed about tomorrow. My talk fits well within the time. Even the brain surgeon laughed at the jokes in it. I had five seamless run-throughs. I think I've got this.

I'm too tired to go down to the hotel restaurant, so I order room service. I eat it on the window ledge, overlooking the city, and allow myself a moment to marvel at the some-times-beautiful state of my life.

Tom and I manage to Skype one another. His little hung-over face appears on my screen, making me smile. The miles that separate us kick my heart back into action.

'Everything hurts,' he announces, his hangover evident in every sallow inch of his skin. His voice is gruff and I can almost smell the sweetness of his breath, even though he's thousands of miles away. 'I hate Vegas.'

I laugh and try not to get distracted by myself in the corner of the screen.

'Hung-over?'

'Hung-over. Jet-lagged. Broken.'

I laugh again and pretend I don't find him kind of gross. We take it in turns to hold our iPads up to the hotel window to see who has got the best view. He wins as he's in the Bellagio and has a view of the fountains.

'My red-eye's in a few hours, so I'm going to try to have

a nap before then. How you feeling about tomorrow, gorgeous?'

I sigh. 'I'm the stupidest person on the line-up, but other than that, I'm feeling OK.'

He shakes his head. 'You're not stupid, Tor.' He doesn't deny that I'm the stupidest person on the line-up though, or maybe that's just me being picky. 'You want to rehearse it on me?'

I shake my head. 'I've done it to death today. Thanks, though.'

'You'll smash it, gorgeous. You always do.'

We dither and dance around our previous argument. I do not bring up strip clubs, or ask if he went to one. It's in my head the whole time though. *Did you go? Did you? Did you go when you knew it would bother me?* But tomorrow is an important day, and, if I bring it up, somehow I know Tom will twist everything so it's my fault. I just don't have the energy to go there and feel worse and be too upset afterwards. So I ask him about the conference, and he asks me what the other speakers are like. He remembers that I'm meeting Taylor and expresses a vague amount of excitement on my behalf. The sun still shines through his hotel window, but it's gone midnight here now and I need to be up at six. Not that I'll sleep, but I guess just lying and staring at the ceiling and freaking out is better than doing that while sitting upright.

'I should sleep,' I say. 'Have a safe flight.'

'Good luck again for tomorrow.' Tom puts his face right

into the camera so all I can see are his nostrils. He starts flaring them for comic value and I do laugh and feel a swell of affection.

'Night then,' I say.

'Night.'

I'm smiling and I'm just about to turn the conversation off, when he says, 'Oh, and Tor? Be careful not to talk too fast. You always talk too fast when you're nervous. But don't worry, I'm sure you'll be amazing.'

*

It is not yet 8a.m. and I've just told Taylor Faithful that I'm in love with her.

'Oh my God, sorry. I've not scared you, have I?'

She laughs. She is smaller in real life. 'Not at all. I'm pleased you like my books so much.'

'Like them? *Like them?* You don't get it.' My hands fly through the air as I try to get her to understand. 'Your first book CHANGED MY LIFE. *Seriously*. It's what made me quit my internship and go travelling, and then it was while I was travelling that I had my *own* eureka moment and wrote my *own* book and, I mean, I can't *believe* we're here. *Together.* Doing a TED talk on the same stage, on the same day. I mean, I even mention your book in my book. I feel like I should pay you some of my royalties. Oh God, I'm babbling, aren't I? You promise I'm not scaring you?'

She laughs again. She gives me her time. Even though

she has just arrived from the airport. Even though she's not had her coffee yet, and Brian's twitching because she needs to rehearse before the doors open.

I still can't believe she's here. Everything is so surreal. And everything was surreal enough already. I'm about to do a TED talk. It will be put on YouTube and will be watched millions of times, even if I'm not very good, because this is TED and these things get views. And now my own guru is here. My very own! And she's behaving exactly how I behave when fans get a bit too intense. She's scanning the room for her publicist; she is not making eye contact; she is laughing, but it's a little bit high-pitched.

Oh no. I am one of them.

I step back. 'Anyway, sorry,' I say. 'I'll let you have some breakfast.'

My mortification at least distracts from my nerves. I sit in the corner, blushing, as I watch Taylor introduce herself to the other speakers, who all behave appropriately. I message Dee, even though she'll get mad at me for how much it will cost her to reply.

Tori: OMFG I JUST MET TAYLOR FAITHFUL AND I BEHAVED LIKE A FUCKING IDIOT FROM HIGH HELL

Taylor's ushered away into rehearsal and I'm ushered away into hair and make-up. They shovel four layers of foundation on, outline my eyes and scrape my long bob into this professional bun that makes me look like I own my shit.

My phone beeps.

Dee: You *finally* met her!? Is she nice!? Are you OK!? I mean, you're like OBSESSED with her, Tor. OBSESSED.
Dee: PS: You're totally paying for this message.
Dee: And this one.
Dee: And this one.
Dee: Play hard to get btw. Win her over the old-fashioned way.

It's not bad advice actually. I smile at Taylor when she returns from make-up but I don't go over. I chat to the other speakers instead. They're such an amazing group of people and we're already so bonded by shared nervousness. I film a video of all our hands held out to show how much we're shaking. I post it to my fan page.

'The doors have opened, guys,' Brian claps his hands as he arrives into the greenroom. 'The first talk will be in about forty minutes. Forty minutes.' He vanishes again.

I turn to Body Language Lady, who is going on first. 'You OK?'

She is green. I didn't know it was possible to actually turn green, but she has managed it. 'I've been sick,' she whispers back. 'What if I'm sick again?'

'Have you eaten?'

She shakes her head.

'Then you have nothing left to sick up. You're empty. It's good.' I have no idea if that's scientifically valid but it seems to calm her. I ask her about her children, to get her mind off the nerves. She has a girl and a boy. The girl is very clever and the boy is very caring. They play so nicely together.

She misses them and cannot wait to get back to Arizona after this whole thing is over. Brain Surgeon joins in. He takes out his phone and shows us his toddler. We say the toddler is cute, we say doesn't he look like you. Taylor Faithful looks over, like she's feeling left out. I want her to come over. I want her to come over so much.

Brian appears again and points at Body Language. 'Lorali, time.'

She stands. Her knees sink towards the floor and it takes visible effort to straighten them again.

'See you on the other side,' I say kindly.

She brushes nothing off her business suit, an outfit that makes it clear she obviously knows what she's talking about. 'See you on the other side,' she smiles back. I don't need to be a body-language expert to know she likes me. We all clap and cheer and I make us form an arch for her to walk through as she leaves. Taylor perks up. Taylor joins in. Taylor is the other side of my arch. We touch hands. I cannot believe we are touching hands. *Taylor. Taylor Faithful!*

Then she walks with me back to my chair. 'So, you like my books, huh?' she starts.

There is the distant sound of applause. Lorali has taken to the stage. My stomach flips, knowing it will be my turn soon. There's a small TV set up in the corner, so we can see how the others are doing. I'm too nervous to look at it, so I just tilt my head at her.

'I really gave myself away, didn't I? I promise you I'm usually cooler than that.'

She laughs and it's filled with warmth. I cannot believe I am here, next to Taylor Faithful. I have so many thoughts. Most of them involve wanting her to really, really like me and for us to really, really connect.

'I hope I wasn't abrupt earlier,' she says. 'I hadn't had any caffeine yet.'

'Oh no, not at all.'

'I was reading your event blurb during my sound check,' she says. 'It sounds like you've been through a lot. Like you've achieved a lot too.'

I wipe my palms against each other, they are sweaty. My armpits also gush out sweat, despite nine layers of deodorant. 'I'm not sure about that,' I say. 'I mean, being around all these other amazing people today is kind of making me think I haven't done much at all . . .' I trail off. *Why am I saying this to her? Why does she care?*

But, oh, she cares. Of course she does.

'That's insane,' she screws up her face 'You can't compare stories and achievements.' She reaches over and takes a glass of water, sipping it with a straw so the red lipstick she is famous for wearing doesn't smudge. 'You could argue I don't help people because all I did was write a book about my own life.'

'But it's so much more than that!' I interrupt. 'I mean, your books . . . they helped me hugely.'

'Well, you see! People could say the same about you. It's not what you go through, it's what you do with it. You were honest about something people needed more honesty about. There's courage in that. That really does help people.'

God, I love her. I love her I love her I love her.

We start chatting like equals, almost like friends. Maybe that's just my projection, but it feels real. My nerves shrivel up, this moment is so good. She asks about *Who The F*ck Am I?* and I tell her my story. Not the polished one that I'm about to go out onto a darkened stage to tell – with punctuated pauses for maximum effect, and jokes I've told a million times over but have to pretend I'm telling afresh. I just garble it all out to her. About how I found travelling so lonely. How I hated most people I met because they kept boasting about how enlightened they were. I tell her how I always thought something was wrong with me – that I was difficult and spiky and unlikeable – until I read her book and realised, no, I was fine, it's just that my boundaries were always being crossed.

'I'd never thought about it that way before,' I gurgle at her. Wanting to ask for a photo, but not wanting to be that dick who asks her for photos when she's trying to relax in the greenroom.

'As I say in the book,' she repeats. 'Anger is neither a positive or negative emotion. It's just a signal that a boundary of yours is being crossed.'

'Exactly!'

We can't have spoken for more than eighteen minutes because we can hear applause. Body Language must be finished. She arrives five minutes later, seeping with relief and glowing with it having gone well.

'I can't feel my face,' she announces as we all stand to clap. Brain Surgeon is up next. I am after him.

'Victoria?' A man dressed in black comes in. 'You ready to be miked up?'

I gulp. I remember. Why I am here. What the hell I need to do in the next hour. The nerves rush back in. I shake. Saliva wells in my mouth. I may very well be sick.

'OK, I'm ready. Hang on.' I turn back to Taylor but she's not there. She's congratulating Body Language. She is giving Brain Surgeon a pep-talk about nerves. There's so much I still want to ask her: Does she ever feel like a fraud? If you tell the truth at the time, but realise later you were wrong, is it still the truth? Does she ever have days when she wishes she could just not be perfect? Although, maybe, she *is* just perfect. But I'm being called. I need to get miked up. I need to swallow this all down and stand on stage in front of thousands and not show even the slightest quiver of self-doubt.

I have to tell my story and it has to be the truth.

'Victoria?' The man calls again.

'I'm coming.'

I ask if I can go to the bathroom. And then, once I'm miked up, I ask if I can go to the bathroom again. This gets all the tech people worried because it means I have to take off my microphone and put it back on again.

'Two minutes,' Brian says. I'm worried he's irritated, but he smiles. 'Happens all the time.'

I hear the huge applause for Brain Surgeon, littered with cheers and whistles. He's nailed it.

I check my bladder is as totally empty as it can be. Thirty seconds. I wash and dry my hands. Thirty seconds. I lean my head against the mirror and take several calming breaths. Thirty seconds. I look up at myself. My face is polished, poised. My lipstick is on point. I really do look like I know what the fuck I'm talking about. 'Because you do,' I tell my reflection. 'Tori, just tell it how it is.'

Time is up.

I emerge into a packed corridor and reassure everyone that I'm fine. They put my microphone back on. They usher me past leads and cables and television monitors and people talking quietly into walkie-talkies. I also can't feel my face, but I'm somehow putting one foot in front of another, even in these heels. Brian walks me all the way to the edge of the stage. He tells me 'you got this'. I get a glimpse of the audience. There are so many of them. I think about how much they must've spent on their tickets; I think about how much they loved Body Language, with her years of experience and her graphs and her facts. All I have are my feelings, and how I made them into a story. The audience hushes, like they know I am there. I am not introduced – that's part of the deal. I just need to walk out into that spotlight and own it.

'And you're on.'

One foot in front of the other. I walk across this giant stage.

I feel the eyes of everyone on me. I stop in the middle. I look up. They wait. The giant red clock starts to count down. All I've done is look up, and I've already lost fifteen seconds. My heart goes berserk, but you probably can't see it beating through all my control underwear.

Speak, Tori. Speak.

I breathe in through my nose. I smile up at them. I deliberately don't look at the clock again.

'Six years ago,' I start, 'if you'd asked me how I was . . .' I wait for the beat. I own the silence. Then I open my mouth and continue '. . . I totally would've lied to you.'

★

@TheRealTori I DID ITTTTTTTTTTTT! Oh, my f*ckers, that was the best experience of my LIFE! I want to do it all over again. My TED talk will be posted next week.

@TheRealTori Look who I met!?!?! Look who I actually f*cking met! Taylor Faithful! Finally! And she was only slightly scared of me! @SpikyWoman

@SpikyWoman It was lovely to meet you too. And you didn't scare me at all! Keep telling your truth x x x @TheRealTori

@TheRealTori From Berlin to Paris – I can't WAIT to speak to all my French f*ckers. I've not slept in two days, but I promise that won't affect my swearing.

★

Tori's *WhoTheF*ckAmI?* Official Fan Page:

To my f*ckers,

I've had the most insane, but the most incredible three days ever. I've done an actual TED talk, I've met Taylor Faithful, sold out my Paris show . . . You guys just keep being my everything. I promise you I will always tell you the truth. That's what got me here. That's what I owe you, for giving me this incredible life of mine.

Last stop, I'm doing an 'intimate' event at the book shop *Shakespeare and Company* for competition winners before I go home. I'm looking forward to seeing you there.

So much love to you all

Tori x x

★

I don't see much of Paris either.

My hotel room is also amazing, yet, again, I'm hardly in it. My skin's breaking out. I've not eaten fresh fruit or fresh anything for three days. Meals are something I stuff into myself at airports, or in the back of taxis on the way to somewhere. It's only been three days but it feels like longer. I yearn for home and Tom and Cat and pyjamas and tea that tastes how tea is supposed to taste. I catnap in the taxi on my way to the bookshop – ignoring the stunning city that gleams in the sunshine.

The store is beautiful enough to perk me up. It's how

every bookshop should be, I decide. With chaotic piles of books that tower to the ceiling and alcoves and nooks to clamber into.

I sit with my legs crossed at the ankle so my knickers won't show in the photos. The intimate crowd of superfans are lovely and kind and laugh in all the right places. There's only about thirty of them, but the intensity of their adoration makes it feel like more. I answer their questions about whether I'm still with Tom and when my next book will be out. Same shit, different country.

I'm just about to wrap it up, when one last hand goes up. 'Yes?'

It's a girl who can't be older than twenty-two. Much younger than my usual readership. She blushes just from me looking at her. 'Can you do a reading?' she asks.

'A reading?' The word stumbles on my tongue. It's been so long since I've been asked to read from my book. In the early days, after publication, it's all I really did. I went to bookshops and not many people turned up and I'd read a few pages to the mostly-empty seats. But as the book grew and the audience grew, the simple act of reading died. It's too intimate a thing to work in giant theatres.

I look to the bookseller to check if we have time. He smiles and nods. We do.

'I've not actually read from my book in ages,' I admit and they laugh. 'OK, a reading. I can totally do a reading. I don't have one planned though. Umm, what bit shall I read?'

'Your first date with Man on the Rock,' she replies, with quiet assertion. 'The bit after you just met him and spent all that time talking on the mountain.'

I raise both eyebrows. 'Oh, OK then. Umm, hang on, let me find it.'

The bookseller has to lend me a copy of my own book, and it takes a further two minutes to find the right starting point. I look down at the words. Is it weird that I haven't looked at the inside of this book for years? It feels surreal that I wrote these paragraphs printed on the page. Like it wasn't me. I've not written anything proper like this in so, so long.

I cough. I look up at the audience to check they're still into this. Their faces are arranged in apprehensive concentration – they are quiet, waiting for me to start. I cough again.

'OK,' I say. I am suddenly nervous. I feel like I'm naked. 'Chapter forty-seven: The Stars are Ours.' I hesitate. I look at the first sentence, printed there, on the page. The most significant date of my life. I raise the book. 'I was not ready for this man,' I start reading. 'I'd had one whole minute of feeling truly free, truly independent. I'd hiked up to that vortex, I'd chucked all my bullshit into it, and I was enough. Finally, I was enough. Then he had appeared, carrying my discarded rosary beads and saying, "Umm, are these yours? They almost hit me on the head." When I got to the motel later, I couldn't fathom how much time we must've spent up there talking. It was *hours*. Conversation spilling out of two strangers, connecting in a way I've literally never connected with anyone before. I couldn't sleep. I couldn't stop thinking about him. This man on the rock.'

I look up to check they're all still interested. They are all still interested. The memory of that week starts flowing into me like warm water. I'd forgotten how intense the whole thing was. How I felt like a rug had been swiped out from under me. But in a good way. A special way.

'He picked me up the next evening,' I start reading again. 'I'd spent the day agonising over whether to cancel or not. I couldn't be in a relationship right now. I couldn't even be on a date right now. This year was for me – just for me. And it had taken me almost all of it to get to where I needed to be. But I couldn't pick up the phone. I couldn't say "I can't meet you tonight." I felt guided by something bigger than me. *Go on the date*, a voice told me. *You will hate yourself forever if you don't go on this date*. I decided though, that if I was going to do this – if I was going to even consider letting a man into my life right now – I was going to do it by being completely and utterly myself.' I smile and glance back up around the bookshop again. God, I was so dramatic back then. So determined for everything to be significant and with a narrative. 'So I didn't dress up. I put on a T-shirt and baggy jeans. I did not wash my hair. I did not wear good underwear. I did not apply make-up. He was lucky I brushed my teeth and applied deodorant – but that was all. I looked at my reflection as I heard his pickup truck roll up outside my grotty motel. "Be you, Tori," I told myself. "Don't be anything else but you."'

The memory of that night stays with me after the applause has died down. After the books have been signed. After I sit, sipping coffee, at Gare du Nord, waiting for the Eurostar to take me back and home to him. It was the most perfect date of perfect first dates. Tom picked me up an hour before dusk. He smelled amazing. He looked amazing. Tanned and youthful. The smile he gave me as I opened my motel-room door . . . Some people wait their whole lives to be smiled at like that. We drove into the desert. I made a joke about him murdering me. He laughed at it – wide and open and with all of his toned stomach. We talked the whole way. There was no empty air, no awkward anything. It was like catching up with my best friend. When we pulled up to a tiny dirt track in the middle of nowhere, all I could see was a picnic blanket and some solar-panelled tealights leading the way to it.

'What's all this?' I asked, not able to comprehend what was happening and how perfect it was.

Tom leaned into the backseat of the truck and removed a hoodie. 'It gets cold once the sun sets,' he replied, handing it over. 'Here, you'll need this soon.'

I pulled it over my head. It smelled of him.

The train pulls in. Everyone scrambles to get on. I wander in a dreamlike state to the first-class carriage and slump, exhausted, into my comfy seat. I listen to the announcement tell me about my upcoming journey – first in French, then in English. And I smile as I remember . . .

The sun set as we sat watching it, drinking beers. The most beautiful sunset I'd ever seen. We talked and talked and talked. And then, when it grew dark, Tom gently extinguished the lights, got me to lie on my back, and showed me the stars. We lay with our heads together as he pointed out the Big Dipper and Orion's Belt. It was like being at the planetarium, but the stars were real. The universe above us was our own state-of-the-art projector.

I still feel overwhelmed by that date when I think of it now. With the suburbs of Paris flashing past me in the window. I remember thinking, *this doesn't happen in real life; nothing this perfect happens in real life.* Tom asked me endlessly about myself and seemed truly bewitched by my every answer. He had this air of magic about him. I felt magic just by being next to him. I could not believe this man had appeared in my life. That he was so gorgeous and amazing and deep and insightful and kind and charming and yet was into me. So, *so* into me. With the stars glowing above us, and with the conversation spilling out into the darkness, I let him kiss me. The most perfect kiss. And I jumped into my life with him – without hesitation, without regret. Only a dawning knowledge that I'd met my One. Yes, the timing could've been better, but they always say they turn up when you least expect it.

I do not read my magazine on the train journey home from Paris. I stare out of the window and remember those heady first months with Tom. Like they are old clothes hidden in the back of my wardrobe that have become fashionable again. I fall in love with him again, alone, on a train, just by remembering what he was like.

I mean, he's still like that sometimes. That's why we're still together. But of course he was more like that at the beginning – everyone always is.

I remember how the second date somehow topped the first. He took me to a national park where the river had carved rocks into natural water chutes. We went first thing in the morning, before the sun had warmed the water, and got the park to ourselves. He took me to the top of a cliff and said that in order to start the date we had to jump into the pool below.

'It's safe,' he kept reassuring me. 'I promise.'

He made me jump first. I remember falling through the air. I remember screaming as I plunged through nothing. I remember how cold the water was. I remember finding Tom's warm body in the pool at the bottom. We clung to one another in the icy water and I remember thinking *I've only just met you.* Yet he looked into my eyes, adrenaline pumping through both of us, and he said, 'Sorry if this is too soon, but I could very easily fall in love with you.' Not one part of me felt it was too soon. We kissed in that icy water, kicking our legs to stop ourselves sinking, not once feeling the cold.

The train enters the tunnel. The views of France plunge into a roaring blackness. An announcement: the buffet car is open. I lean my head against the window and remember it all. I remember how, within a week, we were driving across America together. He knew all the places to go, all the places to eat. He dazzled everyone we met on the way, charming them until we were upgraded to better rooms. He asked me continuously if I was OK. He complimented me constantly and on the strangest of things. 'I love this mole on your toe. I love the way you blush when waiters ask you for your order. I've never met a girl that makes me laugh as much as you laugh.'

The moment we got back to England, he rushed me to his family home to introduce me to his beloved mother.

That wasn't all in the beginning either. He is still that man sometimes. We will argue and I'll scream at him and cry and run out of the house. But then he always pulls out the stops once we've made up. I've come home to first editions of my favourite books. One time, mid-argument, he put up his hand and said 'Let's stop this.' Then he made me pack a bag, took us to the airport and we flew to Iceland. Just like that. We never resolved the argument but we swam in a blue lagoon and Tom managed to use his connections to get us onto a last-minute Northern Lights tour. He held my hand through gloves while we stared up at the dancing neon sky above. 'Remember our first date,' he whispered, his breath crystallising in the air between his mouth and my ear. 'I was so in love with you, even then.'

I look down to find I've been doodling in biro on the back of my glossy magazine. Drawing spirals and hearts and patterns in blotchy ink. I've also written something.

My heart is stuck in a perpetual waiting room,
Looking at the clock,
Wondering when it'll next have an appointment with the
man I know you're capable of being.

I stare at what I've written. I wince. Then I scribble it out and retreat back into happier times.

We draw to a halt in St Pancras far too soon. I'm still lost in the memory of our holiday to Greece, and how we made love in a sandy, abandoned alcove. The sort of sex that you have to call 'making love' because there isn't a better word for it when you connect like that. I shake my head, and pull my wheelie suitcase down from the over-head compartment. My phone beeps to life, realising it's back in its own country – telling me that fact by SMS message in case I hadn't noticed myself. I also have a message from Tom. I get off the train and pull to the side, away from the crowd, letting people flock past me to customs.

I'm so in love with him in this moment that I really need this message to be the Tom I've been daydreaming about.

Bingo.

Tom: Welcome back superstar! How was the rest of your trip? X

Oh, my smile. How it stretches. He called me a superstar! I feel like one because of this message. I glow as I tap out my reply.

Tori: Just got to St Pancras now. So very tired but can't wait to see you! Where you at? X x x

A reply straight away. We have missed each other. We do miss each other. Still. This is important. This is a good sign.

Tom: Really close. I'm watching the game in Kings Cross with Sam and Declan. It's about to finish. I want to show off my superstar girlfriend. Come join us? X
Tori: Which pub? On my way x

I pick up the handle of my suitcase and I wheel my way towards him.

Month Four

Dee Harper and Nigel Tucker are in a relationship

82 likes.

Tori Bailey likes this.

★

I have a pouch.

A band of flab has been slowly building itself a little house just below my belly button. I can't fathom why. I'm not eating any more food than I usually eat. I'm not exercising any less than I usually exercise. I'm even doing sit-ups, though I hate them and never think I'm doing them right and gave myself that back spasm last year after attempting a Victoria's Secret workout on YouTube.

And yet, I have a pouch.

I grab at it when I shower. I stand naked sideways and examine it in the mirror. I spend so much time just staring at my reflection sideways on. I hold in my stomach and see my pouch lessen. I let it go and watch the pouch flop out again.

They told me this would happen.

That your metabolism slows, that you should enjoy being

young and eating what you want when you can. When I was a student I would drunkenly shove a chip butty down my face at three a.m. and yet wake up with a flat stomach that looked good in cropped tops.

Not any more.

Tori: I have a pouch.
Dee: ???
Tori: My stomach. It's grown itself a pouch. I'm so old I am now the sort of woman who needs jeans that cover their pouch.
Dee: Tor, I love you. But please shut up. I've had a fucking pouch since I was twenty-two. X x

I wince at the message from Dee. I can't tell if she's joking or actually hates me. I read it over and over again, trying on different tones of her voice in my head. Things between us have not been as OK as they could be. I can't pretend I've not seen less of her since Nigel. We haven't gone drinking once since the wedding. She's always asking me to do daytime things instead, like coffee, and walks around the park, and art galleries. 'I just think we should try to be more sophisticated,' she says, pretending it's nothing to do with wanting to spend each evening with Nigel. I also feel like I can't talk to her about Tom any more. I feel defensive now that she's all loved-up – like she'll look down on me or something.

I don't know what to do about this pouch. I'm lying in bed and I'm supposed to be preparing for a big meeting with my publisher tomorrow. But I'm grabbing at my spare flesh and jiggling it up and down. I pull it upwards into a happy face and then downwards into an unhappy face. I open the mouth of my pouch and make it talk. 'Why are you so flabby and old, Tor?' my pouch asks in a silly *Sesame Street* voice. 'Where did your youth go?' Suddenly I am inspired. I grab a sharpie and draw cartoon eyes just above my stomach. Then I manipulate my stomach into all sorts of stretched faces and take at least fifty photos of it on my phone.

Tori's *WhoTheF*ckAmI?* Official Fan Page:

To my f*ckers,

I was twenty-five when I wrote *Who The F*ck Am I?*

Thankfully, I am not twenty-five any more. Here is my proof.

I am thrilled to introduce you to my pouch. My thirties pouch. I'm calling him Herman, and he's very pleased to meet you.

At first I wasn't sure if I was a fan of Herman. Herman is a sign that my body is slowing down and chilling out and isn't in its twenties any more. Society may not approve of Herman, fashion may not make Herman-friendly clothing, but I love him. Because Herman tells me my twenties are over! Herman is a sign I've made it through to the other side.

The fact of the matter is that I'm older than a lot of you now. So many of you are still coming to my book for the first time and I love that the book still resonates with people. But I am no longer in my twenties, and I've got Herman to prove it. Let us be your spirit guides – me and Herman. Or send me photos of your own Hermans. Let's celebrate a life where we grow Hermans.

I can tell it's going to be a huge post within ten minutes. The flurry of likes, and heart emojis, and comments telling me what an inspiration I am, come in hard like a blizzard. Herman photos are being sent to me left right and centre. Someone has given their Herman eyebrows. I laugh and send out a request for a Herman with googly eyes. Within half an hour, there are thirty googly-eyed Hermans on my feed. I feel happiness fill me up from the bottom of my toes and up to my scalp. I feel giddy and good about myself and like I am an inspiration after all. Even though I didn't tell anyone that I took over fifty photos of me and Herman and picked the one where I looked prettiest. Even though I put on make-up just to take the photo. Even though I've already Googled exercises I can do to minimise Herman. Even though, when photos of Herman come in thick and fast, I feel good about myself when other women's Hermans are flabbier than mine. Even though, at my TED talk in Berlin last month, I wore control pants to try and minimise Herman. Even though, last week, when Tom grabbed Herman and said, 'this is new', I cried for an hour on the bathroom floor after he fell asleep.

Even though.

'Oh my God, we *love* Herman,' my editor, Marni, says as she walks towards me and opens her arms for an air kiss. I am never sure whether to go for one kiss, or two kisses, or a hug, or a handshake, so I let her guide me into two kisses and accidentally get some of her hair in my mouth. 'We've put Herman on the wall of our office,' she informs me.

I pat my stomach dramatically. 'Thank you from both of us.'

She roars with laughter before kissing my agent on each cheek. 'Can you come in every week, Tori? We need you.'

My publisher's office is made entirely of glass but it's still freezing cold despite the sun streaming through the windows. Air-con rolls out of invisible vents, making me wish I'd brought a jacket. 'Everyone's on the top floor.' Marni takes us through the imposing waiting room to the lifts and presses a card against the bleeper thing. I have never once figured out how these lifts work. There are six of them, and they have no buttons. Somehow the system knows through telepathy which floor you want to get to, and then assigns you your own lift. Marni and Kate, my agent, chat about a recent summer publishing party as we whoosh up to the top floor and emerge with a floor-to-ceiling view of the London skyline. I'm trying not to feel nervous. I shouldn't be nervous. My publishers love me. I've made so much money for them that sometimes I feel like I've grown udders. But, behind their welcoming air-kisses and gushing emails, there is an edge.

An edge that smells like: *Where's your next book?*

They've ordered in platters of fresh fruit and sandwiches cut into triangles. The entire room gets up as I enter and it takes five minutes for us all to kiss each other twice on each cheek. It takes a further five minutes to work out who wants what coffee and how. Everyone smiles at me. Some of the younger ones – in their thick-rimmed specs and dresses worn with Converse – are blushing and giddy. Maybe they've whispered about me coming into the office today. 'I love your book,' one of them says, instead of hello. 'I really *really* loved it.'

I smile and say 'thank you', and then I don't know what else to say.

We all sit around the table and the view really is something. I have seen so many good views since this crazy life of mine took off, but nothing beats the Thames in high summer.

'So,' Marni starts off. 'We're so excited to say that we've fixed your next book into our prime October spot. This gives us just under eighteen months.'

My agent nods. Kate likes the word 'October'. It means your publisher is going to spend money on you to get you into the pre-Christmas promotions. I smile. 'That's great. Wow. It seems so far away.'

'It will come up quickly, believe me,' Marni replies. I'm not sure if she means it to, but it sounds like a warning.

We go through the sales figures of the summer edition and I can tell by how much they're smiling that it isn't selling as well as they wanted it to.

'It's a tricky market . . . pre-orders from bookshops were high . . . the good thing though is that it's perennial . . . we can re-jacket it for paperback next year . . .' When they've run out of steam, they all turn to me with their hands clasped, grins still etched onto their faces.

'So, Kate has been saying you've had a bit of a brain storm?' Marni prompts. 'We're dying to know what your idea is.'

I look over at Kate who nods at me and smiles encouragingly. Even though Kate doesn't like the idea and said she doesn't think they'll go for it. But it's all I have. Somehow, in five whole years, I've not had one decent idea for anything positive and inspirational to write about.

I imagine I am on stage. That I'm giving one of my talks. I am a together businesswoman who knows and understands her brand and her worth and what people want. 'Well, I was thinking,' I start, 'I get so many letters and emails, every day, from people who have read *Who The Fuck Am I?* It's really changed their lives, you know?'

They nod. They know. Of course they know. They're the ones who forward me all the gushing letters on special stationery.

'So,' I say, 'I was thinking, for the follow-up book, we could collect some of the best stories? Make them into an anthology or something? I was thinking we could call it *This Is Who The Fuck I Am.* I mean, the book's all about empowerment, right? What's more empowering than celebrating my readers and the amazing choices they've made?' I am proud of that last sentence. I practised it in front of Tom last night, who said, 'Yeah, it's great. You'll do great', while also looking at his phone.

I stumble into silence and fixed grins and hands clasped tightly on top of the table.

'That's a great idea,' Marni enthuses. 'I love it.'

I wait for the 'but'. I know The But is coming. They're all looking at each other frantically while trying not to move their smiles or eyebrows.

'The thing is,' she continues, 'those books do work. They totally work. But, umm, normally we let a bit more time pass before we release them. Usually as a ten-year anniversary edition or something? It makes for great PR.'

'Oh yes, great PR.' The table nods and agrees and not one of them lets their smile drop.

'But, as *Who The Fuck Am I?* is only five years old, releasing something like this now may feel a little . . . premature? It's a great idea though!'

I bite my lip. I don't know what to say. Because this is the only idea I have. I knew it was nothing but it was all I had. I look at Kate who smiles again. We're all smiling, all of us, the whole room up here on the top floor, even though we're all secretly thinking *fuuuuuuuuuuck.*

'Oh dear,' I laugh. A fake laugh. 'I'm just going to have to think of a new book idea then, aren't I?'

'Well that's why we're all here,' Marni soothes. 'To help. We know how overwhelming it can be.' She pushes the biscuit tray over to me. I don't want a biscuit because I am worried about Herman, but I take one anyway. I hate myself for eating it the moment I've finished it.

One of the younger editorial assistants pipes up, looking

around nervously like she's asking for permission to speak. 'Umm, what motivated you to write your first book?' she asks me directly. 'Maybe we could work from there?'

'I was miserable,' I reply, staring straight at her.

'Oh, right.' She shuffles uncomfortably in her seat and the mood of the room shifts. I forget that people don't like it when you tell the truth in person. They like the truth on TV, or written down so they can read and digest it in their own time. But when you're truthful in person everyone acts like you're farting on a crowded bus while eating an egg sandwich.

'So I guess I just need to make myself really miserable again?' I do another fake laugh, to try and diffuse the belch of honesty. Everyone titters politely. I worry now about what the editorial assistant will tell her friends about me. ('Never meet your idols. She was such a bitch. She wasn't how I expected her to be.') I regain her eye contact as quickly as I can and say, 'Sorry. It's just, I really was miserable. I didn't even think it was going to be a book, I just started writing.'

I'm miserable now, I realise. *And yet I'm not writing . . .*

She blushes. 'No, *I'm* sorry!' she gushes. 'And I should've known. I mean, I've read your book so many times and you're very upfront about your misery in that *brilliant* opening chapter.'

We are now both grinning madly at each other, both insecure, thinking the other one doesn't like us, even though maybe we don't like them. That opening chapter.

Everyone always goes on about that opening chapter. When I was standing on Waterloo Bridge, broke and heartbroken (again), with my hair falling out from the stress of my internship and worried I'd got gonorrhoea after a one-night stand messaged me to say I needed to get tested. Pretty awful. Pretty miserable. Pretty traumatic. Everyone thinks they know all of it, but they don't. There is so much I didn't share. How I only weighed seven stone at the time. Or that, later that night, I drank too much vodka and pathetically took six whole ibuprofen before freaking out and ringing Dee asking if I needed my stomach pumped.

Marni leans forward, sensing the brainstorm waning. 'The thing is, Tori, your USP has always been how honest you are. So, maybe we just need to think of something you can be honest about?'

There is a collective nod. A pre-organised one. They have already discussed this before I arrived. I sit back and wait for them to tell me their idea. I already hate it, because I didn't think of it myself.

'We *loved* your Herman post, and I think one of the reasons it's done so well is that it was the first time you acknowledged you are getting older . . .' She trails off, waiting to see what my face does. I arrange it into Switzerland. 'The thing is, you're bringing in new readers every year, but a lot of your established readership is growing up with you. You were so good at putting into words what it's like to muddle through your twenties . . .'

They're all nodding – they're all looking so very earnest indeed. '. . . so we were thinking you might want to write something about entering your thirties?'

I look out of the window and see London glowing, and showing itself off in the bright sunlight. The glittering Thames looks so beautiful you forget it's a toxic spill of sludge and chemicals. I suddenly don't want to be in this room any more. I want to be outside, my body sticky from the heat. A breeze from the river lifting my hair.

I have nothing to say . . .

But I have to say something.

'Entering my thirties?' I repeat her words as they're the only words I can manage.

Marni is thrilled at my response. 'Yes!' she enthuses, like I've just punched my fist into the air, or clicked my heels in a jig. 'I mean, as a thirty-four-year-old woman myself, I would *love* to know what Tori has to say about it all.'

The intern leans over too. 'And you know your readers are just *obsessed* with you and Tom. It would be great to give them a sequel. I mean, what happened between you and the Man on the Rock?'

Kate turns to check I'm OK. I can see from the blaze of her eyes that she thinks this is a good idea. But she won't admit as much until I've given her a signal.

'I mean,' I say. 'The Man on the Rock clipped his toenails on our bed last night and got little bits of them all over our John Lewis duvet cover.'

Oh, how they laugh. I can see the fillings at the back of

their mouths. I can see their tonsils glow as the sun lights them up through these expensive windows.

'You see!' Marni says. '*This* is what we love about you, Tori. I want to know all about Tori and long-term relationships.'

I haven't said yes and I haven't said I'll do it and I haven't told them I feel dead inside. They don't notice. The table becomes a giddy self-help group of women complaining about all the gross things their boyfriends do. Some of them leave their towels on the floor, some of them fart under the duvet, some of them don't know how to wash up properly. God, aren't they awful creatures? Why do we put up with it? And then the whole conversation morphs into how I can release a book every five to ten years, discussing that particular part of adult life and how basically shit it is. We will have early thirties Tori and late thirties Tori and forties Tori and Tori through the menopause and Tori taking her Rock Boy to the fucking hospice and signing over his power of attorney. Kate cannot believe such a brilliant thing has happened. I can practically see the pound signs in her irises as she asks me what I think. This is unfathomable. I've basically just been offered a lifetime's supply of publishing deals. I'm Charlie fucking Bucket and I'm allowed entry to the factory for the rest of my life, just as long as I pretend I vaguely know what the hell I'm doing.

What the hell am I doing?

I didn't say yes. That's the important thing. That's the thing I hold on to as I emerge from the sleek building made of glass, blinking into the sunlight and turning down my agent's offer to celebrate with champagne. I didn't say yes. I have not signed a contract. I only nodded when they asked for the first three chapters and did not once mention a delivery date.

I stagger around Hay's Galleria, then find myself sitting outside City Hall, trying to regulate my breathing. I stare out at Tower Bridge and watch everyone pass by. Businessmen soaking sweat into their suits on their way to meetings; tourists posing in front of the bridge with selfie sticks; vendors selling ice creams and expensive bottles of water; joggers looking pissed off that their run alongside a major tourist destination is so crowded. Several couples with entwined hands kiss one another's cheeks while pretending their arm isn't outstretched with their phone at the end of it, taking a photo.

Are you happy? I wonder about each and every single one of them. *Are you happy?*

My phone vibrates in my hand and tells me it is Tom.

Tom: Hey, how did the big meeting go?

I don't know how to reply. If I tell him I'm not happy, he will ask why. And then, when I explain, he won't understand why I'm sad. So he will do that thing where he *pretends* he is being sympathetic, but I can sense that, underneath, he thinks I'm being a giant brat. Therefore I'll get mad at him. That anger will then seep into something that happens the following week, when I've realised I can't bury it any longer.

We will have a spat about something insignificant, like what time-slot to get the groceries delivered, and I'll end up yelling *'I'M MAD AT YOU FOR NOT BEING SUPPORTIVE ABOUT MY MEETING.'* And first he'll ask, *'what meeting?'* because so much time has passed. And then, when I explain, he will think I'm crazy for bringing up something that happened over a week ago. And then *he'll* be angry at *me* because he *was* supportive. And then I'll have to try to explain how I know he *thought* he was being supportive but actually I could tell he didn't mean it, and that's actually worse. Then he'll accuse me of putting him in situations where he can never win. Then he'll make that face – the one where I know I've pushed things too far and need to be careful – and I'll say sorry because I can't handle the pure hatred in his eyes. And Tom won't apologise back because he won't think he's done anything wrong. He'll punish me for ever having said anything in the first place. The punishment will include not touching me, or hugging me, or kissing me, but also insisting he is 'not angry' and 'nothing is wrong' for about two weeks until, finally, I have to apologise for being such a terrible person.

So I write:

Tori: It went really well. They want me to write a book a decade essentially until I die! x

Tom: WOW! OMG Gorgeous. That's amazing. I'm so proud of you. X

I take another deep breath and look out at the city skyline. If I can lose myself in this day and how pretty it is, then that is happiness. A fleeting moment. We may all die tomorrow anyway. Most people spend their whole lives dreaming of coming to London. Most people dream of getting books published. Most people dream of having partners at the end of the phone, asking them how important meetings go.

I find sentences pushing their way into my brain – demanding to be listened to. Words arranging themselves into order; feelings tapping me on the shoulder and begging to be understood. My mind is cluttered and busy and I know it won't relax until I let them out. I take a deep breath, rummage in my handbag for the decorative notepad I took to the meeting, and I write:

You can do just as much damage by not saying anything as you can by saying something.

I look down at the words, reading them back under my breath. I feel . . . cleaner than I did before. Like I've just punched an air hole in my own life.

Then I message Dee.

Tori: Had a . . . weird meeting with my publishers. Can we meet tonight and get drunk? It feels like it's been months.

She's at school so doesn't reply until gone four. I'm back at my flat when my phone buzzes. I spent the afternoon lying on my stomach and going through every single tagged photo of myself to try to work out what my life looks like from the outside. I pretend in my head that I've only just added myself as a friend, and try to see what my initial impressions are – of how good my life looks, and how pretty I am, objectively.

Dee: Aww, sorry you had a shit day. It would be nice to have a proper catch-up. Nigel is out at some summer work thing. Dinner?

★

'Have a great time with Dee, sweetheart.' Tom kisses the top of my forehead as I leave. I think, *that's how adults kiss children, not lovers kiss lovers.* But it's still a kiss so I'm taking it.

'What you up to tonight?' I ask him, swinging my handbag onto my shoulder and hoping no one notices it doesn't quite match my sandals.

'I might just take a bath.'

'In this weather?' I am already mad at him because I know he'll use my posh lotion as bubble bath, but I can't remind him not to because he'll say I'm nagging.

'It's never too hot for a bath.' He kisses my forehead again. 'Don't eat too many dough balls now.'

London in summer is hard. Everyone is out and about and loud and brash and drunk and sunburnt and noisy. People spill onto the pavements outside pubs and drink pink cider poured over pint glasses of ice. I take a shortcut through the park and it's even more in your face. There are groups playing frisbee and football, and the thudding of tennis balls being hit around the court where long lines of people wait for their chance to play. I'm exhausted by the time I get to Brixton. And yet Brixton is more rammed and noisy and the heat feels even hotter here. I'm wilting and beyond dewy by the time I reach the cool air-conditioning of Pizza Express. It's mostly empty. Nobody wants to tag themselves into a chain restaurant on a day like today – it is not the done thing.

Dee surprises me by already being here. She smiles and waves as I fluster my way across the marble floor.

'I'm sweating from places I didn't even know it was scientifically possible to sweat from,' I announce.

She wrinkles her nose. 'Like where?'

'My knee-pits. And my vagina mainly. I'm scared my vagina is actually going to leave a sweat smudge on my skirt.'

'It takes a lot to put me off the thought of dough balls,' Dee says, 'but somehow you've managed.'

I slide my way onto the hard wooden chair and pick up the cardboard triangle announcing the summer specials. The waitress comes over and asks if I'd like a drink. 'Yes. Wine! Wine?' I ask over to Dee.

She points to her bottle of sparkling mineral water. 'I'm so dehydrated. I'll stick to this for now.'

'Oh,' I say. I turn to the waitress. 'Umm, OK then. I'll just have a large glass of, umm, rosé, please.'

We're left with our menus, which I don't need to look at because I always order exactly the same thing – the less-than-five-hundred-calories vegetarian *Leggera*. But I wait while Dee pores over hers. She looks a bit different. She's holding herself better, her skin is amazing. I'm about to ask her what cream she's using but remember the answer is probably just: 'I'm happy and in love and having loads of great sex.' Unfortunately you can't buy that and rub it on your face. Not even from Crème de la Mer.

'What you getting?' I ask. 'Have I really put you off the dough balls?'

'Of course I'm still getting dough balls.'

The waitress returns with my wine and I try not to gulp it. Instead I take lots of tiny, frantic sips which still drains half the glass in a small amount of time. She asks if we're ready and we say yes and order. Once she's gone, I'm about to launch into today's meeting when—

'There's something I need to tell you,' Dee says. She is shaking. Her hands are wobbling her glass of carbonated water.

'Rii-iight . . .' I wrack my brains to think what it might be. I arrange my face in the most neutral half-smile I can in preparation. *Oh God. I know what it is, actually. She'll be moving in with Nigel. Of course she will be. And now I'm going to have to pretend it's not too soon.* 'So . . . ?'

She tucks a strand of flaming hair behind her ear. 'I'm pregnant, Tor.'

. . .

. . .

. . .

The dough balls are brought over. Arranged as a moat around the castle of garlic flavoured butter. The waitress, sensing something's up, just plops them down and leaves. 'Oh my *God*,' I say. 'Congratulations!' Dee's crying and I leap up and go and hug her. 'What's wrong? Are you OK?'

She nods and lets me pat her and I hug her again and as I hug her I cannot believe it. I cannot believe. I cannot.

'I'm good. Yes, I'm really happy. I mean, of *course* it was a surprise.' She is talking and I have a smile so etched on my mouth I may as well have put it there with a scalpel. I can't not smile. I cannot let her see what I'm feeling on the inside. Because what I'm feeling on the inside is a free fall into total despair. She is explaining about how the condom split at the wedding, and how she took the morning-after pill but obviously it didn't work. Now she's talking about how good her school is being about it, dropping in that she's already 'practically' moved in with Nigel anyway, despite having a month left on her tenancy contract.

It's so obvious now. So, so obvious. Why we've always met for coffee, not wine. Why her frame has swollen, her rib cage already slightly expanded. Why her skin is looking this good. How could I not have noticed?

'When are you due?' I manage to ask. Because I know what questions to ask when your friends go to the other side of the wall. I have been here before. I know the lingo.

'December,' she admits sheepishly. And the sheepishness is because, when I do the maths, I figure out she's three months gone. *Three months. Three months and she's not told me.*

'Sorry I've not told you,' she says, reading my chaotic mind. She picks up a dough ball and splurges it into the bowl of butter. It oozes around the sides and I'm mesmerised by the sight of Dee eating a dough ball because now she is pregnant Dee eating a dough ball.

Pregnant Dee.

Dee is pregnant.

She chews and swallows and blushes slightly. There is a gap between us now. A space that will grow and grow because Dee's on the other side of the wall. She can still see me and talk to me and we can pretend the wall is not there, but it is. It's been erected in only minutes. Rushed construction workers running out and putting it up while the dough balls were being arranged onto a plate in a circle.

'Tor,' she says. 'I have to say, I've been bricking it about telling you.'

'What?! *Why?*' My mouth is open and my eyes are innocent.

Her voice catches in her throat. 'It's just . . . what I love about our friendship is we've always been honest with each other, and I know how you feel about this sort of thing. I know things aren't great with you and Tom . . .'

There's a pang of pain, like she's just burnt me accidentally with the end of a lit cigarette. *How dare she.* How *dare* she mention Tom when her belly is swelling with socially-acceptable happiness. How *dare* she make that dig. Now.

'Tom and I are *fine*,' I find my voice saying. 'We're in a really good place actually. We talked everything through after the strip-club fiasco last month and it's just what we needed.'

The lie adds another layer of bricks to the wall.

'Aww, that's great to hear! You see! Maybe you'll get pregnant too soon and then we can be bump buddies together.'

Her lie adds a few more centimetres.

'I don't know about that. But I'm really happy for you, Dee, seriously. Shocked as hell, but happy for you.'

She shakes her head, smiling. 'I'm so stupid to think you wouldn't be. Amy told me you'd be great about it.'

I was in the process of trying a dough ball but it drops to my plate. 'Amy knows?' I ask it lightly, casually. I ask it with sugar in my spit. When I want to scream, 'AMY KNOWS!?' Amy was on our corridor in university and Dee and I supposedly hate her. We've ripped it out of her mercifully since she's had two children. Amy updated everyone online about every single day of her pregnancy. Both of them. Like the second baby might grow a bit differently. You couldn't even ignore her if you wanted to. She sent them to our group uni chat too. 'Today my baby is the size of a pea.' 'Today my baby grew a lung.' 'Today my baby can wave its arm around the womb.'

Dee and I had our own private chat going. 'Today I'm worried that Mummy will have no respect for my privacy when I'm born.' 'Today I'm worried Mummy will live-tweet my birth.' 'Today I'm struggling to socialise with other foetuses because I have an overinflated sense of self.'

'She really has been great,' Dee says, wiping away those memories, storing them in a locked box somewhere now her opinion of Amy has changed because she needs it to. 'I had the *worst* morning sickness, Tor. And it's so awful because you can't tell anyone why you're being so useless and exhausted. It *killed* me every time you asked me out for wine.'

I sip at my wine subconsciously. *This wine is all I have left. This is all I have over you now. The fact I can drink wine.*

'So, yes, it was really useful to have Amy to talk to about it. I mean, I know she's sometimes . . . you know . . . but I've been so grateful to her, to be honest. Oh God, and Nigel and Nick get on *so* well. They came round for dinner last week and it was like instant bromance.'

She had them round for dinner. She had them round for dinner. She told Amy she was pregnant and not me because I don't have children and Amy does and she had them round for dinner.

My smile is so wide I'm surprised it's not ripping. 'That's great,' I keep repeating. 'That's great.'

Dee is buoyed by my response and wants to talk about all of it now she is finally able to and I've handled it OK and everything. 'And, don't worry . . .' she reaches over and takes one of my dough balls as I've not touched them.

I hope you get fat, I think, then I blink that horrible thought away, hating myself for thinking it.

'. . . I'm not going to be pregnant like Amy. You will *not* be getting scans posted online.' She smiles warmly. 'I'm still me, Tor. And there is *so* much bullshit around being pregnant that you wouldn't even *believe*. I need you here to listen to me whinge about it.'

I can drink wine, and I am thinner than most of them. That's two things. Two things that people can envy about me. I will not order dessert and I'll really start on those sit-ups to get rid of Herman, and if I work hard for a month, I'll still have August to go around in crop tops and make people realise I'm perfectly OK and I'm successful and in control of my life because I have abs.

Dee launches into her whinging right away, like she's been saving it all up. As she probably has. Moaning about how sick she was. About how scared she was to tell her headteacher. About how physically tiring it is. About how Nigel's parents' first response was, 'that's a bit soon'. About how she's already been to a pregnancy yoga class and hated everyone there because they already had a birth plan. I nod and look annoyed when I'm supposed to, and sympathetic when I'm supposed to.

The pizzas come. I only eat half of mine, and Dee finishes it greedily. A family comes in, dragging two overtired and hot children who smash their cutlery against the marble tables and scream 'I DON'T LIKE PIZZA.' Only months ago, Dee and I would've looked at one another and said,

'I'm never having children.' Now, she just watches them nervously.

'Oh God, my kids won't be like that will they, Tor?'

'Of course not,' I reassure her, even though they probably will be.

However, it is Dee, and I do love her. Tiny granules of happiness for her manage to unleash inside me, giving me the strength to ask all the right questions. How is Nigel taking it? Oh, he's thrilled. Especially as he's almost forty. Is he being supportive? Oh, so supportive. He acted like my servant through the morning sickness, bringing me stacks of toast with marmite. Remember that for when it's your turn, Tor. Marmite is God. Have you had your scan yet? Oh yes, yesterday. And she gets out the photo and I look at it and squeal even though I can't make out a baby in the photo. Have you had any cravings? *Nachos!?* Wow that's hilarious. Did you hear that Amy ate chalk? Have you thought about whether you want a boy or a girl? Oh yes, of course more than anything you just want it to be healthy. But yes, of course a girl. Because we're girls. But boys are cute too, and they're easier when they come to be teenagers. What sort of pregnant do you think you'll get? A little bump? Fat all over? We laugh at all the options. We bring up Kim Kardashian's pregnancy. Dee's pudding is finished and she glows brighter.

The bill comes and I'm saying I'll pay because 'CONGRATULATIONS!' before she brings up my meeting. 'Oh my God, so I've totally dominated,' she says. 'I've not even asked how *you're* doing?'

'Dude, you're pregnant. You've won life-news top trumps today.'

She laughs and pops a mint imperial into her mouth. 'Yes, but as I told you, I don't want to be one of *those* parents. I care about your life. What happened at this meeting?'

It's funny how she already thinks there are different types of people who have kids. I guess that's the sort of thought you have when you're on that side of the wall. Oh, I'm not '*that*' kind of mum, I'm '*this*' kind of mum. They find little subsections and pick the one that most makes them feel the best and therefore it's fine, and they tell all their friends who don't have children how different they are from the other mums. But, on my side of the wall, there are only two categories: people who have children and people who don't. There aren't any subsections for the people who do. They just do, and that's everything to them and their life is changed forever and they're not as much fun any more and won't ever be again. Unless you cross the wall. Then they welcome you with open arms like Amy did. *Oh we always knew you were one of us,* they think.

'It's fine, I was just being dramatic. You know me,' I say.

Dee is not convinced. 'Come on. What happened? Tor, *please*. I'm still me.'

But I don't want to tell her. I don't want to accept weakness when I already feel so weak. I don't want her to go home to Nigel and he'll ask how dinner went and he'll rub her slightly swollen stomach as she says, 'Oh I do worry about Tor.'

I wince as the children drop a knife on the floor behind us, sending a loud clang rippling through the restaurant. 'They just want me to write my next book about turning thirty and all the shit that comes with it.'

'But Tor, that's a great idea. You'd make it hilarious! I would *so* want to read that book.'

'Aww, thank you. I don't know. Maybe the idea will grow on me.'

She doesn't push it and she doesn't really ask for more information. That's the only thing that's different already. She didn't see past my veneer of 'it's all OK'. When she probably would've done in the past. Like a homing missile, she would have followed me round and round, burrowing into me until I admitted all my fears and she could help me with them.

But I guess she has more on now. She cannot be blamed. It's not fair to set people tests and then get annoyed when they fail them.

Brixton is thumping and sweaty when we walk back out into it. Dee explains how vulnerable you feel when you're pregnant and you have to walk through crowds. I guess I've never thought about it before but it makes sense. I walk her to her bus stop, making sure no one bumps into her stomach. She beams at me for the gesture and hugs me so hard when her bus arrives. 'We should totally do dinner soon, the four of us.'

'That would be great.'

Another hug, but the queue to get on the bus is moving along. It's packed and I'm worried she won't get a seat, but she reaches into her bag and removes a small 'Baby on Board' badge. She nervously attaches it to her dress. 'I know,' she says, seeing my expression. 'The first time I put it on I had an existential crisis.'

I watch her get on board and point to her badge and tell someone off until she gets a seat. She gives me a thumbs-up as the bus rumbles off in a fug of exhaust fumes and hissing breaks.

I'm left in the throng of Brixton, alongside all the other people in London who are not ready for what Dee is doing and are instead outside being young and delaying all the thinking about that by tagging themselves into artisan beer houses. I stand and watch the world go by. It's always so chaotic here. The length of pavement from the tube station to the Ritzy cinema is, I swear, the busiest part of London. It's impossible to walk from one to the other without your body accidentally brushing up against at least ten people you will never see again. It's so busy and there are so many people here, drunk and happy from the sunshine and there really are so many of them.

It's a scientific impossibility surely, then . . . that I am capable of feeling this lonely?

I walk back through the park, re-treading the way I came, and yet everything has changed since I was last here. I walk back to my life. My life with Tom. If Dee wasn't pregnant we would've gone on to a wine bar, and then probably another one. I would've come back giddy and light and unburdened and fancy-free and Tom would've been glad to have the flat to himself for an evening. But Dee is pregnant, so I'm walking home at 8.30p.m. The London skyline glimmers in the distance as I reach the top of the hill and pass the tennis courts. The queue has died down and I stop a moment and watch people play. An aggressive male duo thwack the ball back and forth like they're in Wimbledon, not allowing the one remaining couple in the queue to have a turn. I think about happiness and how it's possible to be happy for someone even though their happiness makes you feel sad for yourself. I feel like we need a word for this feeling. There probably is, in Dutch or something. That's a really good idea for my next fan page post actually, but I won't be able to write it for a few days. I can't have Dee thinking it's about her. Even though it is.

When I get in, the flat is quiet apart from the calm voices of *Desert Island Discs* echoing out of the bathroom. 'I'm home!' I call, as Cat greets my ankles. I make my way to the kitchen to decant the pint of milk I picked up from the corner shop. Cat weaves around my legs, almost tripping me, nagging me for food I know she doesn't need. I lose it for a moment. 'FUCK *OFF!*' I yell at Cat, who ignores me, and continues to wind around my legs. I get an urge to kick her.

'Tor?' Tom's voice drifts under the bathroom door. 'That you?'

Feeling guilty, I pour out loads of cat food to compensate for yelling at her. The moment it is in the bowl, she stares at it, unimpressed, and pads off.

'No, it's your other girlfriend!' I call back. He doesn't reply or laugh. Maybe he didn't hear me over the podcast. I stand by the bathroom door for a moment, trying to get myself together before I go in. I do not want Tom to sense my mood, and he's very adept at sensing my mood.

Breathe in, breathe out. In and out.

I push open the door.

I smile.

He's made himself quite the sanctuary in here. He's lit my candles, and poured in my lotion like I knew he would. He looks so cute I don't even mind. The water laps at the rim. His dark hair is all matted with soap; a lazy smile plays on his face. He could be five years old. Well, apart from the gut and the bald patch that we're not ever allowed to bring up, not even as a joke. The love rushes in again. I stand there, arms crossed, grinning at him. He opens his eyes, sensing my presence, or maybe just the draught from the door.

'Hey Tor.' His voice is throaty and relaxed. 'Good time with Dee?'

'Yes.' I want to touch his skin. I want to feel close to him. *God I love him, I love him so much sometimes.* I point to the bath with a tilt of my head. 'Room for one more?'

His eyes squint as he grins. 'Of course. As long as you take the tap end.'

'I always have to go at the tap end.'

'You snooze you lose, sister.'

I step out of my clothes, hoping that he is watching and enjoying me doing so. I take care to wriggle out of my dress slinkily, rather than just tugging it over my head. I stand in my underwear for longer than I should, to give him extra time to appreciate my body. My body that only he gets to touch. That he rarely touches, even though I have sacrificed my entitlement to get touched by other people to be with him. But, when I look down, he's fiddling with his phone to turn off his podcast.

Some water spills onto the bathmat as I gently lower myself between Tom's legs, giving each section of my body time to get used to the hot temperature. I tuck myself between the corner of the bath and the tap and smile over at Tom. He smiles back, his eyes almost half-closed again. My newly cut-back-in fringe is already sticking to my forehead with sweat so I slick it back with my wet hands. You see, this is cute. Isn't this cute? Aren't we cute? We're still a cute couple. We have baths together, like couples do. There's hardly enough room for us though. I have to lean backwards and spread my legs over Tom's chest to fit under the water. Our genitals brush. We only need to re-angle ourselves, and Tom would need to get an erection, and then we could be one of those couples who have sex in the bath. Who get water everywhere and trash the bathroom and gasp into each other's wet shoulders. But Tom doesn't have an erection and now his eyes are completely closed. So I try to relax too, thinking, *See! This is intimate. We can still be intimate.*

Tom opens his eyes and grins at me, his gaze falling over my body. He reaches over and pokes one of my soft nipples with his finger. 'Boobies,' he says childishly.

'Tom!' I cross my arms over myself as he giggles like a schoolboy. 'Seriously Tom, you're thirty-four years of age.'

He wrinkles his nose. He stops laughing. 'For fuck's sake, Tori! Why do you always have to bring up how old we are? I *know* how old I am.'

My mouth falls open and I almost swallow the soapy bath water. 'Tom, you just poked my breast and yelled "boobies" like an actual child.'

'OK, fair point.' He splashes me playfully, but his sudden anger has made my skin itch. Sometimes I feel that he hates me. That his hatred bubbles under the surface like a simmering pot of toxic stew. Last week, after we argued in the kitchen about how to wash up properly, I even *said*, 'Sometimes I actually think you hate me'. He didn't even deny it. He just laughed. *Laughed.* But we're having a bath, like cute couples do. And, to be honest with you, right now this man is all I have left. Dee is pregnant. Everyone is pregnant or married or married and with children. Tom and I will get there too, I'm sure we will. He won't be able to hate me if I give him a child, surely?

It takes me ten minutes to build up the courage to say it. I feel my heart pounding with fear as I open my mouth.

'So, Dee's pregnant.' I don't look at him as I tell him. I

play with the bubbles, cupping them in my hands. I feel his entire body stiffen in the water.

'Woah.'

'Yeah, I know. I'm pretty shocked too.' I pour the foam back onto the surface of the water and look up at him. He's arranged his face into a careful display of impassive. 'I mean, she's only just met Nigel,' I say. 'I don't know how they think this is a good idea. She doesn't know him at all. I mean, you're not supposed to make any major life decisions with a partner until you've been together at least two years, are you?'

Tom hardly shakes his head. His eyebrows are furrowed.

'I mean, remember what *we* were like in the first two years? We were so loved up, but, like, I didn't know you. You didn't know me. Not really. I mean, if you and me ever decide to have kids, we'll really know what we're letting ourselves in for, won't we? But Dee has no idea what Nigel's really like. No idea. None.' The silence roars loudly between my ears. I plunge my hands back into the water and scoop up the remaining bubbles that have gone flat and scummy. I pour them from palm to palm until they are nothing.

'Are *you* going to want to have children now?' Tom finally asks. 'Just because Dee is?'

It takes me three whole blinks before I feel capable of replying. Three whole blinks to push down the anger that rises in my body, the anger that makes me want to smash my hands down in the bath and explode water over him like shrapnel. Three blinks to push away the following comebacks, comebacks that arrive with a wise, authoritarian voice that I'm too scared to listen to because I don't want to upset him: *Maybe I want children because that's a normal thing to want. Maybe I want children because we've been together six years and own a flat together and it should be OK to talk about having children without being labelled as some needy freak. Maybe I am capable of feeling sad and jealous and confused about Dee without getting pregnant as some reflex kick-back. What the fucking fuck is wrong with you? I swear something is seriously wrong with you. I swear this isn't me. It can't all be me. I swear, I swear.*

'Of course not,' I manage.

'Good,' Tom replies.

The air crackles between us, so much so that I'm surprised we don't get electrocuted in this water. There's a mewing at the door. Cat has decided she wants to come in. We both watch as she manages to get her paw into a gap and use that to push the door open. She announces her arrival with a loud *meow*.

'Hello Cat,' I laugh. Tom's smile is back and wide and he's looking at Cat with so much love. She parades up and down the bath mat, purring. Then, with another *meow*, she leaps up onto the bath rim. She pushes one paw into the water, before leaping into the air and scrambling out of the bathroom. The water swirls as we laugh together at Cat. Cat has, once again, brought us back from the relationship precipice.

Tom's head falls back, his smile lazy again. We are silent

apart from the sloshing of water. There are so many things I want to say – bang banging at the door to my mouth, demanding to be let through. But I do not have the energy to fight with Tom, not today. Not when we've only just made up from the last one.

The water has cooled down and is now just warm rather than hot – it's melting away my stress and shock at Dee. I'm beginning to digest this new reality. Breaking it into bite-sized chunks and dissolving it into my future, piece by piece. OK, so she's going to have a child, but she's still Dee. She told me she *hated* it when Nigel put them as 'in a relationship' online. She *did* ask about my day. Her kid will probably be cute and bonkers. And Tom and I will catch up soon enough, and then our children can be friends and hang out after school.

I look at Tom's naked body. How his leg hair expands in the water. At the muscles in his arms; the scar on his thigh from a childhood accident. His penis floats in the water like a lost sea turtle. We're still essentially touching genital-to-genital. Without really thinking, I reach over and lightly stroke his penis underwater, seeing if it responds.

It doesn't. And yet I don't let go.

I lightly grip my hand around it and pump it ever so slightly, like I'm doing it absent-mindedly. I reach out with my other hand and gently tickle the wrinkled conkers of his ball sack. But he's not getting hard and I'm already seeing this failing. His penis floats flaccidly between my loosening fingers. Tom opens his eyes and smiles then firmly pushes my hands off his penis. 'Mmm, that was nice,' he murmurs as he rejects my touch.

The humiliation is instant.

There's the noise of thousands of water droplets rushing towards gravity as Tom stands up and gets out of the bath. He takes half the bathwater with him so it hardly even covers my 'boobies'. 'I'll let you enjoy the bath to yourself a bit,' he says. Like he is kind. Like he didn't just push my hands off his body. Like he wasn't lying just a second ago when he said 'that was nice' – because if it was nice he wouldn't have pushed me off him. I cannot cry until he has left the room. And, even then, I cannot cry in a way that it shows. Crying is even unsexier than whatever it is that I just did wrong. You can't fancy a woman who is crying. I tip my head back so the tears fall around innocent, hideable, parts of my face.

And I get the feeling that Tom isn't even thinking about what just happened.

Month Five

Excerpt from *Who The F*ck Am I?*

What nobody tells you about your twenties is that you lose the methods with which to measure who you are, and how well you're doing. That's what causes so many of the problems. Think about it. From when you're born until you're twenty-one, you've always been doing pretty much the very same thing as everyone around you. The measurements of success are pretty straightforward. *What grades did you get in your exams? A or B or C or D? Have you been fingered yet? Have you started your period? Have you got a boyfriend yet? Or even a best friend?* And, yeah, you may've whinged about 'peer pressure' at the time, but at least you knew what the fuck you were supposed to be doing!

But your early twenties come and then you're all set free on your own gusts of wind. What *is* success? How do you know if you're doing well? Yes, you may have a job and it pays really well and you're earning more than your friends, but you hate it and cry in the loo. Or you *love* your job and you know it's leading somewhere, but you're so broke you're stealing bog paper from the office toilets. Or you're in a relationship and trying to play house but looking at all your single friends screwing their brains out thinking *I should be doing that.* Whereas your single friends spend Sundays alone and hung-over and wish – just wish – they had someone to binge-watch something with. Not enough credit is given to what a mindfuck your twenties are. I just want to be in my thirties! I want to have all that self-belief I've heard is coming my way. I want to know what happens! At least in your thirties you know what happens. That's got to be better than this, right?

★

Extract from Tori's first draft of *What The F*ck Now?*

Hi, my name is Tori and I'm a fucking moron.

I hate the Tori who wrote about her twenties. I hate the Tori who thought her thirties would be brilliant. I WANT MY TWENTIES BACK, OK? Why the fuck did I ever whinge about them?

Oh, yes, of course it's confusing and scary and your flat is shit and everyone seems to be having a better time than you. But you are free. You are so free. And every decision doesn't have massive life-changing consequences. Your boyfriend is a little bit crap? Doesn't matter! You're not going to marry him, are you? Job not great? That's all right! You can still shake the etch-a-sketch and start all over again. Everyone's sporadically honest about how sad they are. You all get pissed together and take turns to cry in the gutter about how lost you feel. Yeah you lose a few cool points for admitting you've messed things up, but you all mess up. It's just a case of whose turn it is.

But in your thirties it's all game face.

'Yes, I'm so happy! Look how happy I am! Look at this huge milestone I've achieved! I'm not going to admit to you how terrified and trapped I feel!' Because, in your thirties, the stakes suddenly get so high. You make decisions that are hard to get out of. So you pretend they're the right ones. Your friends suddenly marry people they've only known a year and buy houses in areas that they always swore they wouldn't and start spouting off shit about school catchment areas. And your eyebrows are raised and you're thinking 'Are you happy? Really? *Really?*' But they won't break. They can't. They've paid estate agents' fees and do you have any idea how much estate agents' fees cost? Nobody will back down. Somehow the gusts of wind we rode on in our twenties have landed us somewhere and we have to make this somewhere work. Because you can't turn back the clock. It's too late now to figure out whether

you're on the right gust or not. And you
don't want people to know you're so stuck,
and so scared and think it's too late to
get yourself out of this situation. You
don't want to fail when everyone else is
supposedly thriving. And, you are happy,
right? Sometimes you're happy, anyway. And
isn't that what happiness is? Fleeting
moments, rather than a permanent state of
euphoria. And as long as it looks OK on
the outside who cares, right? And, you're
confident in who you are now. That is
right. That is the one pay-off you don't
want to exchange for your twenties. But
that sometimes makes it worse because you
know who you are and you know this is
wrong and yet you're doing it anyway and
fucking hell Tor, what the fuck are you
writing? You're so unhappy Tor. You are so
fucking shitting unhappy. WHY AREN'T YOU
DOING ANYTHING ABOUT THIS TOR? WHY WON'T
YOU LEAVE TOM? YOU NEED TO LEAVE TOM. YOU
KNOW YOU DO, SO WHY THE FUCK AREN'T YOU
LEAVING? WHERE THE FUCKING FUCK IS YOUR
FUCKING AGENCY YOU FUCKING SCARED MESS?
HTleah;eshlsruhgshg;osnjkrsbgjkbg;ogn;o

★

Jessica Thornton has posted a picture

DATE NIGHT for me and The Hubby. My man's taking me out for dinner #MarriedLife #Blessed #HubbyDiaries

12 people like this

*

Claire Rodgers has posted a picture

Couples selfie alert! I call this one #DeathByTableFavours

8 people like this

Comments:

Amy Price: OMG – I cannot WAIT for your wedding guys! You two are soooooo cute #goals

*

Amy Price has posted a picture

Saturday night in with the fam #Blessed #Takeaway #FamilyLife #MarriedLife #ILoveMyFamily #SaturdayNightIn #FeelingGood #Breastfeeding #DogsOfInstagram #Weekend #GymTomorrow #LuckiestGirlAlive #BeStrong #Mother #Wife #Peace #Love

★

'Will you take my picture?' I hold out my phone to Tom and try not to notice the flicker of judgement on his face. I walk away from him, to ensure there's enough space between us for a good full-length shot. I have not done all these squats and sit-ups for nothing you know. Herman has left the building. I stand sideways in the mirror each morning and feel good at how flat my stomach is.

'Make sure you get St Paul's in the background,' I instruct. There's another flicker there. He doesn't even try to hide it. I smile and turn my good side towards the phone and bend one leg to make myself look even skinnier.

'Smile then.' Tom presses his thumb to the screen then

hands the phone back. I grab at it to inspect his efforts. He's not framed it properly, cutting off my legs, which pisses me off because I want people to think I have good legs in this dress.

'All right?' he asks. 'Come on, there's a queue.'

South Bank heaves with tourists and more tourists enjoying the sunshine. It's one of those days where London has never been so beautiful and yet it's ruined by how many people are crammed into it. A line of people wait patiently for Tom and me to move along so they can have their photo taken here. It's the best spot on this part of the Thames. You can get both St Paul's and the Walkie-Talkie in the background.

'Let's get a photo of us,' I suggest. We've not had a photo taken together in so long.

'Nah, come on. People are waiting.'

'Just one!' I'm already lifting up my arm and swapping sides with Tom so my good side is showing. I aim the camera down at us so it's more flattering and I smile and look proud to have this man on my arm. 'See, that wasn't so painful.'

Tom's already leading me away by the arm as I check how the photo came out. I judder to a halt. This angle has made my forehead look *huge*, even with my new fringe. And I swear my nose isn't normally that nostrilly. On top of that, Tom isn't smiling. Tom's face isn't doing anything. He's just staring into the camera lens like he's dead inside.

'Tom! You're not smiling,' I complain, feeling rejected

and stung. Tom is hardly listening because he's checking his phone.

'Come on,' he pulls my arm again to the point it almost hurts and slips his phone back into his pocket. 'We're going to be late.'

We dodge through the throngs of people who aren't in as much hurry as we are. They swarm in clusters of carefree happiness. There's a pop-up gin bar with giant novelty chairs made out of shrubbery – because this is London so why not? There's a queue of people waiting to get a photo taken on them, cradling their gin in their hands, trying not to drink it before they get their turn. I wonder when liking gin became a personality trait. And how that paved the way for liking Prosecco to become a personality trait. I want to loiter at the second-hand bookstore under the bridge but Tom pulls me along and I pretend this is funny, even though it feels like he's pulling my shoulder out of its socket. 'What's the rush?' I giggle.

'I don't want us to lose our fucking table,' Tom snaps back.

His *'fucking'* is a verbal warning and I immediately stop being playful. But I can't take it lying down, so I join in the *we-must-get-there-now* game. I pick up pace and storm ahead, pushing people out the way, dodging and weaving through all these humans having a nicer evening than me. When I hit a child with my handbag and don't even apologise, Tom looks at me in disgust.

'What's going on?' he asks. Oh, how he hates me right now. I can visibly see it.

'Nothing!' I shrug. 'I just thought *you* were in a rush to get there?'

He sighs and you could fit the universe in the space of it. We walk the rest of the way in a terse silence that I'm sure he thinks is my fault but I know for sure is his. This is what I think as I walk alongside the love of my life in silence:

Leave him. The wise voice says. *You have to leave him. Why aren't you leaving him? Tori, this isn't going to work out. You must leave him. You are so unhappy.*

We are here. At the little tucked-away French bistro Nigel recommended. Dee and Nigel stand and wave to show us where their table is. I can see Tom approves of the place. It's got high stone-ceilings that rumble as trains pass overhead. He's looking around and nodding slightly.

Leave him. Leave him. Leave him.

We collide with the happy couple and Tom's charm switches on. 'Dee! You're actually glowing. I never knew that happened in real life.' He kisses both of her cheeks, then turns to Nigel and shakes his hand with a strong grip. 'Congratulations, man. And nice to meet you, I'm Tom.'

They both unfurl like photosynthesising flowers under his charm. I've forgotten what it feels like when he's the lighthouse and he puts his beam onto you full whack. I never get his beam any more. He saves his charm for others, but it's a potent force – I'm squinting under the glare of it just by watching him. I grab Dee's engorged stomach and squeal and act delighted when, actually, the sight of it makes me feel weird and surreal. I tell her how good she looks and ask how pregnancy is and say and ask all the things you're supposed to say and ask.

We settle down, screeching our chairs back under the table. I order a bottle of wine the moment the waiter turns up. 'A bottle of Merlot please and three glasses.'

'Four glasses!' Dee pipes up.

I do not know what to say to that, but I sense the table stiffen. Even the waiter looks at her stomach and raises an eyebrow.

'Four glasses,' she repeats.

A touch of frost has fallen when we return our attention to the menus and ask one another if we're getting starters. Dee, never one to allow frost to develop anywhere, says, 'I'm only going to have a trickle. You're allowed a trickle for fuck's sake.'

I'm not sure who she's saying it to. 'Of course!' I jump in. Tom just shrugs. I'd be surprised if he knew even one thing about being pregnant.

Nigel laughs, showing off a mouth made mainly from fillings. 'Of course you can, gorgeous. Nobody says you aren't.'

'Yes they do,' Dee shoots back. 'You have no idea what it's like. I had a trickle last week and someone actually came over to me to tell me I was a bad mother. I've got strangers telling me what I can and can't eat. People are asking me about my sleep patterns and what vitamins I'm taking. I'm not allowed to even carry a shopping bag without some do-gooding meddling twat snatching it off me and telling me it's bad to carry it.'

'Isn't she brilliant?' Nigel asks us, bringing Dee in to kiss the top of her head. 'Isn't she just the best?'

Dee emerges from his armpit blushing and intoxicated by the compliment. 'It's true though,' she protests. 'Tori, you have no idea how awful it is.'

Because you're not telling me, I think. *Because this is the first time you've told me any of this.*

I scan the menu and panic about the clear lack of vegetarian options. Why do French people hate vegetarians so very much? How are they not all constipated with their refusal to ever eat roughage? French women are all so slim, yet, whenever I come home from a trip to Paris, my stomach resembles that constipation advert where she keeps tipping food into her handbag.

Tom leans over. 'You OK with this menu?' he whispers. 'Is there anything you can have?'

I smile at him and grab his leg, giving it a squeeze of affection. 'I'll find something. And sorry . . . about earlier.'

He kisses my forehead in response. 'You're forgiven.'

The waiter returns brandishing the alcohol, and pours a little for Nigel to sip. I'm expecting Nigel to make one of those jokes like, 'Yes, that tastes like wine', as is the custom of anyone chosen to play this weird little game in restaurants. But Nigel takes a small sip and starts swilling it around his mouth like a pro, making unsexy little *slosh slosh* noises. He tips it around the glass and holds it to the light before nodding his head with arrogant quietness. I try to catch Dee's eye to pull a face but she's looking down at her bump and rubbing it absent-mindedly.

The wine is poured and Dee stops the waiter with her hand when he tries to fill her whole glass. But I do see at least six diners watching her do so, and feel a swell of rage for my friend. Dee notices too and holds up her glass to toast them. 'Wine chaser,' she calls across to them. 'Helps take the edge off the skag comedown.'

I erupt with laughter. 'I want to hug you right now,' I tell her. 'I think that is the most perfect thing you've ever done.'

She grins back at me. 'What? What did I do? I wasn't joking, Tor.'

All of us laugh again, even Tom, who has said many a time to me that he finds Dee's humour 'unfeminine'. Nigel entwines his fingers with hers and kisses their fused hands. 'Isn't she something?' he asks us again rhetorically. 'God, I'm the luckiest man alive.'

She rolls her eyes. 'Nigel, I feel nauseous enough as it is.' She smiles as she says it and he kisses her hand again. 'Please kindly do shut up.'

Everyone orders starters but not one of them is vegetarian. 'Just a bowl of olives,' I say to the waiter. I pour more wine into my glass. That first one vanished quickly. I down the second glass within a minute.

Nigel starts explaining his job to us after we make the mistake of asking about it. Tom and I nod and say 'yes, right', although I couldn't honestly tell you what he does for a living, not even if you put a gun to the heads of my parents. It's something in the city, it involves finance, but he's *not a banker*. He's very keen to stress that.

'Darling, nobody cares,' Dee tells him, and the whole table laughs again.

'I still can't believe your name is actually Nigel,' I say. The moment it's out I know I'm already drunker than I thought.

Dee shrieks with glee, and Nigel, to be fair to him, shakes his head and smiles. 'I'm named after an actor from *Chariots of Fire*,' he explains. 'It's all to do with my parents coming from Birkenhead.'

I've forgotten the explanation already because I've thought of a brilliant joke. I lean over the table, excited to tell it. 'You need to be a ticket inspector on a train. Then, when you punch a hole in someone's ticket they can sing to you, "there's a hole in my ticket, dear Nigel, dear Nigel".'

The happy couple laugh. Tom doesn't. He does squeeze my leg under the table – so hard that it hurts – and I'm not sure whether it's a 'that was funny, dear' squeeze or a 'shut the fuck up I hate you' squeeze. I pour the last trickles of the bottle into my glass and wonder whether it's possible it means both.

The food arrives and I order us another bottle of wine. And when I say us, I mean me, because for some reason tonight, oblivion seems like a very welcome option. And you are not a train wreck if you're drinking too much

French Merlot in a restaurant where starters pass the ten pound mark. I toss olive after olive into my mouth and watch how much Nigel loves Dee and how much Dee loves Nigel. He cannot stop touching her. At any given moment there is physical contact. When she speaks, he watches her mouth move with a look on his face of pure adoration. I pour out another glass and pop another olive into my cheek, remembering how Tom used to look at me like that. When we drove across America together after we met in Sedona, I'd catch him just looking at me. Time after time, he'd glance over with the same look that Nigel wears now. It became a game we played. *'What?'* I would ask, whenever I caught him doing it. And he'd smile and say 'nothing'. And then we'd both smile because we knew exactly what it meant. It meant we were falling in love but were too scared to say it just yet. 'Nothing' meant *everything*. These days though, Tom doesn't look at me like that ever. Even if I have his penis encased in my mouth.

Next to me, Tom slurps at a bowl of mussels, and it makes me never want him to give me head ever again. Not that he's given me much head anyway. He told me once that I tasted funny and wouldn't do it again. My glass is empty again. So I fill it. The olives are gone. When did that happen? I push my fingers into the puddle of oil at the bottom of the bowl and fish out small bits of pepper to eat.

The acoustics in here are clattery and voices get lost as they rise up to the high ceilings. Nigel asks Tom about his job and gets excited when Tom says he's a travel journalist.

Everyone is always excited by Tom's job, and by God does he love talking about it and getting them even more whipped up in adoration and jealousy. He and Nigel then get lost in a discussion about all the different places they've been to and get excited when they've been to the same ones. It quickly becomes a friendly one-upmanship of who has the best story about going somewhere in the world. Dee and I pull faces at one another. She's only been abroad once: with me, on an ill-advised trip to Spain when we were twenty-three. We both got food poisoning on the first night and had to take it in turns to shit in the bin when the other one was in the loo.

'The thing that shocked me about Japan was . . .'

'Cambodia? Oh yes. Did you go to the . . . ?'

'The steak in Argentina? Oh yes. Amazing. Brilliant.'

'Oh, that's not my favourite waterfall. My favourite water-fall has to be . . . not very many people know about it . . .'

I drag my chair closer to Dee. 'Remember when we had to take it in turns to shit in the bin?' I ask her.

'I have never travelled since.'

I pick up my wine glass and drain what's left in it. I reach over for the new bottle and pour more in. Our food arrives and stops the men talking about the most authentic place to get good food in Changhai. I had to order the goats-cheese tart even though I hate and despise goats cheese. That is all they had. I try to pick out the goats cheese without Tom noticing as he hates it that I'm a vege-tarian enough as it is. But the bitter tang has contaminated the whole tart so I just mush it around my plate. I steal one of Tom's potatoes and he gets annoyed and tells me I should've ordered my own. There is a third bottle of wine and Tom's looking at me like I shouldn't be being the way I'm being. I think I'm fine personally. I'm not drunk. And even if I am, that is a perfectly allowed thing to be. The food has been taken away and I find myself leaning over the table and promising Dee that I'll throw her the best baby shower the world has ever known.

'There'll be fucking GIN,' I'm shouting at her as she laughs. 'And a Colin the Caterpillar cake.'

The puddings arrive and I've ordered one apparently. I'm so hungry I shovel giant spoonfuls of chocolate mousse into my mouth, hardly even tasting it. The second it's finished, I hate myself. I can picture it travelling through my bloodstream, depositing itself as cellulite onto my arse. I think about making myself sick. Even though I promised myself, all those years ago, that I'd never do that again. God, the way Nigel looks at Dee. It hurts. I never knew it was possible to feel so lonely when you're in a relationship. But, to be fair, Tom is being nice about how wasted I am. Even though I've just spilled the water jug all over the table.

'Feel for me,' he says to the other two. 'I'm the one who has to somehow get her home.' But his arm is around me and he's rubbing my hair like it's all quite cute and he doesn't mind really. He's playing the role of affectionate, 'isn't-she-quite-sweet-despite-this' boyfriend and he could easily get a BAFTA for it.

'They really are the most underrated cakes,' I'm saying to nobody in particular. 'It's not even that they're a caterpillar. It's more that the ratio of buttercream to cake is perfection. I've never met anyone who doesn't enjoy a piece of Colin.'

The French waiter is putting on my leather jacket and I'm asking him why he's not permanently constipated. Dee is cackling with laughter. Tom is saying 'oh dear', but still puts his arm around me as he steers me outside. Dusk has almost fallen. The Thames glitters in the twilight. The heat from the day is almost evaporated but the air still sings with balmy festivities. I'm hugging Nigel. I'm hugging Nigel so tight.

'You fucking take care of her,' I'm saying to him. I am not letting go. I'm repeating it over and over. I'm gripping on to him hard. 'You fucking take care of her, you hear me?'

He expertly extracts himself from my grip and reassures me that he will. I tell him I love him and I'm so happy for them and I start to cry and they all laugh again. Dee hugs me and I can feel her stomach getting in the way and that makes me want to cry harder. I bury my face into her hair. 'I'll get two caterpillar cakes,' I garble. 'Amy will love it.'

'Drink some water before you go to bed, Tor.' She releases my hug.

We say goodbye and I'm waving and watching how Nigel folds Dee in as they walk off. I want to stand here forever and watch them walk away because it could be a metaphor.

'Come on,' Tom tugs at my hand. We turn and stagger back along the Thames.

I thought everything would be OK because Tom was so very lovely in the restaurant. Yet he's hardened right back up again. He drops my hand, he walks too fast, he does not speak to me. I can hardly keep up with him. It's so busy and he's less drunk and therefore has better dexterity for navigating the crowds. I keep colliding with people, saying sorry, tasting wine on my breath. There's a sunset and it's pretty and everyone wants a photo of it and so do I but Tom is too far ahead for me to stop and take one. I do not know where other Tom went. The Tom who seemed to like me only ten minutes ago. The Tom who promised my friend he would get me home safe. I keep picturing how Nigel looked at Dee. I keep remembering Tom saying 'nothing' in the jeep when he really meant 'I love you'. The Tom before his eyes had creases around them, before his stomach started to hang slightly over his waistband, before we knew one another too long to be excited by the prospect of the other's existence any longer. *Where is this going? Why aren't we leaving each other when it's so clear we hate each other?* Oh, I am crying. I have ground to a halt and I'm crying. I watch Tom walk further and further away. He's becoming a small dot, he's merging with the crowds of people who are out here having such a better time than us. I see the back of his tiny head stop when he finally notices I'm not walking alongside him.

He turns and walks back and his head gets bigger and I can see his face is angry but he's trying to pretend it isn't. 'What *now*?' he asks, irritation hacking out like a cough. I am being difficult again, even though I try so very hard not to be difficult for Tom.

'What's going on with us, Tom?' I ask him. I stand there and I just plain ask him. *Why have I been so scared to do this?*

The annoyance on his face evolves into anger – his eyebrows knitting together. 'What? Nothing. Come on, we'll miss our train.'

I am not moving. I am staying right here. With the water glittering and St Paul's reaching up into the sunset. If I'm going to break my heart, I'm going to do it with a view as pretty as this one.

'Do you love me?' I slur at him. 'Properly love me?'

'Of course I do, Tor. Come on. You're wankered and you know it.'

'THEN WHY WON'T YOU MARRY ME?' I find myself screaming.

Pigeons scatter, even the ones with gammy legs. Tourists stop, even the ones who are in rush. In this crazy city where nobody notices anything, my emotional display breaks the social conditioning of London. I'm crying. I'm crying so hard, like there's a switch for my tear ducts that's been switched on. My chest heaves as sobs break through my ribs and expel themselves in gasps. Tom's face bleeds with humiliation. I don't feel guilty. No I don't. *I feel angry.*

'Tor,' he whispers, with such menace I know I should probably be scared. 'Let's. Go. Home.'

I shake my head so hard the whole of London wobbles

behind my eyes. 'I won't go home until you tell me why you won't marry me.'

'I didn't think you wanted to get married,' Tom argues. Crossing his arms. Digging in. Of course he's going to use logic on this.

'I don't believe in stupid expensive weddings, that's different from not believing in marriage,' I counter. 'You wouldn't know though, would you? Because you NEVER LET ME TALK ABOUT IT. Why not? How do I know you're committed, Tom? How do I know you're not going to dump me for some twenty-four-year-old who writes a travel blog about fucking . . . fucking . . . LAOS?'

He grabs my hand and tries to pull me away from my self-made scene. 'OWW!' I yell and a man stops to intervene.

'Are you all right?' He shoots Tom an evil look. That's too much for him. Tom storms off down the river, shaking his head, swearing at people to get the fuck out of his way.

'I'm fine,' I tell this stranger. Even though I'm crying. Even though I can hardly walk straight. I must catch up with Tom. I need to let it all out. We need to talk about this. We can't go on any more not talking about this. People part for me like I'm Moses. You're only invisible in London until you start sobbing publicly, then you're visible enough for everyone to avoid you.

'Tom! Wait!' I yell at him. He does stop, his head bent upwards, like the sky will rescue him from his own live-in girlfriend. I scuttle towards him and manage to catch him up. I pull on his sleeve. I pick up where I left off. I start really crying again. 'You hate me,' I inform him, through my veil of tears. 'Why do you stay with me when you hate me? Why won't you commit? What is wrong with me?'

He's shaking his head. He is not engaging. In multiple senses of the word. 'Tor, come on. You're just upset because you've had too much to drink.'

'No, I've just had enough to FINALLY ADMIT THE TRUTH.'

He yanks me into this little alcove right next to the water and puts his face right to mine. I can smell mussels on his warm breath. 'I *am* committed to you, Tor,' he hisses. 'We own a flat together. I've never cheated on you. We have a cat for fuck's sake.'

'A cat that you like MORE THAN ME.'

'Oh my God, you're *crazy*.' He runs his hands through his hair. 'You're fucking crazy.' He stalks off, leaving me alone. I wait for him to realise I'm not following him but he doesn't return. I slump against the wall, sliding down it onto the grotty floor, and cry and cry and cry. Part of me knows I'm drunk, knows I'm a mess that cannot be reasoned with. The boats passing me in the river blur in my hazy vision. But I am crying because something is very clear. I finally brought up marriage and the future and at not one point did Tom deny my accusations. Oh, he dodged them, he's run from them. But the truth is, he hasn't even considered proposing. You could see it from the shock in his eyes. All those moments – on holidays, or at fancy restaurants

– where I've wondered . . . made sure I was looking nice just in case, imagined what the ring would be like (even though they're a patriarchal statement of ownership that I don't politically believe in, but everyone wants a nice ring don't they?) . . . it has not even crossed his mind.

Christ, I feel sick. I feel really sick. Where is Tom?

I put my face into my knees and cry until there are no tears left in my body. Then, I lift my head.

What the hell have I done?

Tom? Tom! Oh God. He's going to be so angry. He's going to break up with me. My anger floods away and leaves only sickening anxiety. The need to make up for it, the need to make things OK. I can't lose Tom. I'm not sure why, but I can't lose Tom.

I find him at Blackfriars Station, on a bench, his arms crossed, face down. I come up to him. 'I'm sorry, I'm sorry,' I wail at him over and over again, clinging on to him like a traumatized clam. He tries to push me off but I cling harder, burying my face into his chest and getting snot on his shirt – apologising and apologising. The train arrives with a hiss and he, at least, helps me stagger up onto it. Tom sits opposite me, arms still crossed, head still down.

'I'm sorry, I'm so sorry Tom,' I mumble. 'I didn't mean to ruin the evening. You're right, I hate marriage. Fuck marriage. I don't know what got into me. I don't even want a wedding. I don't believe in them. Tom? Tom?'

'Tori, let's just get you home.'

He thinks I'm too drunk. I'm not drunk. I can be sober.

I am totally sober. I sit up straight even though my whole body really wants to lie down. I start making totally appropriate conversation starters like 'Didn't Dee look lovely?' and, 'You and Nigel seemed to get on well.' Tom doesn't engage. The train floor must be so interesting. I really do feel sick. My mouth's doing that watery thing. My hands are shaking. I swallow down a sour-tasting bubbling burp of bile. I can't be sick. That will make everything worse.

Time has passed. I'm back in the flat. Tom is making me drink water. 'I CAN DO IT MYSELF.' I grab the glass off him and pour it mostly down my front. I need the loo. Christ I need the loo. I push past Tom and run to the loo and pee loudly like a man. Whenever I think I've finished peeing, more pee comes. I flush the loo. I stand up. I struggle to pull my dress out from where I've tucked it into my knickers and got a wet stain on it. I look at myself in the mirror.

I have looked better, I will have you know.

My pupils are everywhere. My make-up all down my face. My hair limp and sweaty. I'm so drunk. So fucking drunk. I lean over the toilet bowl and, before I even think about it, I push my hand into my mouth and let the vomit loose. The wine pours out of me, the water pours out of me, the chocolate mousse and olives pour out of me. When it's all gone, when my throat is sore, I grip the rim of the toilet seat for strength.

How do I mend this? How? I've done damage. I'm sobering up enough to know I've done something bad.

When I emerge, my teeth are brushed and my make-up is fixed. I find Tom on his iPad on our bed. He's just in his pants, cooling down from the heat. His stomach swells over the top of them, all full from his dinner. He doesn't look up as I enter. He's just tapping and scrolling, tapping and scrolling.

I am going to seduce Tom.

That's what we need. A good shag. A filthy one because we've both drunk too much so we've lost our inhibitions. This is such a good idea. This will sort out everything. I don't want him to see me as that crying woman begging for marriage by the river. I am not that woman. I may've been her forty minutes ago, but I'm not her any more. I'm young enough and I'm hot and I'm good at sex and I'm wearing matching lingerie and Tom and I are going to *fuck* and it's going to be amazing!

I stand at the foot of our bed. He still won't look up. I shrug out of my dress, so I'm just in my gorgeous expensive matching underwear that only Tom gets to see. He doesn't look up. So I slowly take that off. I'm quite sure I'm the sexiest thing in London right now. I'm now fully naked. I stand there, hand on my hip. I try to flip my hair back but it falls in my eye and it stings actually. *Oww.*

Tom looks up. 'Hey Tor.' He sounds tired and he sounds bored.

'Fuck me,' I say in a voice that is not mine. A voice I am putting on. To distance this sexy naked woman from the one swearing about commitment in front of hundreds of people.

I try to ignore the fact he looks panicked. 'Let's get you to bed, shall we? Sleep it off.'

'Fuck. Me.' I repeat, tossing my hair again.

'Tor, I can't have sex with you when you're this drunk.'

'Suit yourself.' I reach down with my hand and start slowly, deliberately masturbating. It doesn't actually feel that nice because my hands are still cold from where I just washed the vomit off them, but still, I moan. A big porny moan. I once saw Charlotte do this to Trey in *Sex and the City* and it worked for them. And he was incompetent. Hang on . . . wrong word. I let out a bigger moan. I throw my head back. I moan again.

'Seriously, Tor. Stop. Please.'

He will give in eventually. Everything I've ever seen on TV where a girl does this has resulted in the man giving in. Even if it's just hate sex. It's still *sex*. And all Tom and I need to do is have sex. To break the seal. To get back into the habit. To feel like a couple again. I climb onto the bed. I straddle him, still playing with myself. I thrust my naked pelvis into his face so he can see up close what I'm doing. He, at least, puts his iPad down.

That's the only signal I need. I'm on him. Leaning over. Kissing him. Plunging my tongue into his mouth, pushing my boobs up into his face. He tastes of seafood but we're still kissing . . . kissing—

He pushes me off. 'Tor, your breath stinks! Have you been sick?'

OK, so maybe I needed to brush my teeth twice rather

than once. Never mind, you don't need to kiss on the mouth anyway to have good sex. I'll just be Julia Roberts in *Pretty Woman*, she doesn't kiss on the mouth. I move down to his chest, showering it with licks and kisses, pretending he's not repeatedly trying to stop me. 'Tor? Tor!' I tug at his boxers, which aren't full of erection like I expected them to be.

'Tori, please. I'm not in the mood. Get off. Please. Come on. You're so drunk. Tor? TOR!'

He pushes me off gently but I'm too wasted for the movement and I lose my centre of gravity, waving my arms as I fall to the floor with an oomph. I'm off the bed. I'm in a heap on the floor. He's down on the ground. 'Shit, Tor! Are you OK? You just fell like a cartoon.' He laughs nervously.

'You . . . you . . . you don't fancy me any more,' I wail, forgetting instantly that I fell. My jaw shakes with emotion. 'You think I'm disgusting and ugly and you don't want to have sex with me any more.'

He pulls me in for a hug. It's so tight. Almost too tight. 'Look, you're just drunk. I don't want to when you're this drunk. It would be wrong. Can you not see that? Of course I fancy you. I love you. Of course I love you. Look, stop asking me, I told you I love you all right! You need to sleep, you need to. Do you think you can get under the covers? Oh please stop crying. I hate that I've made you cry. Of course you're pretty. Of course. Of course. Yes, much prettier than Dee. I've always told you that. Please just close your eyes, we can talk about it in the morning. Please Tor. Please . . .'

★

Olivia Jessen has shared a photo:

No sleep for Mummy and Daddy because THIS ONE has been up seven times in the night.

3 people like this

Comments:

Andrea Simmons: Oh hon! Sending hugs. It gets easier, I promise. Have you tried Gina Ford?

★

My body wakes me in angry pain.

My head sears like it's been branded. I'm sweating and twisted in one single, sodden, sheet.

Tom is not here.

I flutter my eyes open into the purple glow of early dawn.

The entire room stinks and I have ruined my life.

I'm not sure what happened yet but I know it's not good. It hurts to move my head but I try. I curl into a ball on my side. I see dried vomit splattered down the side of the bed, sprayed in puddles that have hardened on our wooden floorboards. I try to get up but let out a small gasp as I do. It hurts too much. My mouth is so dry. Saharan dry. And yet I feel so nauseous I'm not sure I'll be able to keep any water down. So, for now, I just lie here and watch the sunrise tickle the curtains. I lie here and let the drama of last night break over me like traumatic surf and I stuff my fist into my mouth so I don't scream.

I can't remember it all but I can remember enough.

I remember screaming 'WHY WON'T YOU MARRY ME?' in front of hundreds of people.

I remember begging him to have sex with me.

Have I just ruined my life?

It's just light enough to see through the gloom. I manage to pull myself out of this sick-splattered sheet and stand up. Cat's excited by my early rising. She purrs and meows and winds herself around my ankles as I whisper at her to shut up. I pad tentatively to the kitchen and pass the sleeping lump of Tom on the sofa. Seeing him sets off ten different emotional responses and fresh nausea surfaces, making my mouth water. I concentrate on feeding Cat so she shuts up. I pour myself a glass of water very, very quietly. I glug it down and it sloshes into my empty stomach. I feel sick, but I'm still starving. I smear a thick layer of marmite onto white bread – thinking if it works for Dee's morning sickness it may very well work for my brutal hangover. I tiptoe back to my room, trying not to look at Tom. I do not have the moisture in my body to cry just yet. I know that if I allow myself to start, it won't be easy to stop. I mop up the sick with some wet wipes and throw the stinky sheets into the washing machine.

I wonder if he's going to leave me.

The thought starts small, like a pinprick, but grows quickly, flooding my body with more nausea. He may very well leave me. I have given him more than enough reason. I have broken things that are difficult to repair. I don't know if he's decanted to the sofa because we broke up last night, or just because I vomited all over our bed.

Maybe both.

I perch on the edge of the stripped mattress and eat the bread. My stomach yawns and says thank you for it. The light outside grows brighter by the minute. It burns the backs of my eyes, my forehead thuds in protest. I decide to try to go back to sleep, just for a while. I've taken ibuprofen and my headache will be gone if I can just sleep for another hour or so. I curl up, dragging a clean sheet over my body, and will myself to relax. But, the moment I close my eyes, last night ricochets back.

Why won't you marry me? Fuck me. Why won't you marry me? Fuck me.

I was literally a Madonna-Whore last night. How could becoming the epitome of everything Freud says men want result in such spectacularly terrible consequences?

Have I ruined my life?

It's a dark hour in my head – self-hatred and depression sludging their way in. I'm feeling too numb to cry. I have done something that can't be undone. I've said something that can't be unsaid. I finally asked Tom if he thought about marrying me and it was clear the answer is no.

No.

After all these years. After everything we've shared. He knows me better than any other human could possibly know me, and yet he looks at me and thinks: 'Nope, not for me.' What does that say about me? How terrible must I be to be with?

It's over.

It *has* to be over. *Didn't you want it to be over, Tor?* The voice asks me. *Isn't that what last night was about?*

But now that it might be finished, now that I've made this puke-splattered bed to lie in, I'm realising everything I love about Tom. The thought of no Tom makes my heart feel like it's been thrown into an industrial chicken-shredder. Tom is funny. Tom is ambitious. Tom is charming. Tom is playful. What about that time in Vegas when we won on the blackjack and blew three grand in one night? Or the time when I got my book deal and I came home to our horrid flat to find it filled with daffodils. Or the way Tom holds my hand at scary parties. Or the first time he whispered 'I love you' under the sheets of a hotel bedroom in New York – where he'd taken me as a surprise, to tell me just that. 'I know it's soon,' he said, showering my face with kisses. 'But when you know, you just know.'

I have not, until this morning, until this clusterfuck of a morning, allowed myself to give any thought as to why I am not leaving Tom. Why I'm holding on so tight. And, as sleep is refusing to find me and as shame is thudding in my skull, I may as well.

I push myself up in the unmade bed. God, my head hurts. My eye hurts. But I have to face this. I have to work out what's going on here. There is dried vomit on the floor. My boyfriend has literally just fled from me in the night. I lean over and pick up my discarded laptop and open a blank word-document. I turn down the brightness of the screen until it's practically grey, and, through my splitting headache, I find myself typing.

```
Why aren't you leaving him?
Because I'm scared.
```

That is what bubbles to the top. That is what I write first. Because I'm scared to be alone. I'm scared that no one else will want me, especially as Tom so clearly doesn't. I do not want to be single at this age. I don't want to be out there again. It was bad enough last time but at least I had friends going through it too. I would be the only single one. I'd be the one they don't know where to sit at weddings. I've not met one man that I've clicked with since I clicked with Tom. He may be my only hope.

```
Because maybe this is just what relationships
are like.
```

Another scent of a thought. Love is not whispering romantic things under Egyptian cotton sheets. Love has nothing to do with how besotted you are in those heady first two years. The hormones die off – argument by argument. In time, you discover every single flaw they have, and they discover yours. Your baggage, your insecurities, your gross habits, your nasty streaks. This happens in every relationship, right? This feeling that there's more. The fantasies of what your life would be like with an imaginary different person who doesn't do the annoying shit this real human partner does. It's called 'settling down' for a reason. Because long-term love always means settling. Settling is the key word. I cannot guarantee that I would be any happier with someone who isn't Tom. In fact, I may be even more miserable than I am now. At least I'm adjusted to this misery; at least with this misery I know what I've signed up for.

Tom may very well be the only chance I get for this kind of happiness.

My only shot at marriage and children. Ironic, yes, as he won't talk about either of them, but he's closer than nothing. If I left him I'd be starting all over again. I'd need time to grieve the end of this relationship, then somehow meet someone else I'm compatible with, which will be so much harder as I'm older and all the good ones are taken. Then we'd have to move in together and see how that goes, and on and on, and I may be infertile by the time I've got all that sorted.

Things might get better.

Cat pads in and leaps up onto my bed. She presses her paws in and out and rotates on my lap until she settles. I try to stroke her but she bites me. Maybe Tom and I can save this. Maybe last night will blow everything open and we'll finally talk about all the things we've not been speaking about. I activated multiple land mines and we've fallen through the earth, but it might be just what we needed. We'll go to couples therapy! We'll get an amazing therapist who will talk to us for five sessions and make us realise how in love we are. Then we can have a second honeymoon period and we'll start having mad sex again.

The final reason is more a whisper than a shout.

```
...I still love Tom.
```

I love him so much. When it's good with Tom, it's out of this world good. It's I-feel-like-I'm-in-a-movie good. I have never loved anything or anyone like I love Tom. And I know he loves me. He hates me and I annoy him but he still loves me. If you both love each other that is all you need. You only end relationships when one of you is no longer in love with the other. I push Cat off my lap and tiptoe over to watch Tom sleeping. He's bent at a weird angle on the sofa yet his face is so peaceful. I watch his chest rise and fall with sleep. I reach out and run my hand over the stubble on his face. He leans into it, even in his sleep, and the love rushes in so strong it's like I've been flooded with it.

I have to accept that he may wake up and not want to be with me any more.

The thought fills me with such enormous grief that I let out a weird noise I don't recognise. I run back to the bathroom and empty myself of the toast. I hold the toilet rim, seeping into the bathmat. I cannot leave him. He cannot leave me. Surely anything that hurts this much is the wrong thing? I curl up on the floor, using the bathmat as a blanket, staring at the cobweb behind the base of the loo. This cannot end. I cannot be in this much pain. I don't care if it's wrong, I just need to not lose it.

It's only 6a.m. by the time I step into the shower to wash off my shame. I shampoo my hair twice with volumising shampoo that's specially formulated to work in hard water areas. I put in an intense conditioning mask that will nourish my hair without weighing it down. I sit on the shower floor while it penetrates my hair shafts, smooth on sensitive shaving-foam and shave my legs with a razor head containing five blades and a 'Goddess' moisturising strip. I tidy up my triangle of pubic hair. I have enough that I can still feel like I'm a feminist, but not so much that I'm one of *those* feminists. I exfoliate my face with a scrub that doesn't use the plastic beads that kill all the fish, and, when I've washed out my conditioner, I finish on a cold rinse to lock in shine and close my split ends. I dry my body with a clean towel and rub organic coconut oil all over my skin. I step into the yellow summer dress that Tom always says he likes. I apply light-reflecting foundation and under-eye concealer. I use a yellow-tinted primer on my eyelids so they look less red. I apply only minimal make-up after that. A lip tint, some black mascara to my curled lashes. A stroke of blusher to my cheeks. When Tom wakes up, I will not be the mess he had last night. I am together Tori. I am *let's-talk-about-this-and-then-laugh* Tori. The Tori I'm looking at in the mirror doesn't believe in weddings. She doesn't need an expensive ring to know a man is committed to her.

It's only 6.45a.m. by the time the bedroom is cleaned and aired. The vomit is hiding in the washing machine. I save the word document I wrote into a crammed tax-folder in the depths of my saved items. I call it 'Dee's Baby Shower Planning'. I write while I wait for him.

Tom doesn't wake until ten. It is the most agonising wait of my life. I run through every single possible alternative of our first interaction. I rehearse what I'm going to say. I reapply my lip stain. I tie my hair back in a ponytail because it makes me look younger. I hear him shuffling around the kitchen and I quickly close the word document and open a game of solitaire. My laptop is balanced on my outstretched legs and I've almost won when he appears in the doorway.

He just looks at me.

'Hi,' I say.

'Hi.'

I've never felt further from him. The entire dynamic between us has shifted with just one evening of me telling the truth.

'I'm glad you're OK.' His voice is so hollow you could curl up and hide in it.

'Tom, I'm so sorry.' I stand up and walk over to him. I want to touch him but I'm not sure if it's allowed. 'I don't know what got into me. I just drank too much. I don't want to get married. You know me, I don't believe in any of that nonsense. And, it must've been embarrassing and . . .'

He holds up a hand to stop me. 'Tor, it's fine,' he says.

'It is?'

How can it be fine? I set off a grenade.

'Look, you were just wasted, that's all. You had too much to drink because Dee's pregnancy is freaking you out a bit. It's fine. It's nothing. Have you cleaned up the sick?'

I nod solemnly. I was not expecting this to be fine. We need to talk about it. Surely we need to talk about it? 'Are you not mad at me?'

I swear I see him roll his eyes – ever so slightly – before he says no. But he still says no.

'I am really sorry.'

'I know.'

He squats down and starts pulling running clothes out from the drawer built under the bed. He shoves a T-shirt over his head. He pulls on his special running socks. I watch him carefully tie his Adidas trainers. 'I'm going for a run,' he says, unnecessarily.

'OK.'

I follow him to the door like a puppy who doesn't want his owner to leave. He turns the knob without looking at me. 'I love you,' I call after him, my throat catching. He stops. I cannot cry. I am together Tori. I have red lip stain on.

Finally, he turns. 'I love you too.' He leans in to kiss my forehead and I keep my eyes open to watch his facial expression. His eyes look right past me, unfocused, like he's trying to make a Magic Eye pattern reveal its secrets.

Then he turns.

Then he is gone.

Month Six

Taylor Faithful's Fan Page:

<u>ARE YOU A DIFFICULT WOMAN?</u>

Do this simple relationship test to find out.

Answer yes or no to the following:

- Does your man regularly bring up imaginary glory days of your relationship and ask where 'Old You' has gone?
- Does he claim he is impressed by your career success but then goes quiet whenever you mention a new milestone?
- Are the things he used to love about you at the start of your relationship the things he now continually asks you to stop doing?
- Does he get really excited on the rare instances you bake for him?
- Does he use a minor insecurity you've admitted to him as ammunition in arguments? And, if you ever try to tackle him about his behaviour on anything, by the end of the discussion has it been decided that it was your insecurity that was to blame, not his behaviour?
- Do you worry a lot that you're such a crazy woman and that no one else will want you?
- Are you called 'needy' when you ask for essentially anything from your relationship?

- Do you sometimes feel like he's embarrassed by you at social events? Do you see him wince when you talk?
- Does he boast about fancying strong-willed women, while his celebrity crushes are actually all on fictional film characters who are docile as fuck?

Answered 'Yes' for three or more? Congratulations! You are NOT a difficult woman. You are just in a really bad relationship – probably with a narcissist.

Here's the thing guys: *every* woman is difficult. *Every* woman is spiky. And you need to find someone who wants to hang decorative freaking baubles off your spiky bits, not try to sand them down until they're smooth.

3645 likes.

Tori Bailey likes this

Comments:

Tori Bailey: Amen sister! :) :)

*

Google search: Am I in a relationship with a narcissist or have we just been together a long time?

*

Nigel Tucker

Look at my glowing golden girl and her golden glowing bump in this autumn light. I am the happiest man in the world right now.

24 likes.

★

Dee: DO NOT JUDGE ME FOR NIGEL'S STATUS UPDATE. HE'S GOT SYMPATHY PREGNANCY HORMONES I THINK.

Tori: I have no idea what you're talking about.

Tori: Golden girl . . .

Dee: I hate you, right? You know that I hate you.

Tori: I hate you too Golden Girl.

Tori: The Golden Girl on the Train

Tori: The Golden Girl with The Dragon Tattoo

Tori: Hey now, hey now, what's the matter with the Golden Girls just wanna have fun now. Come on.

Tori: Who run the world?

Dee: I hate you.

Dee: . . .

Dee: Golden Girls?

★

I have a young friend.

She is twenty-four and we met when she interviewed me about *Who The F∗ck Am I?* for a 'zine' she has launched. She was very nice when I politely asked her what the hell a 'zine' was. She has taken me out dancing.

The music here is incredible and I don't even have to pretend as much. We are in a basement somewhere just off Covent Garden. The toilets are disgusting but the cocktails are insane. There are over twenty-five different types of gin to choose from.

'This is my friend Tori,' Tiff yells at her friends over the thud of the music. 'She's written an amazing book about how fucked up it is being in your twenties.'

The cluster of young people cheer and all put their grotty glasses forward to toast me. One girl disentangles herself and launches at me, smacking into me for a hug.

'Oh my God, are you Tori who wrote *Who The Fuck Am I?*' she squeals into my ear. The sweat from her face is now partly on mine. 'I can't believe it! I tried to get tickets for your London show but it had sold out.' She grabs at my shoulders, her eyes moist with excitement. 'That book changed my fucking life! I swear I've read it a million times. I was working in finance before I read it. I was twenty-two and so stressed and miserable and I earned a lot of money but it wasn't where my heart was, you know? Anyway, I read your book and now I work for this zine with Tiff!'

I smile. I switch into professional Tor mode. The one who is humble yet powerful. The Tor she expects me to be. 'I'm so happy my book had that impact on you,' I tell her, hugging her again because she's pulling me in and I don't have a choice. 'It's so important to follow your dreams.'

I worry about her as I go to the bar. How is she ever going to afford a mortgage if she works for a *zine?* If she wants a baby, I bet the zine has a really bad maternity package. Finance would've been a much better long-term option. She'd have got regular pay rises and job perks and, by the time she was my age, would be on well over eighty thousand pounds. Being bored in your job is not cool, but she'll one day realise it's much more uncool to be constantly worried about money and still be in a flat-share aged thirty-three. I pay for a round of shots to secretly apologise to this girl. I've not done a shot in forever but I've not forgotten how to do it – how not to wince, so you look like one of those cool girls who can handle alcohol. I tip back two Jägerbombs and yell at the group, 'I HAVE A FUCKING WEDDING TO GO TO TOMORROW,' and they all cheer me like I've announced I'm going to prison in the morning.

I am dancing now. It feels so good to dance. I move my body and I swirl and I twirl. I giggle and I cup my hand over people's ears and yell stuff into them and we both laugh. The youth glows off my new friends. Their skin is so plump and smooth. Their bodies are so taut and look good in the current fashions. Some of them are in couples and some of them are single but none of them are worrying whether this is The One or if they're going to die alone. I cannot tell you how good it feels to dance to music when you know there is no chance of 'Agadoo' cropping up at some point between ten and eleven. Or that some dude is going to pop up with a fiddle and a kilt on and demand I strip the willow. I only dance at weddings now, I realise. Apart from tonight, I only move my body to music when I am at a wedding. That awful, in-an-awkward-circle 'yes, we look just as bad as our parents used to' dancing that weddings inspire. My counsellor is right. Tonight is just what I need.

Oh yes. I have a counsellor now.

Tom and I finally, finally, had a talk. A talk about our relationship. About us. About what is going on. About why he won't have sex with me.

I broached the topic. I followed all the advice online. I did not bring it up at a bad moment, or in bed. I used 'I feel' statements rather than 'you always'. We were walking around the park to admire the first twinges of autumn – it's best to talk to men when you're walking along side by side because their hunter-gatherer caveman instincts favour side-to-side communication.

God I love this song. Tiff holds my hands and twirls me

round and round and we're all laughing and d'you know what, I don't think one of them is thinking I'm old at all.

Oh yes. So I brought things up with Tom and I was just about to suggest couples therapy when he came out with it all. He admitted it was clear that I was very unhappy and he'd noticed how thin I was getting and how I was projecting all my own personal unhappiness onto the relationship. Which wasn't what I was thinking at all. But after he had given me lots of evidence and reasoning, I was left thinking he could actually be right. I brought up the sex thing, and how he would never touch me and he admitted, he finally admitted, it was happening. And, again, he had a very convincing argument that I'd become too needy. And that he was worried about me and felt sorry for me because of all my unhappiness and that it was very hard to be aroused when you were feeling sorry for someone. He couldn't find me sexy because I was too needy. 'That is normal,' he said. 'You would be worried if I wanted to have sex with you right now.' So, now I have a counsellor – Anne – and we've had two sessions. She asked me why I was there, and I told her I needed to sort out my eating and stop being so needy so my boyfriend would love me again and she seemed to find that very interesting. Anyway, here I am because of her. She has suggested I'm too hung up about the number of my age. Yes, there are biological factors to consider when you hit thirty, but that doesn't mean I have to limit my friendships only to people who are in their thirties too. So I'm here with Tiff, and yes I'll get another round in. Yes, I have some tissues in my purse because the toilets have run out of loo roll. God, her skin. Why didn't I appreciate my skin when it was like that? Why was I so busy being miserable and writing my book when I could have just been looking at my skin in the mirror and stroking it and pushing it to see how firm it was?

I've stopped dancing and I'm having a very intense conversation with Tiff about weddings. I'm smoking again apparently. I've really missed smoking. Why did I ever quit when it's such a brilliant thing to do? Tiff smokes roll-ups and I swear that's so cool. She has rolled me one and I'm smoking it.

'The first wedding is really exciting,' I tell her, spelling indecipherable words in the darkness with the glowing end of my cigarette. 'You can't quite believe that you're grown up enough to be doing all this yet. You spend ages planning what to wear and the whole thing is a huge novelty. It doesn't seem real. You all get so drunk. It's so much fun, the first one, Tiff. It's so much fun.'

She's nodding. 'I've got my first one next year. I'm so excited. It's my housemate's from uni. She's a Christian so she has to get married to have sex.'

We laugh and we suck from our papers wrapped around Golden Virginia.

'Enjoy it,' I tell her. 'You'll have a great time. But this is the start of the trickle, Tiff. Have you ever been in a tropical rain storm? It starts with a few, welcome droplets from the sky. In your twenties, weddings are like that. A few pitter-patters of bride raindrops. Then you turn thirty and BAM—' Tiff jumps as I yell and almost drops her cigarette —'the downpour of weddings hits you, soaks you through instantly, Tiff. And do not forget the hen dos. Every single weekend you'll be dragged to overpriced cottages or pole-dancing lessons or hilarious activities where you make fucking pants. You will feel dead inside whenever you see an L-plate. Then there are the weddings themselves. You'll eat so much chicken, Tiff. You'll eat chicken wrapped in ham almost every Saturday from April until September. You'll have so many packaged-up sugared almonds you'll find them at the bottom of every handbag for the rest of your life.'

Tiff sucks at her fag, her eyebrows furrowed. There isn't any wrinkling between them yet. Sooner than she thinks her face will stay like that, even after she relaxes it, like a creased piece of paper you try to flatten out again. 'I don't want to get married,' she declares. 'I'm never going to do it. Do you know they did this study and found men are made happier by marriage, but women end up less happy?'

'Amen, sister.' We chink our roll-ups in the dark like they are champagne glasses.

I am back inside and I can hardly hear myself speak. I'm leaning against this gorgeous man's long body and we're shouting at one another.

'I think it's so amazing that you write books.' I can feel

his groin pressed against mine. This is the hottest thing to happen to me in at least three years.

I throw my head back, laughing. 'You think that now. But if we went out, you'd resent my success in time.'

He shakes his head, maintaining direct eye-contact throughout. His eyes are green. He's wearing the most adorable glasses. He is so well dressed and his skin. So young. I want to reach out and touch it. I do. He smiles and leans his face into my hand. 'I like successful women who know what they want,' he calls into my ear. His breath is hot; my entire neck tingles. Every part of my body is pinned against the exposed brickwork of this club. 'I'm a feminist,' he says simply. 'How can I not be?'

I shut my eyes, feeling the room tilt. I open them. He is still there. 'I've never heard a man call himself a feminist before,' I admit. 'My boyfriend says the word itself is sexist.'

He leans so close that he can whisper. 'No offence,' he says, 'but your boyfriend is clearly a dickhead.'

I am so close to cheating on Tom. I just need to turn my head and this boy will kiss me. I just need to turn my head and I will have done something that is so big and so permanent that Tom and I will be annihilated within a second. I know it would be such a good kiss. I've not felt like this in so long. Powerful and sexy and playful and fun.

'How old are you?' I ask him. I'm not sure why I ask him.

He smiles, pushes his adorable glasses up his nose and presses his body closer into me. 'Twenty-three.'

I let out a shrill laugh. 'I'm old enough to be your . . . your . . .'

'Sister?' he offers. 'You're not old anyway.' He leans closer and closer. I can't be certain, but I think I can feel his erection through his jeans, pressing against my thigh. 'You're so hot.' His lips are almost on my lips. He's holding them there, seeing if I respond. He's not pushing it or plunging his tongue into my mouth uninvited like the boys I remember from my twenties, the modern feminist boy that he is – and he really is still just a boy. Our foreheads are the only part of our faces that are touching. I am so full of desire. I can't believe someone wants me. The thrill it gives me. The unashamed thrill. Tiff catches my eye as I look over his shoulder. She gives me the thumbs-up before launching her face into the face of another young gorgeous man. But I can't . . . I can't do this.

'I have a boyfriend,' I remind him. Our lips meet just from me speaking. My entire mouth tingles. I hate myself for saying it. I hate Tom for existing, inconveniently, in this moment. The boy withdraws. I realise I don't even know his name. He leans back slightly so he's no longer pushing me into the wall. I worry now that he's going to vanish. Find another girl, one who is young and unburdened with long-term partners and shared cats. But this boy doesn't vanish. He takes my hand and leads me to a quieter part of the club and we have brilliant conversations about poly-amory and whether it's the future, and the flawed institution of marriage, and the crisis of masculinity. When he goes to the bathroom, I sink into the disgusting sofa and marvel at him.

Tori: Men under twenty-five are the answer.
Dee: What are you doing up at 1am? We have the wedding tomorrow. I'm only awake due to heartburn because I'm a fat mess.
Dee: WHAT MEN UNDER TWENTY-FIVE?

I smile and tap out a reply. Tiff pulls away from her conquest and gestures with her thumb to check if I'm OK or not. Her hair is laden with sweat but she still looks gorgeous and spritely. I make an A-OK sign and return to my phone.

Tori: I'm clubbing Dee. With twenty-somethings. I KNOW. But OMG the boys! They're so enlightened and sexy and educated about women and sexy and interesting and sexy. Did I mention sexy?
Dee: I hate you for going clubbing with fit men without me.
Dee: I hate my heart for burning so hard. I've not slept in forever. Fuck this fucking baby.
Tori: Sorry about your heart. I have literally no advice to give you. But I can send you a photo of the hot man who's trying to convince me polyamory is the future.

The boy emerges from the bathroom, smiling. He comes and sits right back down next to me. Even though I wouldn't kiss him. Even though I'm the oldest person here by about six years. 'Yeah, so I'm starting my Masters next year in Gender Studies,' he tells me. 'I want to specialise in the early socialisation of children and how much is nature and how much is nurture. Because, if you think about it, gender doesn't exist in a vacuum, does it?'

'Can I take your photo? My friend Dee wants to know what you look like.'

'Oh, yeah, of course.' He switches from gender campaigner to selfie pro within an instant. I lean my head up against his head and think just how good he smells. I hold my arm above my head to give us a better angle and then smile with my chin down. 'Let me see,' he says, taking my phone off me. 'Oh, not that one. I don't like that one. Let's take another.' He takes charge of my phone and holds it at a better angle and I try and replicate the smile I just smiled because I looked good in the last photo and I'm worried I won't look as good in this one. My phone flashes. We inspect it. We are both tolerable. I send it off.

Dee replies almost instantly.

Dee: WHERE ARE YOU? I'M ON MY WAY! I've now got loin burn as WELL as heartburn.

I show him the message and we laugh with our heads together. His hand is on my leg and that is technically cheating I guess, but it feels so good. To have a man who wants to touch me. We whisper to one another over the music.

'What do you think it's like to be in your thirties?' I ask him.

He takes my hand and stretches out my fingers one by one before entwining them in his fingers and squeezing.

I've not held hands in so long. 'I think you know yourself better,' he replies. 'But I think you're sad that you didn't feel like that when you were young. I think you mourn the waste.'

I shake my head, smiling. I lean my forehead to his. I could still kiss him. This moment could still happen. I'd be the cheat. I'd be the Bad One in the relationship. Tom could throw everything he wants at me and I'd just have to take it because I cheated and cheaters are scum and we all hate cheaters. Tom could be the victim. I could be the arsehole. Tom would love that. He'd be devastated but the self-righteousness would really help him along. The music thumps the walls and it pulses through my body. I am standing on top of a tall building and I'm thinking about throwing myself off without a net to catch me. There's always a net to catch you in the movies, even if you can't see it yet. But life isn't a movie.

My phone buzzes. I have to let go of his hand to see what Dee has written. We lean in together to read her reply.

She's taken a selfie from below her bump. Her pyjama top is pulled up and the underside of her face is just visible above her swollen breasts and her vein-splodged stomach. She sucks her finger suggestively.

'DON'T CHA WISH YOUR GIRLFRIEND WAS HOT LIKE ME?'

We laugh. We really laugh. All my affection for this boy flies over to Dee – who is remarkably still Dee, even when she's pregnant. I stand up. I extricate myself from the first man to pay me any attention in years. It is late and I'm too old to stay out any longer. Also, I have yet another wedding in the morning.

Tiff notices. She comes over. Her lipstick is smudged from kissing a man who has now vanished. She is not bothered about it at all. More men will come. She's not ready for anyone to be The One yet anyway. It would ruin everything because they would change too much in her twenties, and then she'd be facing a break-up at the socially-inappropriate-age-to-be-single of thirty.

'You going?'

I bring her in for a hug. 'I am. Thanks for inviting me.'

'Dude. Any time. And let me know how the new book is coming.'

The boy follows me through the throng of people to the rickety staircase that will take me into the cold air. He follows me outside where the young congregate and smoke and giggle and take photographs of themselves having fun. I know that they're not really having fun. I travel the world giving talks about how it is never what it looks like. But, despite all that, I feel a pang. A pang that part of my life is over and it will never come back.

'It was really great to meet you,' I tell Boy. I reach out for a hug, just a hug. 'Thank you for giving me hope in men again.'

He twists his face so we are almost kissing for the third time. He bites his lip. 'Come back to mine,' he whispers into my ear.

I pause.

'I can't.'

'You can.'

I close my eyes and smell him one more time. I wonder how good he is at sex. I don't even care actually. It would be sex. I would actually have a man in bed with me who wanted to do something with this body of mine.

'I . . . you know I have a boyfriend.'

'Come back to mine then. He'll never know. Come on. You want it, I know you want it.' I pause because I do. I really do. Then he says, 'We'll have to be quiet so we don't wake up my parents, but they won't mind you coming back.'

I stifle a laugh. The fantasy coughs up a lung and then dies on the pavement. I do not laugh. I lean in and very gently brush my lips with his. I cup his young face. 'Not tonight,' I say. And I turn and walk away.

I feel my swagger. I am one of those cool women in TV shows who walks away from men who fall for her without looking back, even though she knows they are watching. I am powerful, I am sexy, it's all going to be—

'Fucking prick-tease cunt!' the boy shouts at my back.

★

It hurts to wake up. It hurts to be in the shower. It hurts when I see the state of myself in the mirror. Even with all the light-reflecting foundation, even with my special creams, even with my dress from Whistles that glides tastefully over the bits of me that I want glided over.

Tom thinks it's hilarious that I went clubbing with a bunch of twenty-year-olds.

'HOW'S THE HANGOVER?' he yells into my ear as I struggle to keep down my free-range poached eggs on rye toast.

'You're not funny,' I reply, as he kisses me on the forehead. Always on the forehead.

The wedding is in London, which is brilliant because we don't have to pay a fortune to stay overnight and we can get there by tube. Let me tell you about how this wedding is different. It is different because Harry and Claire have managed to arrange the whole thing in less than a year. Isn't that spectacular? It's different because they have tiered cheeses as their wedding cake, because they totally love cheese. That is a defining characteristic of their entwined personality. It's different because Claire wears a plain dress to show off her very expensive designer yellow shoes, because Claire loves shoes and that is a defining characteristic of her personality. It's different because their own daughter, Bonny, is the flower girl, because they did not get married before they had children – because they are modern like that. The ceremony is in a registry office because Harry hates organised religion to the point he's almost religious about it and that is a defining characteristic of his personality. We sit with Dee, who really is every cliché you hear about pregnancy and blooming. With her long red hair and her huge pillowy boobs, she looks almost like a Raphaelite painting. I squeal and hug the rest of our university friends while we wait for Claire. They say it's been too long and it's such a shame I had to miss the hen do as I was in Berlin but that they saw the TED talk and isn't it exciting all this book stuff. Amy looks stressed. Her toddler, Joel, pulls at her dress as she balances her baby on her boob. Her husband, Nick, not doing enough to help. He and Tom complain quietly about all the football they are missing to be here today.

We quieten as Claire walks down the aisle – until Bonny drops the basket of rose petals upside down and we all laugh. That will be a story they'll tell her for the rest of her life now. As they make their vows, I try not to think about the fact that Harry screwed someone else from his office four years ago when Claire was pregnant. I still don't know how she forgave him. She even moved in with Dee for two months to punish Harry enough until she forgave him. But they look happy enough, pledging their life together.

I have to be very careful not to look at Tom in case he interprets it as me wanting to get married.

After the ceremony and throwing confetti and getting our photos of all of that bit, we hop on the tube to get to the reception. They've hired out a whole gastro-pub and filled it with roses. Stacks of bread with dipping oil adorn most tables and I leap onto them and soak up as much of last night as I can. Dee joins me by the bread and we stuff it into our mouths. I even block her while she downs half a glass of my prosecco.

'If one more person comes up and touches my stomach', she threatens, necking her glass, 'I swear I will fart on them.'

'But I touch your stomach all the time.'

'You're my best friend, you're allowed. But honestly Tor, six people have grabbed my belly already today. Some weird uncle of Claire's even held his hand there until it kicked! And I'm supposed to just smile and let it happen because of the miracle of life or something.'

'Is there any way of setting up some kind of electronic device that shocks people who do it?'

Dee dips another chunk of bread into oil and swallows it whole. 'It's easier just to fart on them. I've got so many farts just desperate to come out.'

The back of the pub has huge floor-to-ceiling windows leading out into the beautiful-for-London beer garden. We watch as Claire and Harry pose for non-traditional shots with their non-traditional wedding photographer who has tattoos and everything. He's very excited by Claire's yellow shoes and has her standing on a picnic table to get some proper shots of them. Dee and I watch Harry and Claire touch each other between set-ups – how they laugh so hard the corners of their eyes wrinkle.

'Do you think Nigel would ever cheat on you?' I ask her, still watching out of the window and remembering those months Claire spent crying in Dee's kitchen.

She laughs. 'He hadn't had sex in three years when I broke his seal. Chance would be a fine thing. Why? Do you think Tom would?'

I shake my head and stop eating the bread because I've had three slices now and I don't want to get fat. 'No. It's the one thing about him I've always been certain of. His dad cheated on his mum then left when he was young. He's really . . . weird about it.'

In fact he'd break up with me if he knew about the boy from last night – even though nothing really happened. I sigh and suppress all the emotions last night triggers. 'Do you think you'll ever marry Nigel?' I ask.

Dee takes another slice of bread but squishes it into a ball rather than eating it. 'We've talked about it,' she admits. 'I don't see why not. I mean, we're going to have a baby. Marriage is less of a commitment than that.'

I cannot believe they've *already* spoken about it. Like it's a natural path to walk down, rather than one I constantly have to pretend I'm not dragging Tom along. I feel envy boil through my arteries. I think *it's not fair*. I think *they hardly know each other*. It sounds terrible to admit this, but I always thought I would get married and have children before Dee. I was with Tom and we were stable and committed whereas Dee was the one who was shit at rela-tionships. And now . . . now. God! Being in your thirties is like a game of Snakes and Ladders. You may think you're beating everyone, but you're only one dice-roll away from falling down a snake and suddenly coming last. And the person stuck on square four may randomly land on a ladder and suddenly overtake you in this game to get everything sorted before your ovaries go kaput. That's a really good analogy actually. I should put that in the book I'm hardly able to write. The book I've given myself a month off social media for so I can finish it in time. It's not helping though. My word document is still mostly blank. I just can't think of anything to write. I keep worrying about Tom reading it and what he'd think and how I don't want to have another argument. I think about that snake on the board – that arsehole snake you get around square ninety-seven that takes you right back to the start. If I break up with Tom, it will be like sliding down that really long arsehole snake. Whereas Dee has just shot up that motherfucking huge ladder and the finishing square is in sight. But I don't have any more thoughts because the uni lot are running over to us, their hands outstretched to caress Dee's bump.

'Oh my *God*, Dee! I swear it's the perfect shape,' Sally says, rubbing Dee's tummy like it's a Magic 8 Ball. Sally was in the room next door to me in halls. She once went out clubbing in just a bra and knickers and a pair of bunny ears. Her child is sitting with Amy's child by the soft play area. 'Not long to go now! When are you due?'

'Christmas. It's going to be one of those babies who has a complex about its birthday,' Dee says.

They all crowd around and take it in turns to touch it. Dee rolls her eyes at me when she can see nobody is looking.

'Have you done pregnancy yoga?'

'Are you planning a home birth?'

'God, the thought of not being in hospital if something goes wrong.'

'I was in labour for two days. When it was over, I looked in the mirror and I'd burst every single blood vessel in my face from straining.'

'I ripped so badly I had to sit on a rubber ring for two weeks. It's never been the same down there.'

'My contractions stopped just as Clara crowned. I had to lie with her head stuck for two minutes until the next contraction kicked in. I needed a lot of stitches after that,' Amy adds.

Dee grabs my hand and squeezes it. Hard. I try to butt in, but it takes a while for Amy to finish her story about how the gas and air wasn't connected properly during her second labour.

'Think of all the babies being born right this moment,' I interrupt. 'Thousands of them coming into the world just this minute. All completely fine.' I turn to Dee. 'Whatever happens, it will be over in a day.'

'Mine wasn't,' Amy pipes up. 'I was in labour for forty-two hours.'

Dee squeezes my hand even harder, pulverising my fingers. I blink and reach for the kryptonite I keep in my handbag at all times. 'But you wouldn't change it, would you?' I ask all of them, unleashing my weapon and chucking it into their faces. 'I mean, having children is worth it, right?'

They are quiet for half a second.

'Oh God, no. They're the best thing in my life.'

'It's worth it, Dee. The pain is totally worth it. Then you have a gorgeous baby for the rest of your life.'

They turn to me, their prickles up and quivering, for even daring to suggest there's any moment, any moment at all, when they wish they hadn't had their beautiful gorgeous children.

'It's so powerful, Tor. You won't understand just yet. But when you and Tom get there.'

'Finally!' Amy shrills, laughing as she tips her head back to swill more champagne down it. She's on at least her fourth glass. Nick is on babysitting duty tonight.

And it's Dee's turn to squeeze my hand to give me strength.

I twirl and shake hands and introduce myself and make polite conversation with a bunch of people I will never see again. We lie suspended in this day, all here to witness Claire and Harry wed, before we disperse forever and are never collected in this exact variety of humans ever again. I am well-practised at mingling.

'Didn't she look beautiful?' I say, when I run dry. 'Wasn't that moment where Bonny tipped the basket over just the cutest? Oh, yes, yes, I am that woman who wrote that book. Thank you. Your niece loves it you say? Well that's just made my day, thank you so much. Me? Married? Oh no. That's my boyfriend over there though. Six and a half years. Yep. Oh no. Not yet. But maybe one day.'

Tom is behaving well enough. This is only the second time he's gone to the loo to check the football scores. He comes back smiling, so some man he has never met, and who probably has sex with underage teenagers without consequences, must have kicked a ball into a goal. I'm rewarded with physical affection. He puts his arm around me as we wait to be told where we're sitting. He laughs and hugs me tighter when the uni lot cluster together and share stories of our drunken antics in university halls.

'Tor, do you remember in first year when you stole that fridge from the boys' corridor?'

'I'm still not sure how I managed to pick it up and carry it.'

We all roar in a circle and Tom pulls me in and kisses the top of my head and I melt for what this must look like from the outside. We're pestered with questions about when Tom will 'finally make an honest woman out of me' and he takes it well enough. We reminisce about the nights out we had, and the fancy dress costumes we made, and the pasta with tomato ketchup we used to eat as a meal. We're bonded forever by these stories of being young with nothing to worry about but three hours of lectures and getting a two-one that nobody asks you about from the moment you graduate. Nigel, of course, is hearing all of these for the very first time. It's casting a further bewitching spell. He rubs Dee's tummy and he smiles at the best story about her – the one where she stole the DJ and made him come back to ours for a party. Considering everything, I'm in quite good spirits. There is something relaxing about a wedding, where every hour of the day is catered for. No surprises. Just a paint-by-numbers day. It's nice to see my friends, even if I am totally the odd one out now, and it's going to be an OK day actually, until . . .

Until we look at the seating plan and I'm not seated at a table with my friends.

'What the hell?' I mutter, checking the chart again. The seating plan is arranged according to cheeses because Harry and Claire really like cheese. Didn't you know? Dee, Nigel, Amy, her children, and everyone else are on Gouda. Whereas Tom and I are seated miles away on Brie.

'Oh no,' Amy coos behind me. I can smell her sweet champagne breath. 'Tor Tor you're not sitting with us!' Then she turns and swans off without much of a thought about it because she's still seated with her friends.

Dee is suitably outraged. 'What the fuck?' she whispers to me. 'Is this because you didn't come on the hen do?'

'I couldn't! I was in Berlin. I was doing a TED talk for Christ's sake. Isn't that more important than spending seventy quid to make cocktails in Tiger Tiger?'

'Not according to Claire,' Dee steers me to one side. There's too much of a crowd around the chart and she's wary of her bump. 'She made at least five snide comments that night about how you're "obviously too important to come to her little hen do".'

'Ergh! Bitch. I don't want to sit without you!' I wail at Dee.

'I don't want to sit without *you*,' she hugs me. 'Tor, if one more person tells me their horror birth story, I think I'm going to explode. Which will apparently hurt less than labour.'

'Can everyone please take their seats ready for the bride and groom,' booms the voice of the guy who's been picked to politely order people around all day. Dee and I hug one last time then I take Tom's hand and cart him over to Brie. We're clearly on the odds and sods table. The sleazy uncle that Dee complained about is seated alongside an assortment of other people who have absolutely no common link at all. Tom and I throw ourselves into it because what else can you do?

'How do you know the bride and groom?'

'Oh, you work with her? That's great.'

'You and Harry volunteer together? I did not know he volunteered. Where for? Oh, the local atheist centre. Oh yes, organised religion. Terrible stuff, isn't it? Jeez.'

We just about cover everyone before we have to be upstanding for the bride and groom and the newly-weds arrive like rock stars while we applaud them. We sit down and everyone tries hard not to eat their bread roll before the soup arrives. I keep glancing over at Gouda wistfully. The offspring are sitting at one end, playing miraculously well with their provided paper and crayons, as the adults laugh and bond without me.

'Who do you support?' Tom asks the pervy uncle. And I lose him too, as they compare their opinions about the start of the season and their teams' chances. The work colleague next to me is very excited that I've written a book and she's looking it up on her phone.

'Woah, it's on Amazon and everything,' she squeals.

'Crazy, isn't it?' *It has sold over two million copies.*

I watch Tom drink heavily, see the telltale signs of his intoxication begin to creep in. He will start to over-gesticulate soon. Then he will become overly affectionate. Next, he will think his dancing is brilliant. Then, he will switch to whisky and start explaining whisky to anyone unlucky enough to be near him. Next, I'll have to be very very careful what I say because he'll read into everything and use it to start an argument about how I've changed so much since we were younger. I stick to water.

There is pudding. There are speeches and toasts. 'She looks so beautiful today.' The bride wipes her eyes. The transition from speeches into disco comes a little too quickly and nobody is ready to dance yet. The cleared floor shimmers with rotating disco lights and the DJ pretends that we aren't ignoring him as it stands empty apart from a few kids using the space to skid around. Harry and Claire are at that point where the bride and groom go round and say a small word to each and every one of the guests. Tom keeps leaning in to kiss my cheek, right on schedule. I smile at him and hope he stays in this type of drunk for longer than normal. I rotate back to Dee as soon as the table is cleared.

'Your table looked like it was having fun,' I say to everyone, in a pointed way to make them realise it is weird I wasn't sitting at it. But it's not their rejection so they don't notice.

'Oh, it was great,' says Nigel. 'I heard all about your crazy landlord from your second year.'

'Ahh,' I nod. 'Lock-your-bedroom-door-Malcolm.'

Nigel laughs loud and wide. 'That's the one! Brilliant!'

I still feel left out, even though we're all standing together

229

again. Because I'm trying to work out why I was sitting at a different table. Yes, it was probably because I missed the fucking hen do, but she won't be able to admit that to herself. Why else was I clustered away from them? And, as Dee and I have always come as a pair, why wasn't she paired with me?

Because I have not had children and they have.

That is what decided it. Even though I held back Claire's hair when she vomited on the night bus. Even though I was at every twenty-first party, every ball, every boring night watching *Neighbours* for the second time that day . . . I am on the other side of the wall now.

'TORRRRRRR-I!' Claire calls and I turn to find her walking over with her arms flung wide. 'You actually made it.'

I wrinkle my nose as she hugs me so she can't see it. 'I made it.'

'It's so, so lovely to see you.'

'You look beautiful,' I tell her, because that is what you always tell them. 'I love the shoes.'

She points her toe out. 'I know, right? And, they're so much better than blowing all my money on an expensive wedding dress because I can actually wear them again. Oh, I'm so glad you came.'

'Why wouldn't I come?'

She doesn't reply to that. I've won my point, so I amble on. Complimenting her on the ceremony, thanking her for the lack of goats cheese, and she laughs. She pulls me in for another hug. 'Oh, hon. About the tables,' she says. 'You didn't mind not being sat with the others, did you?'

I make direct eye contact as I smile. 'Not at all.'

'There just wasn't space, what with all the children. And I know how good you and Tom are at mingling. Tom, especially! Harry has such a man crush on him. Where is he anyway?'

'By the bar.'

'Oh I must go say hello. I guess it will be you guys next, won't it? Though we all need to get together when one of us *isn't* getting married. It's hard when we all have children though.'

She is already off. Hugging Dee next. Grabbing her bump. 'Oh, it's coming up, isn't it? How are you feeling? I had the *worst* labour with Bonny . . .'

The night rides on. It gets dark. Parents who drew the short straw take the children away. Amy drew the long straw and she is more than overcompensating. I watch people line up and do shots. Tom is leaning against the bar explaining whiskey to Nigel, who is also into whiskey, so they are out-explaining each other. People are finally drunk enough to dance and even drunk enough to dance to *Love Shack*. Dee and I sit in the corner – the islands of sober in an ocean of adults drinking to escape the lives they feel trapped in. We wave as the uni lot moves in a little circle. Amy has placed herself in the middle and spins while they dance around her. God she is happy without the children. Not that she'll ever admit it. I feel quite calm. This month off social media suggested by my counsellor has been illuminating. After the first day or two of withdrawal, I've settled into it. It's nice not to have a thought, instantly followed by *that would make a good post*. When that famous singer died last week, I didn't have to pretend I liked or knew his music more than I did. I did not have to image-search for a meaningful lyric he had written and then post it quicker than others to get the most re-posts. I just thought *Oh, so-and-so is dead,* and got on with my day of not being able to write anything. Even now, as Dee sticks out her ankles and demands I rub them, I'm not thinking *I should take a selfie of this, isn't it funny?* I'm just here in the moment and glad for it. It's only a month off. I need to be on those sites. Unfortunately, it's a key part of my job.

It gets later. Tom is at the bad stage of drunk.

'Why aren't you dancing?' he demands. 'You're being rude.'

'I'm looking after Dee.'

'Come dance.' A slow song starts. Robbie Williams. Tom pulls me to him and we dance slowly as everyone shouts the lyrics at the top of their lungs and points towards the ceiling. Tom also shouts along – even though he once referred to Robbie Williams as 'the mother of all cunts'. He pulls me into his sweaty armpit and I hate him for a moment. He is a disgusting sweaty mess and he looks old and he really needs to lose some weight and I hate the way he treats me and I hate him for not loving me enough and

I hate how he explains whiskey and I hate how he looks in that suit and I hate the way his sweat smells and how his recent burp floats into my face and smells of beer and vegetable samosas and whiskey. I feel a sudden urge to get away from him. To have him not touch me. I pull myself out of his armpit. Undeterred, he grabs Nigel instead, who is also singing 'and down the waterfaaaaaaaaaaaaaaaall'. I weave my way through the pathetic mess that we have all become and practically run to the bathroom. For quiet. For space. To wash my hands. To wash Tom off me.

Amy is in the bathroom.

I find her alone, sitting on the loo with the seat down, her arm outstretched, and taking several selfies. She's pulled down her dress so she has a better cleavage. She is doing a duck face.

'Oh my God, Tor.' She staggers up. Man, she is drunk. Her voice is slurring, her eyes are all over the place. 'We need to get a photo.'

She drags me back into the toilet cubicle and it takes her three tries to even get the camera up on her phone. She pushes me to her left, which means the photo will be on my bad side. We obviously have the same bad side and she has won the battle of who gets to hide it from the camera. 'On the count of three. One, two, three.' I smile like I'm having the best time in the world because I know that Amy will post it instantly and everyone I know will see it and I want them to look at the photo and think how well I'm doing. We both crowd round the screen to examine ourselves.

'For God's sake, I look so *old*,' Amy moans with pure despair. 'Look at the state of my eyes.'

'You don't look old,' I protest, silently pleased with how the photo has come out for me and hoping she still posts it.

'I've not slept in years.' She puts her phone back into her clutch bag and slumps against the wall of the cubicle. 'I've not been on holiday anywhere that doesn't have a fucking soft play area. Do you have any idea how much of my life I spend in soft play, Tor? *Any* idea? I have a degree in Sociology, but all I can tell you is where the good soft play is locally.'

I'm not sure what to say to her. Her eyes are rolling back in her head now. I sense a puke brewing. I want to message Dee to tell her to get in and help but I left my phone on the table. Amy *always* did this at uni – always drank too much, always got too emotional, always ended up needing at least one of us to look after her. For a moment I'm back in that carefree time, with my feet sticking to the floor and the loud bass thudding through the gross toilets with no seats on them.

'But you seem so happy,' I tell her. 'All the photos you put up . . .'

'I *am* happy, I am . . . I am . . .' She's almost saying it to herself now. 'I'm so lucky. So lucky. It's the most beautiful thing having children, Tor. The most beautiful.' I roll my eyes as I stroke her hair. Saying 'there, there' and wondering when I can leave. I try to tune out her incoherent mumbling. 'Joel is such a menace, but a good menace you know? He's got a good heart. And Clara. Her smile just lights up the room, you know? The whole room. Everyone says so. I mean, it's hard, Tor. No one tells you how hard it is. Relentless. That's the word. Relentless. Nick and I haven't had sex in ages of course. He's always nagging me. Push push push. But I've just not been interested since the birth . . . I hope he doesn't have an affair. And I've always been so jealous of you . . .'

Hang on.

'Jealous?' I ask disbelievingly.

'Yes,' she admits. 'You're always swanning off, all over the place. You always wear nice outfits that match. I just have one jumper that I feel nice in. Just one.'

I shake my head. I reject her words. I can't believe them. 'Things aren't always as they seem,' I manage to get out.

'Ah, come on. You and Tom have the perfect life, the perfect flat. You both have great jobs, you go on all those trips away.' Her voice borders on anger now. Bitterness. I see a little bit of *my* medicine she has to swallow – my projections and my posts and my photographs and how they make her feel. It makes me feel slightly less guilty for the multitude of bitter, nasty, judgemental thoughts I have about her. And this is all very revealing and all very interesting and everything but the moment has passed now because Amy is gasping, 'I'm going to be sick.'

And she swings her head into the toilet bowl.

I hold her hair back for her.

We never talk like that again.

Month Seven

Lizzie Jones

Jake and I are so happy to present little Ewan to the world. Two weeks late, 9lbs and 7ozs, but very worth it for the chubbiness of those cheeks. Georgia is already smitten, as are we.

324 likes.

Tori Bailey likes this.

*

Claire Spears has posted a photo album containing 287 photos

'Who says you can't go backpacking on your honeymoon?'

231 likes

Tori Bailey likes this.

*

Dee Harper has posted a photo.

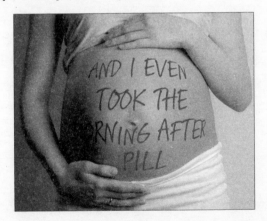

Caption: Don't know why my headteacher deemed this scary costume 'inappropriate' for the school Halloween party . . .

32 likes.

Tori Bailey: I LOVE YOU SO MUCH

*

Extract from Tori's first draft of *What The F*ck Now?*

<u>Lies We Tell Ourselves</u>

How much do you need to lie in order to make a long-term relationship work?

Not only to your partner – *no, of course I don't think your friend is good-looking. Yes, it's fiiiiiine for you to go out tonight, I don't mind! Masturbate? When I have you? Of course not!*

But how much do you need to lie to yourself? *I really do love them. I honestly don't mind. I am lucky to have them.*

I'm supposed to be telling you the truth, so I guess that means telling the truth about the untruth. The denial and the suppression and the covering up that needs to exist in order to wake up to the same person every single morning and not want to smother yourself (or them) with a pillow. ~~OR MAYBE THIS ISN'T RIGHT, TORI? HAVE YOU THOUGHT ABOUT THAT? MAYBE OTHER COUPLES DON'T NEED TO LIE TO ONE ANOTHER AND TOM AND YOU ARE JUST FUCKED UP AND WRONG.~~

★

I have this really good sexual fantasy on the go.

In it, Tom cheats on me, which means I'm free and single, but without any of the guilt. And the person he cheated on me with is much less pretty than me so I'm not even insecure about the fact he cheated. He begs me for forgiveness but I say no. I go clubbing with Tiff and meet a really attractive rich banker, but, like, he's not like other bankers. He volunteers for a children's hospice too, or something like that. I've not figured that bit out yet. Anyway, he looks amazing in sharp suits and he's instantly bewitched by me. Every single thing I do and say further bewitches him. He takes me on incredible dates in incredible restaurants. I plan my imaginary outfits for every single one of these dates, including shoes, handbags, make-up and how I will style my hair. In one, I'm somehow wearing a dress exactly like the green one Keira Knightley wears in *Atonement* when she has sex with James McAvoy in the library. At the opera, I wear red like Julia Roberts in *Pretty Woman* and he gets us a box and, somehow, in this fantasy I actually like opera and don't find it boring and pretentious. The red dress is off-the-shoulder by the way, in case you are wondering. Hang on, I'll get to the sex in a minute. Sometimes I've fallen asleep by the time I've got to this point in my sexual fantasy. It takes me so long to plan all my outfits that I zonk out before I've even had a chance to masturbate. Anyway, finally, when we've been on enough dates that the sexual tension is almost unbearable, this man books us into that hotel at the top of the Shard. The moment we get into the hotel room, the atmosphere changes and suddenly he's not a gentleman any more. He's rough and wants me so much it's insane. We rip each other's clothes off as we stagger around the luxury room while he murmurs constantly how beautiful and sexy I am, and how he has never once been this aroused by anyone or anything ever before. He reaches down and touches me and knows exactly how to touch my clitoris and I get wet much quicker than I've ever done before because this man is so perfect and good at sex. Then he takes me onto the balcony and bends me over it and pulls up the skirt of my dress (blue, vintage, with a skirt made of netting, a bit like the one Carrie wears in Paris in the last ever episode of *Sex and The City*). With the entire city of London stretched out below me, we have sex from behind. Anyway, the sex is rough and, even though I've never once enjoyed sex from behind in my entire life, somehow in this fantasy it feels really good and I don't feel objectified or worried about the size of my arse or anything. We both come at the same time – naturally – and fall onto the huge hotel bed made with white crisp sheets. He doesn't fall asleep or lose interest in me now he's got what he wants. Instead, I play with his chest hair and we talk about our childhoods and he opens up to me in a way he's never opened up to anyone before. And he says, 'Tori, there's something about you. I can just open up in a way that I've never opened up to anyone before.' Then we kiss slowly. We stroke each other's faces and feel each other falling so much in love. The kiss slowly builds to a really passionate one and then we make love on the hotel bed, really tenderly and slowly. He looks into my eyes with each thrust like he cannot believe his luck that he gets to thrust into someone as amazing as me. And I cry, the sex is so beautiful. We both orgasm again, even though I can hardly ever come through penetrative sex. But this man is so perfect and so good at sex and I realise it wasn't my awkward body that was the problem, it was just that all the other boys I've slept with were shit in bed. But I don't have to worry about that any more because this man is here now and I'll never have bad sex ever again. He will love me unwaveringly, and never lose his sex appeal, and never once fancy another woman. We'll have sex at least three times a week, even when we're old. And we'll be that couple that everyone is jealous of.

★

I masturbate when Tom is sleeping. Or when he pops out to get us milk. Once I was masturbating in the shower and he barged in to brush his teeth and I had to pretend I was 'just washing that area' and he pulled a face and said 'gross'. Anne, my counsellor, has told me to masturbate by the way. It's my current homework. She says I can't force Tom to be in touch with his sexuality right now but I can at least focus on my own sexuality. I am a woman and I have sexual needs and I have a right to be in a relationship where they are satisfied.

She likes to talk about Tom a lot, my counsellor, even though that's not what I'm supposed to be going to her for.

'So, how's your week been?' Anne asks me at our session today. She is around forty and I like her very much indeed. I walk to her Victorian conversion flat every week and spill my heart out while admiring her mahogany furniture.

'OK,' I say. It's what I always say. Initially. 'I met my new nephew this week. His name is Ewan. He's so cute.' I dig in my pocket for my phone and pull up some photos to show her.

'He's very sweet,' Anne comments neutrally. 'I love that Babygro. So, what was it like, meeting your new nephew?'

I sigh and remember all the feelings. The huge rush of instant love. My heart growing more room. The way Lizzie's house felt – like it was a home, like it was safe. The way Ewan smelled and how I couldn't get enough of it. The way holding him made my womb do this thump like the glass of water in *Jurassic Park*. I blink the feelings away and stare at the huge mahogany cabinet Anne has. How did she even get it up here? She'll never be able to get it out again. 'It was great,' I reply. 'It's weird though, how primal the whole thing is. My sister's doing well . . .' I pause, weighing up whether I can say what I want to say. I don't want Anne to think I'm shallow and selfish. She senses my hesitation and crosses her ankles the other way and waits.

'This is going to sound stupid but I put a photo of me

and Ewan up on my personal page. As you do. Just one shot. Captioned with something like "So happy to be an auntie again." And, well, normally I mostly post career type stuff to my personal page, as that's the thing that's going most well in my life I guess.' I cough and shake my head. 'Well, this post about being an auntie, it got so many more likes than any of my other posts. I know it sounds stupid, but it really upset me.'

I shake my head again and make a face at Anne, to show her I'm aware that I don't think this is a real problem. But, because I'm paying her and everything, Anne doesn't say 'Dude, that is not a real problem. Get over yourself.' Instead she says, 'Why do you think it upset you?'

And even though I knew that question was coming, it takes me more than a moment to construct a reply. 'The thing is,' I say, twisting my hands. 'I don't actually boast that much about my career on my personal pages. I think it's crass and everyone knows my deal anyway. People are past the fact that they're excited by my success, so, at first, I thought it might just be jealousy, or them thinking I'm boasting, but I'm really careful not to boast . . .' I trail off and look out of Anne's bay windows. Her counselling room overlooks an oblong of communal gardens that back onto several other oblongs of communal gardens. The trees are starting to turn their leaves. They are half green and half the colours of autumn – like you've whipped back the changing room curtain before they've finished.

'Do go on,' Anne says.

'But I do post the odd career thing when it's something really important to me. Like when I did the TED talk,' I continue. 'And, well, it's always a bit tumbleweedy when I do. I get a few likes and a few comments but mostly it goes very quiet. But, yesterday, when I said I'm an auntie and I post a photo of me holding a baby, it goes mental. Likes and hearts and comments . . . and it's such a noticeable difference, Anne. I'm not making it up. Tom says I am but I'm not.'

God, I'm annoyed now. This really has annoyed me. I can feel the toxic sting of hate and anger burn in my fingers. *It's stupid*, I tell myself. *Stop being so stupid, Tor.* But I cannot switch off my reaction to this. I cannot pretend that I don't feel betrayed.

Anne is deciding what to say next. She looks out of the window for one moment. She pulls her marigold cardigan further over her shoulders. I know she's supposed to be neutral but I sense she's on my side on this. She isn't married and she doesn't have kids. I could tell that much by how nice her furniture is. We are on the same side of the wall. I don't think I could have a counsellor who was on the other side, quite frankly.

'What does it mean to you, Tori? To have your friends like things that you've posted? What does it signify?'

I squeeze each finger one by one. I shouldn't have brought this up, it's silly. I'm spending seventy quid to learn to be less needy and to stop losing weight. My BMI has gone into the 'unhealthy' zone, which I secretly think of as the 'ideal weight' zone. Instead, I'm wasting this time talking

about people not liking my status updates. 'A like means
. . . well . . . it means you've done something good enough
for people to make that subconscious decision to actually
click on the tick. Think about it. Think about what you like
or do not like when you're online. You scroll through so
much and you don't like everything but you do like some
things. It's a subconscious thing . . . what prompts you to
hit the screen with your thumb twice. It's so . . . subtle,
but it reveals a lot. What makes you scroll past something
and what makes you pause long enough to let them know
you approve? That you're willing to have that very small
interaction with them, ultimately letting them know you
validate that particular choice?' I hear the rumble of the
downstairs flat's central heating clicking in. I hear it clunking
up the pipes. 'That's what it means. Well, that's what I think
it means anyway.'

'And you are upset that people subconsciously validate
you holding your nephew more than your career achievements?' Anne asks, making a small note in her book.

I nod and I'm not sure why I feel so very much like
crying. 'Yes. Because it means that everything I've achieved
means nothing unless I have a baby . . . I know that's what
these friends must think. I know that's what they must use
against me. Maybe not consciously, maybe they don't ever
even talk about it. But, in the whispers in their head, they
will be thinking *Well, she's met the Queen and sold two million*
copies but she's not had a child, has she? That *must* be the
subconscious thought otherwise why would they like me

247

holding my nephew more than my screenshot from my TED talk?'

'Do you want a baby?' Anne asks, out of the blue.

My mouth falls open uselessly. Nobody has ever asked me this question.

'I don't know', I admit. 'How are you supposed to know?'

She shrugs. My counsellor actually shrugs.

'If I want one,' I say, 'I want one for the right reasons. I want one because I want one. Not because I think it will bring Tom and me closer together, not because everyone fucking else is doing it, not because I feel insecure that my life isn't being validated by people I actually don't like that much,' I tick this all off on my fingers, 'not just because I may as well, as a backup, otherwise I'll regret it when I'm forty-eight, not because I think it will give my life meaning, not because I want to dress them in cute outfits, not because I don't want to get abused in the old folk's home.'

I run out of breath and I grind to a halt.

'Well,' Anne says, making more notes. 'It sounds like you've thought of lots of good reasons *not* to have a baby.'

I lie back in the brown leather of her sofa and cross my arms. 'I think I do want one . . . soon . . . I wish I could talk about these things with Tom,' I admit. 'I wish I could have this conversation with him.'

'So you and Tom haven't discussed children?'

'Not really. He says he definitely wants to have them some day. But "some day" is always this pie-in-the-sky in the future. It was fine four years ago, and even three years ago. But I find it . . . weird he won't let me talk about it even now. I mean, shouldn't I be allowed to talk about it?'

I've asked her a question which is a silly thing to do because she never answers them. Even though I know she knows the answer. Anne keeps all her answers bunched close to her chest and only reveals one once I've figured it out myself.

'Do you want to be in a relationship where you can discuss children?' she asks.

'Well, yeah. I'm not saying I definitely want them, but it would be good to at least talk about it. I think he does want them but . . . but . . .' I feel the tears starting, the emotion throbbing in my chest, catching in my throat. A salty tear spills down my face and probably messes up my mineral foundation. 'I worry he just doesn't want them with me.'

She leaves another silence.

'If that's the case, then I don't understand why he stays with me,' I say.

'Why do you stay with him?' Anne asks.

'Because I love him I guess.'

'You guess?'

I let out a sigh. 'I do love him, it's just so hard.' The tears keep coming. Anne hands me a tissue and I dab at my face and then twist it into knots. 'It's hard that we always argue. It's hard that he won't let me talk about the future. It's hard that he seems . . . let down whenever I'm myself. I'm exhausted by us constantly treading on each other's toes, and arguing, and both of us saying "I didn't want to fight" and "me neither" but somehow we end up fighting anyway. I resent him . . .' It spills out in my monologue. The truth. A golden pearl of it that could ruin everything.

Anne spots the pearl. She picks it up off her antique rug and holds it up to the autumn light. 'You resent Tom?'

I nod. I dab the ruined tissue at my face. 'This is stupid,' I say, balling it into my fist. 'I'm not here to talk about all this. I'm here to be less needy. I'm here to sort out my eating. It's nothing to do with Tom.'

Anne raises both eyebrows. 'Do you not think perhaps your neediness is triggered by Tom's behaviour? That you're not the only one creating this situation?'

I think about it. 'I brought that up with Tom, but he said it wasn't that,' I reply. 'He argues it can't be him, because I didn't used to be like this in the past.'

'But you were younger then. You didn't need commitment then.'

'I guess.'

Anne takes a fresh tissue from the box and hands it to me without mentioning it. I take it from her and wipe under my eyes, blow snot into it with a loud, unattractive splutter.

'It's OK to want commitment, you know?' she says. 'I know you pride yourself on being a strong woman, but you can be strong and still want a partner to meet your needs.'

I let out a slight sob and try to push it back down inside. I can't unleash these emotions. I can't. I don't know how to push them back in again once they're out.

I think of those likes under the photo of me and Ewan. I think of how many more there were than normal. 'If I lose Tom,' I say quietly, 'I lose more than just Tom. It's everything Tom stands for.' I screw the tissue up in my palm, ruining this one too. I twist it into tiny spikes. I rip bits off and roll them into balls that get lost down the side of the sofa. 'And what about my fans?' I ask her. 'Tom is my happily ever after. Tom is my plotline. Tom is the thing they hold on to knowing it's all going to be OK in the end. I was a mess when I met him . . . a mess. My whole career depends on people thinking I know what I'm talking about. If I lose him, they won't trust me any more.'

Anne is quiet. Anne is thinking.

Anne eventually says, 'I thought your career was built on you telling the truth?'

I give that breakthrough the moment's silence it deserves.

'That too,' I say. 'But . . . well, I tell the truth *and* I also have my shit together. That's the package. People only listen to the truth if they think you're . . . successful.'

'And what does successful mean, Tori?'

'I don't know. Having it all.'

'But what if you had it all and you weren't happy?' she presses. 'Is that still success?'

I laugh and wipe my nose with the back of my hand. 'You're making my brain hurt!'

I think about the word 'success'. I think about how often people use it about me. About how my time with that word is running out because the goalposts are changing. If I don't get married and don't have children then soon I will be seen as less successful. Even if my new book sells ten million copies, my lack of a man loving me, of that man spunking into my womb and growing a person, will deem me unsuccessful. 'Because it came at a cost, didn't it?' they will say. And don't pretend for a moment that they won't say it.

'I guess true success,' I start to say, nervous I've got the answer wrong. 'True success is living the life you want to live and not caring what other people think.'

Anne gives me a look. The look says 'bingo'.

'I want my boyfriend to love me more than he does,' I admit.

'You cannot control how much Tom loves you.'

I raise an eyebrow. 'And now you're going to say something all Oprah, like "But you can control how much you love yourself".'

Anne gives me another look. This look says 'bingo'.

'I don't think I'm brave enough to leave him.'

'Maybe not today.'

'What if I'm never brave enough? What if I waste my life when there could be someone so much better out there?'

'Then that's what you've chosen to do. You have to take responsibility for that choice.'

'What if there is no one better?' I ask. Like she's a psychic. Like she knows the answer. Like she's got someone better hiding in her mahogany cupboard, just waiting for the moment I say 'I'm leaving Tom' to jump out and go

'Surprise! Here's your reward for being brave. I love you wholeheartedly. We're going to have great sex and I'll never once criticise any part of your personality.'

'You're unlikely to meet anyone else when you're with Tom,' Anne says.

Her eye twitches above my head at the clock. Our time is running out. As always after a session, I feel no different. More confused than anything. Tom doesn't even approve of me going to counselling any more. 'You're always weird with me afterwards,' he complained the other week.

'Why is Tom not leaving me?' I ask, even though we have no time to go there today.

'Let Tom worry about Tom,' Anne says. 'And you worry about you.'

*

FEMME FATALE FESTIVAL PROGRAMME

HEADLINING: **TORI BAILEY**
'STAND BY YOUR MAN' October 30th 7p.m.-8p.m.

The bestselling author of *Who The F*ck Am I?*
is our special guest in this panel event
about how to make long-term love last.

@WhatTheFckFanGirl @TheRealTori This is a joke, right?

@RealityBabes @TheRealTori Umm, since when did you become a 1950s housewife, Tori? I expected better from you

@LizLizLizzy @TheRealTori STAND BY YOUR MAN?!!? I THOUGHT I KNEW YOU

@JenniferJJ @TheRealTori I was looking forward to your new book but I'm going to boycott it if it's a marriage manual – just so you know

@RandomFacelessEgg @TheRealTori Feminism is cancer

*

From: Tori@WhoTheFckAmI.com
To: Jenny@Hawkpublishing.com
Subject: Femme Fatale Festival

Hi Jenny
How are you? Good I hope?
This is a bit of a tricky one, but I've just seen the schedule for this year's Femme Fatale Festival and I'm a bit thrown by my event. It says I'm down for a panel discussion called 'Stand By Your Man'? I know the title is deliberately tongue-in-cheek, but I'm still a bit confused as to why I've been booked. *Who The F*ck Am I?* doesn't have a man in it until the last chapter! Has there been some kind of mistake?

Thanks for looking into it.
Tori x

*

From: Jenny@Hawkpublishing.com
To: Tori@WhoTheFckAmI.com
Subject: RE: Femme Fatale Festival

Hi Tori

I'm good thank you, and yourself? Writing coming along nicely? Everyone here is so excited to read your new manuscript!!

Regarding FFF, I'm sorry you have concerns but I think it's a really good opportunity. This was actually an event pitched by us. We want to start re-positioning you in the market, and think this is a great place to start. And, yes, of course the title is tongue-in-cheek! I'm sure you've seen the outrage about it online already. Great publicity! Of course, when the event actually happens people will realise it's not about that at all. It's just going to be a friendly chat with other extraordinary women about heterosexual relationships and how to navigate them when you're a kick-ass femme fatale such as yourself!!!

I hope this has alleviated your concerns somewhat. Feel free to ring me if you have any further questions.

Kindest regards
Jenny

*

From: Tori@WhoTheFckAmI.com
To: Jenny@Hawkpublishing.com
CC: Kate@Nightingaleagents.com
Subject: RE RE: Femme Fatale Festival

Hi Jenny

Thanks for getting back to me so quickly. I've CC'd my agent into this just so she knows what's going on. I hope that's OK?

I have seen the backlash to the event. I've had to come off my accounts today because I'm being trolled. A lot of them are fans and readers. I think if you're going to make an event tongue-in-cheek you may need to be clearer about it . . .

I really don't want to be difficult but I feel very uncomfortable with this event. I am an expert in being true to yourself and finding strength in yourself, not in long-term heterosexual relationships. It would be great if we could look at this situation quite urgently as I don't want to damage my brand by pretending I'm an expert in something I'm not.

Sorry if this email has made things more confusing, not less confusing.

Regards
Tori

*

From: Kate@Nightingaleagents.com
To: Tori@WhoTheFckAmI.com
Subject:

Tor, what's going on?
I've just been CC'd into an email with you and your publisher about the FFF? Everything OK? How are those chapters coming along?

Kate x

*

From: Tori@WhoTheFckAmI.com
To: Kate@NightingaleAgents.com
Subject:

Kate
I'm so angry at Hawk! They've shoved me onto some fucking piss stain of an event and they won't cancel it. I'm going to pull out and I thought things might get messy so I cc'd you in. I can't BELIEVE they think it's a good idea to have me up on stage, spouting off about how in love I am!? Do they not understand my brand at all!? FFS. The whole thing is a mess. I'm so embarrassed.

Tori x

*

From: Kate@Nightingaleagents.com
To: Tori@WhoTheFckAmI.com
Subject: RE No title

Tori, are you free for me to call you ASAP?
I'm sorry you're upset and I'll speak to Hawk about it.
However, FFF is a huge opportunity and you have a great
relationship with them. It would be a bad idea to upset
their scheduling this late on. Also, regarding your brand.
I thought you were happy with how we were moving this
on? *What The F*ck Now?* is all about your thirties, not
your twenties, and about you and Rock Man's relationship.
I do agree with Hawk that this is a good place to let your
readers and fans know this.

But of course I don't want you to do anything you're
uncomfortable with. Please let me know when I can call you.

Kate x

*

From: Tori@WhoTheFckAmI.com
To: Jenny@Hawkpublishing.com
Subject: RE RE RE Femme Fatale Festival

Hi again Jenny
I'm really sorry if I've confused everyone with these emails.
I think I just got thrown by the online backlash and freaked
out a bit. I hope I've not been too much of a headache.
I've had a chat with Kate and I can see why you've pitched
me in this way. It's a really good idea actually! I think I

just got the wrong end of the stick. So, please don't worry. I won't pull out. I'm looking forward to unleashing this new brand of Tori on the world.

Anyway, looking forward to seeing you next week at the festival.

Tori x

*

Tori's *WhoTheF*ckAmI?* Official Fan Page:
To my F*ckers,
I'm SO EXCITED about this year's Femme Fatale Festival in London. Who's coming? I'll be speaking about monogamy and the complexities of modern relationships at the *Stand By Your Man* event at 7p.m. Yes that IS a tongue-in-cheek title so calm yourself! I've not been dragged off to Stepford overnight. With that cleared up, expect much swearing, hilarious anecdotes of the banality of long-term love with Rock Man and . . . drum roll please . . . AN ANNOUNCEMENT ABOUT MY NEW BOOK! Only a few tickets left so go go go.
458 likes

*

What sort of outfit projects the message that you are a strong, independent woman who is exploiting the fact she's in a hetero- normative relationship to further her career?

That is what I'm thinking as I stare at my vast cupboard of clothes.

Do I wear a smart dress? Does a dress, one of those tight corporate ones in bright colours like purple or red, balance femininity with independence? Or should I wear a trouser suit? I do not own a trouser suit, but I have a few hours before I become a national hypocrite to buy one.

I repeatedly go through my rails, pushing clothes from one end to the other like the act will magically dislodge a perfect garment I missed the last eight times.

I cannot believe I am going through with this.

'I have nothing to wear!' I shout to Tom. He doesn't hear me though because he's watching football with his headphones on. The headphones are something new we are trying as a compromise on how much sport he watches. Tom watches the football with his headphones on, while I curl up next to him on the sofa and watch something on my iPad with *my* headphones on. That way we can spend quality time together without having to talk, or even have our brains in the same reality. Sometimes, he even rubs my feet as he watches the football that I can't hear.

I pull on a menagerie of different combinations and examine my body from all angles. This is never the best of ideas because then I focus on all the bits of my body that I don't like. Like my shoulders, and how they're a hint too bulky. Or the top two inches of my thighs and how they bulge out. I used to be able to cover my thighs with longer tops but it's not been fashionable to wear a long, flattering anything for two years now, and every top in the universe ends just above the belly button. Oh, I don't want to be doing this event. Everything about this event is wrong. Everything about this book is wrong. Everything about my relationship is wrong and I'm about to sit on a stool, in front of four hundred people, and pretend the exact opposite. I pad about our room in my underwear, rifling through drawers for a perfect jumper I know doesn't actually exist. I'm on the verge of giving up and just turning up in my pants when I get a blurt of inspiration.

Taylor Faithful.

What does she wear? I remember she looked amazing in Berlin, and she was talking about her husband then. I will just copy her. She will know how to utilise a trouser suit.

I flop onto my stomach and open my laptop. This disrupts Cat who lets out an annoyed mew and opens one eye lazily to give me the biggest of all cat glares. 'Oh get over it,' I mutter, as I type in Taylor's name and pull up her page to look for photos of her past events and . . .

And . . .

NO.

I let out such a loud yelp of despair that Cat scatters off the bed.

Dear Spiky Women,

I hope you respond to this post with grace and sensitivity. My friends, my dear friends, it is with great sadness I announce that my husband and I are separated.

Some loves last forever, like evergreen trees. But other loves are only one cycle of seasons. A spring full of hopeful

*bloom, a summer of hazy sun, an autumn where the leaves
fall even though you don't want them to, and a winter where
the branches are empty. Sometimes, after these winters, you
can find spring again. The buds can grow back, the blossom
will return. But sometimes you only get the one season. And,
in this amazing, beautiful, challenging relationship between my
husband and me, we have only had one season.*

*I do hope you can respect our privacy at this difficult time.
I am grieving something I'd never thought I'd grieve but I
know there is my own personal spring waiting for me around
the corner. Until then, the only way out is through and I'll be
taking a break from this account indefinitely.*

See you on the other side, you spiky, wonderful people.
Much love
Taylor x

Tom runs into the room, his eyes wide with panic.

'What is it? I heard a scream. Are you OK? Oh my God,
Tori. What's happened?'

'It's . . . it's . . .' I cannot talk. My mouth cannot function.
The shock has rendered me incapacitated.

'What is it? Tor!? Is it Dee? Is she OK? Talk to me
Tor!'

I cannot. My heart is sliding down to my ankles, my hope
has strapped on an explosive vest and it's not even demanded
a ransom before blowing itself to pieces. 'It's . . . it's . . .' I
point to the screen and Tom snatches the laptop off me,
reading under his breath. He lets out an angry exhale.

'Tor! I thought someone had fucking died.' He shoves the laptop back at me.

'You don't understand,' I manage to get out. 'I feel so let down . . .'

He's shaking his head. 'I honestly thought something terrible had happened,' he mutters.

'I didn't mean to scare you,' I get out. 'I was just shocked, that's all.'

His anger is hardly contained, it is seeping out of him. His fists are clenched.

'Just don't freak me out like that again, OK?' he says. He slams the door behind him and it shakes the room. I am too many emotions now. I read the post again and feel bitterness crawl under the gaps of me.

I trusted you.

I Google search her name to see if I can glean any more information. I need to know everything and then maybe I can understand it. Maybe I can rework my blueprint for forever happiness which was her blueprint for forever happiness. There are a few small news stories about it. She's just about famous enough for this to be vaguely newsworthy.

Self-confessed 'difficult' lifestyle guru, Taylor Faithful, has announced she is divorcing her husband of seven years. In a short post to her fans, Taylor confirmed her split. Her bestselling memoir *Spiky Around The Edges* has sold over three million copies.

There's nothing else. No additional information. I try to think of any reason for this divorce that I can live with. He's had an affair? But why would he have an affair if he truly loved her for being a difficult woman? Does that mean if you're a difficult woman you're one day too difficult to love and so men go and shag some basic woman as an act of defiance? Or did they just drift apart? Like everyone does. Does everyone drift apart? I can feel myself spiralling even though I need to be dressed and preened in an hour's time. I don't know what I'm wearing yet, and I've not done my make-up. I will need to put on three different creams before I even start my foundation and they each take about five minutes to sink in between applications so I should really be getting a move on, but I can't. I feel . . . I feel . . .

Dee answers her phone right away. 'I'm too fat to give you advice on what to wear to this thing,' she says. 'I hate you for not having a giant blubber ball tied to your stomach while I can only wear a sack.'

'You're not fat,' I say. 'You are blooming and gorgeous and pregnant and it won't last forever. And that is not why I'm calling.'

I hear the angry crunch of her eating crisps down the line. 'What else has happened?'

I pause, hoping she, at least, understands. Though I've been scared to tell her my problems lately. They all seem insignificant compared to her heartburn and her worries about childbirth and if she'll be a good mother.

'Taylor Faithful is getting divorced. She just announced it online.'

'No way! Your guru?'

I nod into my phone, so relieved she gets it. 'Yep. Basically, if *she* can't make it last, we are all screwed. I can't believe it. I'm traumatised, Dee, totally traumatised. She's been lying to me this whole time!'

Dee laughs. 'She might not have been! This may have been a complete shock to her too.'

I shake my head into the phone this time. 'No. She must've known something was off. You always know something is off. There must've been at least one time where "It's Too Late" by Carole King or "Foundations" by Kate Nash came on the radio and she found herself weeping and then had to pretend to him she was only crying because she was on her period.'

'That's a very specific example, Tor. I wonder why the hell you came up with that . . .'

'Shut it.'

Dee laughs and then goes, 'Oh bugger. I've woken up the baby. Calm down in there! Seriously foetus, please, *oww. Oww.* Leave me alone. Stop kicking.'

I change the phone to my other ear as I examine my crows feet in the mirror.

'Kicking again?'

'Yep. Nigel keeps making jokes that it means it'll be good at football and I keep hitting him. If it's a boy, I refuse to let it be good at football. I am not spending my Saturday mornings in some freezing field somewhere. Oh, hang on, it's calmed down now.' She pauses and takes a breath to eat more crisps. The crunches echo down the line and I wait for her to swallow.

'She was my hope,' I wail. The shock repeating on me like reflux. 'My one hope. She was tricky and spiky and yet she still found a man to love her forever. Now she's alone.'

'Hey!' Dee says. 'How is she your only hope? What about me and Nigel? I got disciplined at work for my Halloween costume – that's spiky too, thank you very much. And he loves me for exactly who I am.'

I bite my lip. I'm glad we're on the phone so she can't see my face. 'Apart from you,' I say, rolling my eyes to myself. Sorry, but Nigel and Dee have only been together for seven months. I cannot base any relationship idol-worshipping on couples who've only been together seven months. They're off their tits on serotonin right now. 'You know what I mean though anyway. I just . . . I thought I knew her. I feel duped!'

'So she needs to stay in an unhappy relationship forever, just so you can believe in her book?'

'Umm, yes.'

Dee is quiet a moment. 'You still seeing that counsellor?'

'Yes, why?'

'Well, you may want to repeat back what you've just said to her. It will make her day. The *depth* here, Tor, the depth!'

I shake my head. 'Don't, Dee,' I plead. 'I'm about to talk

to a room full of people about how happy my relationship is. They're calling me an "expert" in the programme. Just because I am in a relationship, that somehow makes me an expert. And now I've just lost the one rock in my entire attitude towards love. It's a joke. My whole life . . . it's a joke. I'm even considering buying a trouser suit.'

'God, Tor. Things really are bad, aren't they?'

I feel tears threatening to spill and push them back in with my thumb. I don't have time to cry and let my skin calm down enough to apply the first batch of cream. I'm already going to have to skip out some stages. Also, Tom will get annoyed at me for crying. Again. He says I'm falling apart too often. He calls it 'a bad habit'. 'I don't know, Dee. I've got a bad feeling about this event. About this book. About everything.'

'Tor, it will be fine! You're going to be great, you always are. As for Tom . . . well . . . don't think about it right now. But if Taylor can leave . . . well, you may want to think about that. But, for now, just get through this event first. You'll be amazing. You're the strongest person I know.'

I laugh. A short burst of it that takes me by surprise. 'Seriously?'

'Yes! You don't buy into nonsense because you're insecure and overcompensating. That's why we're friends, remember? But it takes strength to reject all the things the world tells you to be.' Another crackling sound as she takes another mouthful of crisps. 'You show me that you are strong every day. So today is going to be fine. And your relationship . . . whatever happens with that, Tor, you *will* be fine, because you are strong and you are fighting for a life you deserve.'

'Why are you so much better at cheering me up than Tom?'

She laughs. 'Because I'm a woman. Because I've been socialised into knowing that showing your emotions is a healthy, natural response to stress. Because you're not trying to have sex with me. Because I've known you longer. Because, if I piss you off, you can just not see me for a few days until we've cooled down, but you wake up to Tom every single morning.'

I take in a deep breath. Like Anne has taught me to. Because apparently, alongside all my other problems, I'm not even breathing properly. 'Thank you,' I say. 'For talking me down off the ledge. Again.'

'Any time.'

'How are you anyway? All good with the pregnancy?'

She cackles. 'Well, let's see. I've not slept in forever. I'm so fat I don't possibly understand how there is any space left for me to get fatter, but I've still got weeks to go. I can hardly get through a day at work without napping. And, if I allow myself to think about it, I worry constantly about bleeding out in childbirth and/or my child being Kevin from *We Need To Talk About Kevin* because maybe it will cry too much and I won't bond with it enough so it will become a psychopath and kill everyone in high school and I know it will be all my fault.'

I undo a pot of moisturiser. 'Just never let your child get really into crossbows.'

Dee laughs. 'You see! This is what I need. Practical advice! Nigel just keeps telling me I'm being unreasonable.'

A tiny chink. The tiniest of chinks. The first thing she's ever admitted, suggesting she and Nigel aren't completely perfect and shagging all the live long day. It's terrible how reassured I feel. 'Men always think women are being unreasonable. But, hey, who lives longer?'

Dee's laugh gurgles down the line and I let my stomach dissolve into relief. It's OK. I don't need Tom to calm me down when I've got Dee. We put too much pressure on our relationships anyway and then wonder why they break. You can't rely on one person to fulfil all your needs, so it's *fine* that Tom doesn't fulfil all my needs. In fact, it's good I've recognised that. That probably makes us happier and healthier than all those couples who are so loved up and everything to each other that they'll have to die at the same time like in *The Notebook*.

Co-dependency. That's what that movie is about. A morality tale about the dangers of co-dependency.

'Don't you have to put on a trouser suit now and tell a room full of people how happy you are?' Dee asks.

'Oh buggery. I've not even put on my primer yet.'

★

I arrive late and flustered and not happy in the outfit I ended up choosing.

'Sorry. I'm so sorry,' I blurt out to my publicist, Jenny, instead of hello. She's waiting for me outside the British Library – shivering in her trendy chequered coat.

'It's OK. We've still got an hour. I love your dress,' she says.

I wrinkle my nose because I'm still not sure about it. She gestures to a glass door and I clop in on my heels. Gorgeous Femme Fatale posters adorn each red-bricked wall, and lots of pulled-together women with good taste in spectacles loiter and hold Paperchase notepads.

I'm weaved through the throng like a cross-stitch needle. We pass a long queue of women sitting on the ground. 'They're queuing for your event,' Jenny squeaks. 'Some of them have been here for hours.'

There's a ripple amongst the crowds as people start recognising me and whispering their discovery to their friends. I receive lots of toothy smiles as they try desperately to connect with me in some way as I pass. *'Did you see her? She smiled back at me!'* I imagine them saying to one another.

We push through to the green room which, I can tell you, always sounds so much more exciting than it ever is. The room groans quietly under the weight of a very busy day. It's mostly empty. A few people are sitting, silently tapping on their phones. The bottles of antibacterial hand gel on each table are almost used up. There's a crumb-laden corner where the catering must've been. It now holds only two crumpled bags of cheese and onion crisps. Jenny panics. 'There were sandwiches. I promise you. They were here an hour ago.' And I tell her not to worry because I have already eaten, even though I haven't eaten. I am glad because this means I can skip dinner without it being my fault, because there were no sandwiches.

'There's wine though!' I say, spotting the bottles of it in the corner and making my way over. 'This festival has its priorities exactly right.'

Enough random people in the room titter at my joke, revealing they've all been listening to me. I pour myself a large glug of white as red wine yellows your teeth and I'm about to be in twelve trillion photographs. A pretty woman with a black ponytail approaches, holding a notebook in one hand. 'Hi, Tori. Nice to meet you!' She stretches out her hand. 'I'm your chair for the panel event. Anika. I write for the *Guardian.*'

I put down my glass of wine and reach out to shake her hand. 'Hi Anika, it's lovely to meet you too.'

'I have to say, I'm a *huge* fan,' she admits from behind her thick-framed glasses. '*Who The Fuck Am I?* helped me through the big break-up of my early twenties.'

I nod wisely and sip the wine. 'Ahh, yes. The *we-met-too-young-and-we-want-to-have-sex-with-other-people-even-though-we're-so-compatible-and-we're-taking-it-for-granted* break-up.'

Her eyes shine. 'Exactly the one!'

I tilt my head and drink more wine. 'I'm so pleased my book helped you,' I say, practically robotically, even though I do mean it. I'm ushered along to a table and I'm still holding my wine glass as I meet the other two panellists. We shake hands and compliment each other on each other's work even though we probably didn't know we all existed until a week ago. I feel the alcohol working its magic, soothing and dulling my nerves. It's going to be OK actually. I've done so many events before, I am good at this, this is what I do. I pour myself another glass of wine. Jenny looks worried. But I'm not. I'm better with a tiny bit of wine in me. I'm funnier, I'm sparkier. My filter is diminished and it's my lack of filter that got me booked in the first place.

I have to do a last-minute wee and it's only then I notice I have red lipstick all over my teeth. Nobody thought to tell me and I feel a twinge of humiliation as I wipe it off in the mirror. I can't handle it when anyone has lipstick on their teeth. It is the ultimate sign someone doesn't have their shit together. But I found it in time and I reapply and blot and I tell myself it's all going to go great. I get miked up and flirt with the sound technician who has to clip the little thing to my boob.

'This is going to be fun,' I tell Jenny and wonder why she looks worried.

Then we're being summoned by someone wearing a black T-shirt and carrying a clipboard and it's time to follow her in a line like we're at primary school. I peek out from behind the stage curtain and see that it's fit to bursting. Row after row is chock-a-block with dewy-eyed women. Earnestness rolls off them like mist off the sea. They are checking the time; they are wondering when it is going to start; they cannot wait to hear what us experts have to say; they want to know all the answers. Then we're being told we're on and I'm walking out into bright hot lights and the eager sea foam claps and whoops, and it's only when I sit down on my stool that I realise I'm still carrying a topped-up glass of wine.

'Hello, hello everyone,' Anika says to the crowd. Very pro, very confident. 'And welcome to the controversially-titled event *Stand By Your Man*.' The audience giggle. Wow, Anika is good. Addressing the controversy right away. Letting them know that we know. 'I'm delighted to introduce our panel tonight. On the far right, we have Lisa Ainsbury. Journalist, playwright and self-confessed "shagger of the whole city of London".' The audience laugh again as Lisa waves all like 'yeah, that's me'. 'Lisa's award-winning play was an autobiographical examination of her break-up that she processed through lots of casual sex—'

'It's a tough job,' Lisa interrupts, 'But someone's got to do it.' Everyone laughs again. I laugh too. Maybe a little bit too late. Oh well.

'But, last year,' Anika continues, 'Lisa met the love of her life and is now engaged to be married. She's working on a new stage show called *I'm Stuck With This One Penis Forever?*'

Oh, how they laugh and applaud and think *hahahahaha well done Lisa*. When everyone's finished clapping Lisa's existence, we move on to the dude sitting next to me. 'In

273

the middle we have Liam Singer. Liam is the founder of The Good Guy Project: a web-based advice platform for men struggling with their masculinity.' Everyone politely claps him while I try not to roll my eyes. I'm sure he has good intentions and all, but I just cannot handle men who get applauded for not being an arsehole. It should not be rewarded, it should just be a given. 'Liam's been with his childhood sweetheart since he was fifteen years old,' Anika informs us and everyone coos, and melts in on themselves, and I have to think *for fuck's sake* rather than say it out loud because I'm miked up.

'And, finally, I'm very excited to introduce our third panellist, Tori Bailey.' Oh, yes, thank you, they are certainly clapping harder for me than the others. I get whoops and I get cheers and I already feel much better about everything thank you very much. 'Author of the bestselling *Who The Fuck Am I?* and inspirational speaker, Tori has been with Rock Man since the end of the gap year that inspired her book.'

'Six and a half years,' I add, because I want everyone to coo about Tom and me like how they cooed for the others. They oblige. Everyone coos. And I feel temporarily less empty inside. For ten whole seconds actually.

'*Who The Fuck Am I?* is a defining book for any woman in her twenties,' Anika says. 'But Tori is here today to talk about what's next. In fact – drum roll, please – Tori, I believe you have a very special announcement for us, don't you?'

I look to my publicist who is sitting at the side with her hands clasped together. This is the moment. The big moment. I cannot take this back once I open my mouth and say it. 'Yes, I do,' I say smoothly. Because I am a professional, I even put down my wine glass. 'I'm really excited to say that I'm writing a new book. It's called *What The Fuck Now?* and it's all about your thirties and long-term relationships and how to still fancy someone after you've had to sit on their stomach one night to help them get rid of their trapped wind.'

I get the most laughs. Brilliant. Everyone is so excited. *AHAHAHAHA. I win, I win.* I drain my glass of wine and feel pretty damn brilliant about myself. Dee was right. I am strong. I am hard core. I am good at this. I've not even written this book yet, even though the first draft is due in a month, but it will be fine because look how much they yearn for my lies. Look how much they don't care about the truth. I am the emperor and they really want my new clothes to be real. Sometimes I think they want my new clothes to be real more than I do.

It takes a while for everyone to quieten down from the excitement of this bullshit book announcement and, eventually, we launch into the questions.

'So, expert panel, what does monogamy mean to you?' **Lisa:** It means working through the hard bits. It means knowing they will make you stronger. It means connecting on a deeper level.

Liam: It's growing together, not apart. And that is so beautiful.

Me: It means picturing someone else when you're having sex as it's the only way to still be aroused by them, but never, *ever*, telling them.
AHAHAHAHAHAHAHAHAHAHAHAHAHA
HAHAHAHAHA
HAHA
HA.

'Now, tell me, do you have to be happy in yourself before you can be happy in a relationship?'

Lisa: I mean, of *course* you have to be happy with yourself. That's the only way. When I was having all that casual sex, I thought I was happy, but I wasn't. It was only when I was truly happy with me – just me – that my fiancé popped out like magic. It's like the universe knew.

Me: < interrupting the applause > So single people aren't happy with themselves?

Lisa: That's not what I was saying.

Me: Then why were *you* rewarded for being happy with yourself, but not *other women* who are happy with themselves?

Lisa: Umm.

Liam: I mean, I get what Lisa's saying. My wife and I met when we were fifteen and we still love each other so much. When you meet that young, of course you're not totally happy with yourself, but that doesn't mean you can't still be happy in a relationship. We've grown together, that's what I love about us. I'm happy with *us*, not just me. Us is more important than me. I think that's what 'real love' is.

Me: But what if your wife got hit by a bus tomorrow? Then what? Because it could happen. It could totally happen. You could always end up alone, even when you're together with someone. They may get cancer or hit by a bus or have a midlife crisis and leave you and start another family with someone fourteen years younger. You can only control you. You cannot put your happiness into another person. You can . . . can . . .

Anika: OK, right . . . moving on . . .

'Can you be a feminist and be in a heterosexual relationship?'

Liam: Well, as you all know, I'm a proud feminist.

Audience: Wooo! Go you! < applause >

Liam: And what I love most about my relationship with my wife is how totally equal it is . . .

Me: Oh my God, so you clean the toilets?

Liam: Umm . . .

Me: You've actually, in the course of all your years together, scrubbed your own shit off the porcelain?

Liam: We have a cleaner so . . .

Me: Who cooks the Christmas dinner?

Liam: Well, my wife likes cooking so . . .

Me: I bet she does.

Lisa: I'm a feminist and you can totally be one in a hetero-sexual relationship. Totally. It's so important. Me and my fiancé are in a completely equal, feminist, relationship.

Me: Are you on the pill, Lisa?

Lisa: What? Umm . . . that's a very personal question.

Me: Or the coil? Or the injection? Or that thing they put in your arm that makes everyone get fat and go crazy? Are you taking hormones because your fiancé doesn't like using condoms?

Lisa: I don't see how . . . anyway, he always says he would take the male pill if it existed.

Me: That's a very easy thing for him to say considering it doesn't exist. And never will because, God forbid, hormones give men side effects.

Audience: < applauds >

Anika: So, Tori. You're a proud feminist. Are you saying you and Rock Man are in an equal relationship?

Me: < pause > I don't fucking know anything any more.

Afterwards, the general politely-put-by-my-publicist consensus on the event is 'um . . . well . . . all publicity is good publicity'.

I can't remember the rest of it, to be honest. I just remember being sad when my glass of wine was finished. And the moment I wasn't able to stop myself pulling a face when Lisa told her super-cute proposal story. Half the audience laughed, and half took to the Internet to tell me I'm a bad person afterwards. Jenny keeps promising me it went 'really well'. Liam asks me for a drink afterwards because 'your questions have revealed parts of my privilege I'd never realised before'. He clearly thinks one discussion with a drunk angry women will help absolve him of his guilt.

'I can't go for a drink,' I slur at him. 'Just promise me you'll go down on your wife every so often and clean the fucking toilet once in a while.'

He laughs. I can tell he hates me when he laughs. I picture him getting into bed with his wife tonight and saying, 'I met the most awful woman tonight. Just awful. I feel so sorry for her boyfriend.'

Lisa and I hug and pretend we're friends and I say I can't wait to see her show. Even though I will never see her show. She says she can't wait to read my new book. Even though she will never read my new book. Because we are women and women always have to pretend they like each other and support one another otherwise they are bad feminists. There is no signing afterwards – Femme Fatale policy. Which is just as well because I run to the green room toilets, pull my tights down, and scratch the top of my thighs until I draw blood.

Month Eight

Tori Bailey has created an event:

Dee's 'Mother's Ruin' Baby Shower – November 15th 2.30-5.30p.m.

Hey everyone,

So it's a bit last minute – I'm still in shock that Dee is having a baby – but let's get the gins in and all hang out and do baby shower stuff at mine. Bagsy I'm the one who's allowed to buy her a Sophie the Giraffe!

16 people are attending

Comments:

Amy Price: Hey Tor, it's not clear from this invite if babies are welcome at this baby shower. Am I allowed to bring Joel and Clara? Otherwise I can't come because I won't be able to get a sitter this last-minute.

Tori Bailey: Whoops, didn't think of that! Yeah, of course they're welcome!

Claire Spears: Phew, I was about to ask the same thing.

Sally Thomson: Me too!

*

Google search: 'Baby shower ideas'

Results:

'Why not cut out pastel-coloured squares of paper and get people to write their mothering advice on them? Then you can put them into this beautiful box for Mother Hen to look through whenever she has a tizzy moment!'

'Baby piñata! You can buy one in the shape of a stork, and then fill it with dummies, and teething rings and all sorts of other baby goodies. Just make sure pregnant mummy is careful while swinging that bat!'

'Bless the baby. Buy a candle for all of your guests, light them, and get everyone to say a blessing for the baby. This ritual is a super-cute way to bond the party. And they can even keep the candle to take home as a party favour!'

'Why not get everyone at the shower to put their thumbprint onto a picture to make into a unique piece of art to hang in the baby's room?'

'Pin the sperm on the egg!'

'Baby bingo!'

'Who can change the doll's nappy the quickest?!'

'Bobbing for nipples!'

Google search: 'How the fuck do you bob for nipples?'

★

If you type the words 'baby shower ideas' into a crafting website's search bar, the appropriate word for what happens next is 'clusterfuckingfuck'.

'No way,' I mutter to myself as I scroll through the death of feminism. 'This is satire, surely?'

I have never found the words 'basic' and 'bitch' so hugely necessary to be used together. Who the hell comes up with this stuff?

Oh, and don't get me started on that thumbprint thing. When did thumb-printing become linked with socially-acceptable life-goal celebrations? I mean, who cares if the government snoop on us when we are willing to give up our individual thumbprints whenever we go to an event in our thirties? It's only a matter of time before our sentimental 'thumbprint art' is released to the government for 'our own safety'. There will be a news story about a serial killer who was tracked down because, even though they'd covered up every single trace, they'd still had to shove their thumb into some pink ink at Jenny and Ben's wedding to add to the 'love air balloon'.

Calm down, Tor. Deep breaths. Click off. Click off.

Dee won't want any of this stuff anyway. I order in ten takeaway pizzas. I buy three big bottles of gin. I even order a *giant* Colin the Caterpillar cake from the catering section of M&S and, when it arrives, I'm so excited I take fifty selfies with it. I decide to make one baby-showery decoration, just to stop all the mums bitching about me afterwards. The least repulsive thing I can find is bunting made out of Babygros. I reckon if I hang it over the sofa then Amy won't be able to make bitchy comments about how I obviously wasn't the right person to host this. I buy a pack of cheap, gender-neutral Babygros from Primark, some ribbon and tiny pegs, and, an hour before everyone is due to arrive, I'm on the carpet figuring out how the sodding hell to make it look like the photo.

'What. The. Hell. Is. That?' Tom steps over my efforts on his way to the kitchen.

I stare down, dismayed. The Babygros just won't peg onto the ribbon stiffly. They're kind of dropping forward in a chaotic row. Tom laughs and puts his hands on my shoulders. 'It looks like there used to be babies inside but they were vaporised away or something,' he says.

'That's exactly the look I was aiming for,' I reply. 'The remnants of genocide.'

He laughs harder and bends over and nuzzles his head into my hair. He obviously finds this endearing.

'Tor, I'm actually quite afraid. What did you do with the babies?'

'Stop it! I'm copying the instructions but it's just not working.' I hold out my iPad to show him the craft page and that makes him laugh even harder. After five solid minutes of ripping the piss ('maybe stick with books, not babies') Tom peels himself away to the kitchen.

'You're not helping,' I mutter the moment he leaves. I sigh long and loud. Everyone's arriving in an hour and I can't have this Babygro massacre hanging over the sofa. I unpeg the clothes and think of what else to do. Maybe I can thread the ribbon through them and hang them up that way? I shove the ribbon through each arm of the Babygros, pegging each sleeve so they don't slide into each other. This will work, this will totally work.

'Voila!' I hold them up to Tom. He stares at my upgraded creation then leans forward onto his knees and laughs harder than I've seen him laugh in years.

'What? What is it?'

'Tor . . . Tor . . . Oh my God . . .'

'What?' His laughter is contagious and I giggle even though I don't know the joke yet.

'It . . . it . . . it looks like you've crucified the Babygros . . . oh my God . . . oh my . . .'

I take another look and the threading of the Babygros has, indeed, created a . . . 'biblical' look. Their arms stretch out painfully while the chests slump forward. I've crucified a Babygro. I did not know that was possible. 'I'm going to go to Hell,' I say. 'I'm the least maternal woman in history and I'm going to go to Hell.'

Tom kneels down next to me and lifts up a Babygro. 'Father forgive them,' he booms, making it speak. 'For they know not what they do.'

We collapse into giddy shared hysterics. We lean our heads together and laugh until we've sprained our stomach muscles. We *do* love each other. We *do* find our way back to each other, every time. I mush my lips into his neck, inhaling his smell that I know so well. He buries his head into my hair. We unclasp from one another and turn our faces so the tips of our noses touch. Tom smiles and it reaches his eyes. He moves a thumb across my cheek. 'I love you, Tor.'

Oh, my smile. How it grows.

'You never say it first,' I say, because he doesn't.

'I do!'

'Rarely.'

I wrap my arms back around him again and squeeze so hard. 'I love you too,' I whisper, clutching on to him, clutching on to this moment.

Tom stands abruptly. 'I need to get out of here before all the hysterical women arrive,' he says. 'When's it safe to come home?'

I pretend I'm not upset that he broke off the hug. 'Six.'

'I might be later than that. There are two games on today.'

'OK,' I say. 'Cool.'

'Save me some caterpillar.'

'I will.'

He squeezes my shoulders again and then he is off to go and find his coat and scarf and gloves and hat and everything else you need to leave the house at this time of year. I slip the Babygros off their ribbon and artfully drape them around random spots of our living room. They look a bit 'Salvador Dali melting clock' but it's better than nothing. Tom comes in to collect his keys from the kitchen counter.

'Much better,' he says, examining my handiwork. 'Right, I'm off. Have fun, gorgeous.'

'I don't know if "fun" is the right word to use about a baby shower.'

He smiles, but this one is not his real smile. 'Just don't get all broody and then start a fight with me when I get home, promise?' He says it like it's a joke but it is not a joke. It's a command.

Tom has left before I have the chance to tell him as much.

★

'Sorry I'm early,' Amy says, as her toddler, Joel, shoots through my front door like a Tasmanian devil. She kisses me on both cheeks, which is quite impressive considering she has her baby, Clara, in one arm and a giant bag in the other.

'Hello, it's OK. I've just finished setting up.'

'Mummy? MUMMY? Where are all the toys?' Joel's voice demands from the living room.

'I TOLD YOU. TORI DOESN'T HAVE ANY TOYS,' she shouts back. 'Sorry,' she says. 'I did warn him you wouldn't have any. He's used to there being a box of them around everyone else's houses because they have children too.'

I grin through my teeth as I take her coat and plop it onto the bed in the guest room. I close the door behind me, as I've done with every other door in the flat – the passive-aggressive way of letting parents know their children are not allowed in.

Joel's already poked his finger into Colin's arse when I

get to the living room. 'Sorry Tor. They're just *so* obsessed with chocolate at this age. Can we cut him a small piece, please? To keep him going?' And before I can say no, and that Dee's not even seen it yet, Amy lifts the knife, cuts a slice, wraps it in kitchen roll and rewards her child for his bad behaviour. I smile and do not say anything because you are not allowed to say anything to parents about how terrible their children are. Especially, *particularly*, if you do not have children yourself. This is the rule.

'Gin?' I ask, watching every single crumb of chocolate cake falling out of Joel's mouth onto my cream carpet.

'Tor! I can't! I'm breastfeeding.'

'Oh. You were drinking at the wedding, so I thought . . .'

'That was a pump and dump day. Can I have a cup of tea?'

'Of course.'

I leave Amy with her baby propped on her knee and her toddler ruining my carpet and put the kettle on. I'm worried I won't have enough milk if everyone wants tea instead of gin. I've only got about a pint left. It never occurred to me people wouldn't want gin. *What does pump and dump mean?*

'I like your Babygros,' Amy calls after me. 'They're . . . umm . . . cute.'

I stick my tongue out as I tip in the teabag and add water. 'They were supposed to be baby bunting, but it didn't quite go to plan,' I call back.

'Oh, cute! I've made that before. It's a bit tricky at first, but I got the hang of it.'

I stick my tongue out again. 'Yeah, I guess. I don't know. I've just been soooooo busy with my *career* I only had time to make it this morning.' When I arrive back with a milk and two sugars, I'm surprised to find my living room full of things I did not buy. 'What's all this?' I ask, looking at bags of nappies and baby food and stacks of things and wool and stickers.

'Oh, I thought it would be fun if we played some games.' Amy holds out the nappies and tubs of baby food. 'Can you help me pour the baby food into the nappies so it looks like poo? Then we can make Dee eat it and she has to guess the flavour. Isn't it hilarious? Do you have a spoon?'

I'm holding the nappies dubiously just as Clara starts howling. Amy coos and tucks down her jumper and pulls out her engorged breast. I try not to watch as her giant red swollen nipple misses and hits Clara's eye. I never, ever, want my nipple to look like Amy's nipple looks right now. Like an udder. *Oh my God, it's actually an udder. I've never thought of it like that before.* 'Come on, Clara. Be good for Mummy. I know you want it. Come on, come on.' There's a *waa* and then a silence and then a suckling. Clara has successfully attached. I'm about to go and retrieve a spoon when I hear Joel say 'Whoops'. He has the biggest grin ever on his pudgy face and Colin Caterpillar's chocolate arse is now all over my carpet.

'Oh no! *Joelly*. That's not how we eat, is it? Sorry Tor. I'd help but . . .' Amy gestures towards her suckling baby. 'You don't mind getting a cloth, do you?'

I smile through my gritted teeth and think things can't possibly get worse. 'Of course, Amy,' I say. 'I'm on it.'

Things have got worse.

Nobody wants gin. Gin was a stupid idea. Everyone is either breastfeeding or trying to lose weight since they stopped breastfeeding or are still pregnant or look at me in horror and say, 'It's only the afternoon, I have to put the kids to bed yet.' I have to leave the flat in the carnage of three toddlers, five babies, twelve mums and a very very very fat but very very very happy Dee to get milk from the corner shop. The pizza, at least, is going down well. And Joel now has Bonny, and Sara, some primary teacher's daughter, to keep him company. This mother understands how to deal with toddlers and has set up a hula-hoop filled with toys and set them the task of staying inside the hoop. They're delighted and sit quietly with books, which is totally brilliant as it gives everyone the calm needed to talk endlessly about their babies.

'Oh, Atticus didn't sleep, didn't sleep *at all* for the first six months. I thought I was going to go crazy.'

'Oh, my Evie was like that. Except she had silent acid reflux so we didn't get her to sleep through until nine months.'

'Look at her sitting up already. She's very advanced for her age. I know every parent thinks that, but she really is very advanced for her age.'

'Have you registered with a nursery yet? Oh, yes, it's never too soon. Especially not for the good ones in London. I signed up Bonny when we got our three month scan.'

I keep trying to make eye contact with Dee, but she is inundated with advice and adoration and attention. Her massive bump is the altar and the women throw themselves onto it. They hold it and rub it and tell her what a very good size it is. They drink tea and offer her advice on everything, from how to sleep with the bump, to telling her she will not sleep again for six years, to how to lose the baby weight. For women so worried about baby weight, they are all eating a lot of Colin and pizza. I was worried I'd over-ordered but almost everything's gone. The mothers are easily divided into two categories weight-wise – the ones who have 'taken it too far' and got too skinny again too quickly, and the ones who have gained a bit too much weight than is considered healthy. Neither win. I stand against the wall and marvel at the sting of jellyfish comments whipping around my flat.

'Oh, I don't know *how* you have time to go to the gym. I can't leave Clara, she just cries and cries without me. What can I say? I'm an attachment Mum.'

'I've cut out sugar. It's not just for me, but the kids too. It can get into the breast milk, did you know?'

'Oh, I couldn't breastfeed. We tried. But she wouldn't take. Yeah, I know. I worry about allergies too, but it's not like I didn't try . . . Bottle feeding is good because it involves the father too. He didn't feel so left out which can happen with breastfeeding. So actually, it's really bonded us as a couple. You hear, don't you? How it can impact a relationship in the early months but not us. Every cloud, eh?'

A gravelly voice next to me. 'Do you have any more gin?'

I spin and smile at the woman asking the question. I think her name is Sandy – I remember Dee telling me about her. She's the assistant head at Dee's school and her favourite colleague.

'Yes! Someone else who is drinking gin,' I whisper. 'Come this way. Make me feel better about my life choices.' I steer her into the kitchen where it's just far enough away to talk freely.

'I'm Tori, by the way,' I hold out my hand and she shakes it. 'I'm Dee's best friend.'

'I've heard all about you,' Sandy replies, smiling. I really like her outfit. She's got a floaty see-through blouse on with dark skinny jeans and proper good boots. 'You're all Dee talks about in school. You're the writer, right?'

I shrug and pour us both a large measure of gin. 'Yes, I guess I am,' I say.

Sandy takes the gin and tonic gratefully and clunks half of it back without even damaging her red lipstick. 'I've not read your book I'm afraid. I feel I'm a bit too old for it.'

I like how she's come out and said it. That she hasn't pretended she's read it, which lots of people do. '*I'm* too old for it too now,' I laugh and take a big slurp of my drink. I'm allowed the calories because I've not had any cake.

'How old are you?' she asks.

'I turn thirty-two next week. You?'

'Thirty-eight.'

I check her hand and see there is no ring on her finger. No diamond someone saved up for so it can be posted online and other people can judge it. Given to her in a way that demands a narrative so you can tell everyone *exactly* 'how he did it' over and over until someone else gets engaged and it's not your turn any more. We drink our drinks in companionable silence and listen as the conversation filters around the corner. It's moved on to working arrangements now.

'Well, I'm lucky that they let me back three days a week.'

'I just couldn't make the cost of childcare add up.'

'The thing is, there's no more important job than being a mother.'

'The early years are so key. You've got to be there.'

Sandy has finished her drink. She holds out her empty glass. 'Can I have more gin?'

I smile at her as I take it and replenish. 'I like you,' I tell her.

'I don't normally drink like this, just so you know. I just find these things . . . tiresome. I'm surprised Dee had one to be honest.'

'It was my idea,' I say. 'I thought I would make it different but it got hijacked.'

Sandy giggles. 'I can tell. Don't get me wrong, I like children. And I know a couple of really great kick-ass mothers, but . . .' Sandy's teeth clink against the rim of her glass '. . . I just can't help overhearing conversations like this and thinking "men don't have these conversations", and feeling like there's something weird going on.'

I'm nodding so hard, I'm liking this woman so very much. 'We should probably go and rescue Dee actually,' I say. 'She made me promise I wouldn't leave her alone for more than five minutes.'

We find her blindfolded and being force-fed baby food out of nappies. Amy shrieks so hard my eardrums almost burst while half the room film it on their phones.

This is followed by a bracing photocard game of 'Porn or Labour'. At which point, Dee, bless her, politely claims she needs a wee and stays weeing until the game is finished. I go and check on her and she gives me a hug. 'Tor, if one more person tells me how awful labour is and I kill them, do you mind if I get blood all over your cream carpet?'

We return in time to see what the ball of wool is for. Cutting off lengths of it to wrap around and guess the size of Dee's bump. The only game in history where women can openly comment on and guess the size of a woman's stomach.

Finally it's time to open presents and Dee *oohs* and *ahhs* at the Babygros and other useful things that are explained to her by mothers. 'We couldn't live without ours' is said so many times. By the end, you can hardly see her over the mountains of delicately dyed tissue paper, towers of nappies and plastic things that help with something-or-other, and lots of framed shit off NotInTheShops that is covered in storks.

It gets to the time where I start passive-aggressively looking at the clock, but nobody notices because they're too busy asking Dee when she plans to get her bikini wax.

'Her what?' I ask. I start aggressive-aggressively picking up the mugs so all these women will get out of my house before Joel makes another stain on the carpet.

'You have to get a wax before labour,' Amy tells me, like I'm stupid.

'That's an actual thing?'

Dee nods at me in a way that says 'don't worry, we'll talk about this later'.

'But . . . but . . .'

Olivia sways her baby gently to try and get it to sleep. 'You don't want the doctors and midwifes to see your pubes!' she says. 'I got mine exactly a week before my due date. That's what I'd recommend, Dee, just in time.'

'What would have happened otherwise?' Sandy asks, swaying gently because she's drunk four gins. 'They'd have shoved your baby back in and refused to deliver it until you'd got a landing strip?'

I start laughing and grip Sandy's arm in appreciation. 'Oh my God! I always thought the landing strip was for men going down on you but it's for . . . it's for . . .' the laughter has me in its grip now. 'But the landing strip is for the baby so it knows where to come out!' I dissolve against the wall.

'I'm not getting a wax,' Dee tells the room. They gasp even louder than when she said she was considering a home birth. 'You've all spent today telling me I'm definitely going to shit myself during labour. Shit is worse than pubes, I reckon. So I may as well save myself forty quid and spend it on the therapy I'll need for PTSD from the terrible childbirth I'm apparently going to have.'

Sandy and I are the only ones who are laughing now, by the way.

We muddle through the resulting awkward silence. And, at the very least, it encourages everyone to get up and thank me and leave my house. Dee hugs me exceedingly tight when it's time to say goodbye.

'Thank you Tor.' We can hardly reach each other over her bump.

'You sure you don't want to stay and hang out?'

She shakes her head. 'I'm overdue my third nap of the day. I have to get at least five in before bedtime.'

I kiss her cheek. 'I'll drive over tomorrow and drop off all your gifts. You don't want to be without that chapped nipple relief cream.'

'You're kind sometimes, aren't you?'

*

Amy Price has shared a photo:

HAPPY BABY SHOWER DEE! Gin and chocolate cake and presents – oh my! Can't wait to welcome this one to the mummy club x x x x x

★

Sandy's the only person who offers to stay behind and help clean up – the only one without a baby to use as an excuse not to. I close the door and smile shyly at her. The flat feels unnaturally quiet, as spaces always do after they've been crammed with people. Mess litters every surface – paper plates harvesting chocolate crumbs, nappies filled with baby food, stray bits of wool everywhere – and there's Joel's stain on the carpet to deal with.

'Gin?' I ask Sandy.

'Gin,' she nods.

We crank on the radio and pull out bin bags and put everything in them, even things you're supposed to recycle really. Then we treat ourselves to another drink. We stack all the mugs into the dishwasher while she tells me about the school and how you run one and how the government are ruining the industry and there are no good teachers left.

'I cried when Dee got pregnant,' she admits with a slur in her voice. 'Not in front of her obviously. But she's one of our best and the thought of finding a replacement for her, on top of all the other stress, was just too much. I went home and cried for two hours.'

'She's coming back though, isn't she?' I slam the dishwasher door shut. 'She told me she's planning to come back full-time? Nigel's so minted they can afford nursery.'

Sandy smiles at me like she feels sorry for me. She bites her lip for a moment, and it must be a good lipstick she has on, because none of it sticks to her teeth. 'She won't come back full-time,' she replies. 'She thinks she will, they always think they will. But everything changes the moment the baby comes.'

I go into the living room and sit abruptly on the sofa. I raise my gin to my mouth. 'Dee's not most people,' I tell Sandy, who joins me.

'I know she isn't,' she replies. 'But . . . I've worked in teaching a long time. Their priorities change when the baby comes, the hormones kick in. Some of their friends from NCT don't go back, so they feel guilty and neglectful if *they* do. I mean, maybe Dee will be different, but I'll be surprised.'

I'm not sure why I'm angry all of a sudden. I'm not sure why I feel like Dee has suddenly betrayed me, and woman-kind as a whole. She's not even done anything yet, and it doesn't affect me whether she goes back to work or not anyway. But I realise I'm judging her. Already judging her. I'm horrified at myself, and Sandy can tell.

'I didn't mean to upset you,' Sandy says, sensing I've gone away somewhere in my head.

I look up at her. 'You didn't. I just . . . I don't know. I'm really happy for Dee, I am. But, she's my best friend and I don't want things to change.'

'They will. They have to.'

It's seven. Sandy is still here and we're drinking cups of tea to sober ourselves up.

'Christ it's dark,' I say, leaning over the sofa to draw the curtains. 'I always forget how depressing winter is.' My foot slips and I land face down on the sofa with an *oomph*. Sandy bursts into a cackle and I join her, laughing into the leather. I've had so much fun with her. I've not checked my phone once.

'When's your boyfriend getting home?'

'God knows.' I'm struggling with the motor skills required to get up. In the end, I go for a ninja roll sideways that gives me so much extra thrust, I'm able to get onto both feet. 'Whenever he's finished watching all the football games to delay spending any time with me.'

Sandy raises one eyebrow as she takes a sip of tea. 'You guys have a fight or something?'

I settle in a chair at the dining table and shake my head, looking at the smudge of chocolate stain that remains on the carpet. 'Oh, I *wish* we could have a fight,' I say. 'I wish he could yell at me at least once. It would be reassuring to know I evoke any strong emotions in him whatsoever.' I pick up my mug of tea. I take a sip. I allowed myself one sugar as a treat because I didn't have any cake. It tastes comforting and exactly what I need but I know I'll hate myself for the sugar when it's finished. 'I know being single is awful,' I tell Sandy. 'And that the grass is always greener, yadda yadda yadda. But I do get jealous that single people have still got all the good bits of falling in love ahead of them. The butter-flies stage and the brilliant sex stage and the stage where they still look at you like they can't believe their luck rather than looking at you like they can't believe you didn't live up to the hype they imposed on you.'

Sandy shakes her head laughing. 'Tori,' she says into the steam of her tea. 'Being single isn't *awful*. I mean, it's hard sometimes, yes. But it's not the worst thing in the world.' She pauses, uncertain what to say next. 'I mean, it's not as bad as being in the wrong relationship.'

'I don't know,' I counter quickly, not sure why. 'The things Dee told me about some of her dates. It sounds like carnage out there.'

'Oh, I'm not denying that. Dating can be brutal. The moment I hit thirty-five, my number of matches dropped because all the men put that as their limit, even if they're forty-two.' Sandy closes her eyes for longer than a blink before looking right at me. 'I mean, there are a lot of arse-holes you need to wade through, and it can be pretty exhausting and some days you just feel like giving up . . . Can I have another cup of tea? I'll leave soon, I promise.'

I smile at her. 'Of course. I need another one too. And stay as long as you want.'

Sandy stands with me while I boil the kettle. She compliments me on my hilarious mugs that Tom doesn't find funny. I'm drinking from a Lionel Richie one that says *'Hello? Is it tea you're looking for?'* and Sandy's drinking from the Adele one – *'Hello? It's tea.'* We pour in milk and I don't have sugar in this one because I had sugar in the last one and I shouldn't have had that as it is. We sit back down again and pick up where we left off, like we are friends who have known each other forever.

'When I first started dating again,' Sandy continues, 'at first I was horrified at the state of all the men. I had some comically awful dates and started to worry something was wrong with me.' I'm gripping the handle of my mug so hard I'm surprised it doesn't fall off. I cannot imagine any man not wanting to fall in love with Sandy. I am already half in love with Sandy. She laughs. 'But then I got the hang of dating and learned how to dodge the crazies. And now it's really quite fun. I mean, obviously I've not met The One, but I've met so many interesting people I'd never have met otherwise. Dating gives you this opportunity to get a little glimpse into someone's life. It's great if you're nosy. The thing is, after a while, something just clicked. I stopped worrying and caring and just focused on me and my own life and what I wanted to do and now I *love* being single.' Her face breaks into a smile. She is telling the truth, I can feel her telling me the truth. 'My head feels so much lighter, you know? I was in a terrible relationship in my early thirties and I sucked myself dry worrying about how *he* was, and what *he* was thinking and what *he* meant when he said this. I would be having a lovely day, then one argument with him would lead me into total free fall. But now . . .' she takes another slurp of her tea '. . . now, I feel about ten stone lighter, and I'm so much happier. Don't get me wrong, I still hope I meet someone, but I also know I'll be fine if I don't, you know? My life is mine, totally mine. And, on good days, it's mad how empowering that can be. I'm not saying there aren't hard days though . . . God, sorry. I'm really going on. Blame the gin! Anyway, I guess none of this is relevant to you. I mean, you've got Tom, haven't you? Well, if things are OK between you?'

'Yes, I've got Tom.' I say. I take a sip of my tea but I don't taste it. My eye started twitching right from the moment Sandy used the words 'sucked dry'. It's like a little clockwork monkey has got out a mallet and smashed a nerve. I remember how, the other day, I was euphorically giddy because Taylor Faithful told my publicist she wants to read my new book when it's done. Tom got home and I was being silly and dancing around the kitchen, saying 'Guess what? Guess what?', all springy and bouncy and just how he likes me, but apparently the rules had changed because he didn't like me that day. 'What's got into you?' he asked, practically in disgust. And, when I told him, all he said was, 'Well done Tor', but with these dead shark-eyes, and all the euphoria vanished as I started to worry what was wrong with him, and whether I'd upset him, and I kept asking him if he was OK and he kept saying he was fine, but he turned on the football and didn't talk to me all night and I cried in the shower so he wouldn't see my blotchy face.

Sucked dry . . .

'So being single in your thirties isn't terrible then?' I find myself asking before I even know I'm going to ask it. The smile Sandy gives me in return is so warm that I could almost tan in it.

'No, Tori. You might actually find you're quite happy . . . you know . . . if you ever decided—'

'To leave him?' I interrupt. *I can't believe I've said it. I can't believe I've said it out loud. I mean, of course I won't leave him. I love him. But, I've said it out loud.*

Sandy nods. 'Just something to think about.'

★

82 people commented on Tori Bailey's wall:

Jessica Thornton: Happy birthday Tor! Hope you have an amazing day and that Tom spoils you rotten x x x

Dee Harper: I refuse to accept you are 32. You are still 19 and you've just been sick in your handbag so the taxi doesn't fine us.

Sandy Carson: I am wishing you a happy birthday online. This makes us proper friends, don't you know?

Someone From School I Never Speak To And Yet We Are Online Friends: Happy Birthday Tori. I hope you have a great day x

★

    Document: Dee's Baby Shower Planning
It is my birthday and I'm dreading having
sex with Tom later.
    We've not had penetrative sex since his

305

birthday, in February. And, before then, we'd not had penetrative sex since my birthday. We almost had sex last Christmas after my publisher's big party, but he was too drunk to keep it up so we passed out on the sofa instead.

I know it doesn't make sense to be dreading having sex with Tom when I spend all my time complaining that Tom and I don't have sex any more. But I am. Because this sex won't be sex he's having with me because he fancies me and he just can't not. It's dutiful sex. Sex we must have because having sex is something couples do to each other on their birthdays. And, though Tom has come up with plenty of seemingly valid reasons for why we don't have sex the rest of the time – reasons like he is tired, or I put too much pressure on him, or I am needy, or he's worried I've secretly stopped taking the pill to trick him into getting pregnant (oh, yeah, that happened, last month. Anne threw a fit.) – even Tom can't deny birthday sex. If you don't have sex with your partner on their birthday there really is a problem with you as a couple and neither Tom, nor I,

want to be a problematic couple. We just
want it to work.

God, the sex is going to be so fucking
awful. I hope I get flu between this
morning and tonight so we have a really
valid reason not to have sex.

★

Tom wakes me with a cup of fresh coffee from the good
deli next door.

'Happy Birthday gorgeous,' he singsongs.

I blink a few times into the dull grey November light,
turn around and smile at him. 'Morning.'

He presses the hot drink into my hand and ruffles my
hair affectionately. He peels off his jogging bottoms and
climbs back into bed. The cold air from outside lingers on
his legs. He picks up his own cup of coffee and we relax
back together in our pillows, sipping and watching the
steam spiral up to the ceiling.

'Thirty-two,' I say. To no one. To him.

'Hey, spring chicken. Thirty-two is better than thirty-four.'

I sip my drink which is too hot and burns the tip of my
tongue, scalding off some rather vital taste buds. 'But it's
not the same for you. You're a guy. You don't have a use-by-
date stamped onto your genitalia.'

'Let's not go down this road, Tor. Not today. Let's just
have a nice day.'

Cat counter-attacks the comeback souring in my throat. She leaps onto my legs and starts clawing at me through the winter duvet. We laugh at her and watch her and marvel at how funny she is and what a personality she has.

'Ready for your present?' Tom asks.

'Oh yeah! Of course!'

He leaves me with Cat and returns with a small oblong box. I kick my legs, disrupting Cat, and say 'presents presents presents' like I'm a cute child. He smiles like he actually likes me. Tom puts his arm around me and I snuggle into his shoulder. I open the card first – it's an arty one with daffodils on the front.

I open it up to read inside.

Dear Tor,
I really fucking love you.
Happy Birthday
Love Tom x

'Aww Tom,' I burrow further into his shoulder, feeling the love kick-start again. I picture him choosing the card in the shop, I picture him sitting with a pen deciding what to write.

'It's true.' He kisses me on the top of my head. 'Now, come on! Open the present.' His excitement radiates off him while I try to hide my disappointment it's not a small, square, jewellery box. Even though I didn't think I wanted one. Even though I didn't know I was maybe expecting one, until the wrapped box came out in this size and shape.

'What *have* you got me?' I use my fingernail to get under

the Sellotape. I push back the folded flap of wrapping paper. I peer in. It's a black box made of silky cardboard. I'm none the wiser until I totally rip off all the paper and turn to the front of the box.

It's a vibrator.

A very expensive vibrator.

'It's a vibrator,' I say, as Tom laughs and congratulates himself.

He pulls me in for a hug while I stare at the box in my hands. 'Well, you're always banging on about how we never have enough sex,' he says. 'So I thought this would help.' He's smiling as he says it.

Here are the orgasms you were after. I won't feel emasculated about you wanking to get them because I picked out the device myself.

'The lady in the shop said they're really good.' He kisses my head again. 'Are you proud of me? I went into an actual *Agent Provocateur* and everything. I even asked for advice. I'm a new man!'

I can't bring myself to take it out of its box. I'm using all I have not to cry on him. The thing is, this is him trying. I know him so well and I know this is him really, really trying. But his trying is breaking my heart.

'You'll have to hide it tomorrow when your parents come over for dinner.' He picks it up and waves it around comically. 'Sorry I can't come to that by the way. I'm so bored of going to Copenhagen. We'll have a nice dinner tonight though, won't we? Oh, Happy Birthday Tor.' I'm engulfed in yet another hug. I manage to squeeze him back, just enough so he won't suspect anything. But if I don't get out of this room very very quickly, he will see me start to cry. Then I'll have to explain why and he won't understand because he thought he was trying so hard. I feel like I need to reward his trying, even if he got it so very wrong.

'Thank you Tom,' I manage to say, without even a quiver of grief in my voice.

You have to leave him, you have to leave him, you have to leave him, my brain is shouting. I gulp. 'I'm going to have a shower.' I kiss him right on the lips and dislodge Cat from my legs, stumbling over to the en suite.

'Tori?'

I turn back and find he is spread out on the bed, hand under his head, leg bent. A bit like how Rose poses when Jack draws her in *Titanic* – except Rose hadn't got a giant pink dildo out of its box and hilariously shoved it between her legs.

'We can use it later tonight.' He wiggles his eyebrows.

It is my birthday and now I am really dreading have sex with Tom later.

★

I get a facial. Because they're always telling you to and I'm panicking about the two lines that have appeared between my eyebrows. They lie like a sideways equals sign. On the plus side, they provide the perfect measurement of when to finish plucking my eyebrows. On the negative, I'm fucking shitting old.

And stern.

My face has always been all angles, which is jolly nice when you're growing up and you can turn the best angle towards a camera and people tell you you could be a model. But now these angles are ageing badly. I'm going to be one of those pointy old women that make you jump if they emerge from the fog holding a poisoned apple or something. I wonder if there's any way to put on weight, but only on your face?

'How is my skin?' I ask the very expensive facialist. 'Is it OK?'

'Do try to relax,' she replies, bundling my face into its fourth hot flannel.

'I gave up smoking,' I tell the flannel. 'When I was twenty-five. So I'm hoping that helped with everything.'

'I'm going to apply a moisturising mask now. It will need to sit for ten minutes while I give you a neck and shoulder massage.'

The mask feels cold on my face but my, it's good to be touched. Even if it's by someone you're paying to touch you. I close my eyes and imagine the mask burrowing into my sideways equals sign, plumping it up, erasing it. The facialist's fingers deftly stroke upwards and around, they zoom in on the sides of my nose, clogging it with special magic mask. It's not like I don't want to grow old, I just want to do it in that graceful way everyone always bangs on about. Where you don't get Botox because that is weird and cheating, but your wrinkles are kind of in the right places and glow and look all mature and sophisticated.

'What does Helen Mirren put on her face?' I ask the facialist.

'We'll go through products at the end of the session. Do try and relax.' I don't know why she's being so snippy. I mean, she started this ruddy thing by using some evil camera that 'diagnosed' my face, pointing out everything that is wrong with it in the photos, and then telling me off for not using sunscreen properly in my gap year. 'Sun protection is so important,' she told me, even though it's obviously too late for that advice unless I now make a fucking Tardis. And if you've managed to conquer the complexities of time travel and then only use it to go back and shovel sunscreen onto your face, rather than murdering Hitler, well, then, I think that says a lot about you as a person . . . Maybe you could do both though . . .

Anyway, what I'm trying to say is that this facialist woman shouldn't freak me the hell out by telling me everything is wrong and then tell me to relax. A lavender-scented mask is not going to undo the words, 'Oh yes, there's a problem area here'. But I lie back and try to listen to the dolphins whistling. It's so warm here in this little black cocoon she's made for me. It's almost relaxing as long as I don't think about the designer vibrator waiting for me when I get home.

After an hour of being stroked and poked, lathered and slathered, I am seated up and shown my face again in the mirror.

'Woah,' I say.

The facialist laughs.

I can't get enough of my face. I turn from side to side, look up and look down, and wonder if it's possible to get it to stay like this forever. It's so pure and clean. She sits me down and shows me all the products I need to buy to get this at home. There is a cleanser and a mask and a moisturiser and an eye cream and a lip balm and a retinoid something-or-other. She tells me everything I've been using is wrong.

'But it can't be, it's all organic!'

'No no no. You need *this*.' She places bottles into my hands with such urgency that I end up spending an extra hundred and fifty quid, on top of the extortionate amount I spent on the facial.

I emerge into the West End and smile at everyone so they can see how glowy I glow. But, within two seconds, I remember I am in London and they'd ignore me even if I was bleeding and holding my blown-off arm out to them. I take myself to Selfridges and wander around aimlessly, picking up handbags and looking at the prices and putting them down again. I go to the book section to check they have mine in stock. Only one copy, but still. I move it to the front of a display.

I feel very alone by the way.

Tom's on deadline and can't meet me until tonight. Dee is away with Nigel for one last mini break before she's too pregnant to move. I'm not seeing my family until tomorrow because Lizzie couldn't get a sitter for today. Even then, she can only come up for two hours because she's breast-feeding. I aimlessly ride the tube back to Brixton and decide to walk back through the park. It's so cold that the morning frost lies suspended on the bits of grass people haven't walked through yet. No one is playing tennis and you can hardly see the city through the dense November fog. It clings to the trees and buildings – I can only see people when they're five feet ahead, emerging through the murk. I sit down on a bench, shivering as I stare out at the fog.

Thirty-two.

When I was younger I could hardly imagine being this age. It was just a blur of assumptions anyway. Of course I'd be married and have children in a house of some kind by then. But of course. That's just what happens.

You have your career, I remind myself. My glistening golden career that so many would kill for.

You have Tom.

Maybe, tonight, we can talk about the future. We'll share an artisan-bread basket and I can say something really simple, like, 'I know we both want to have children at some point, but maybe it would be useful if we actually talk time spans?' And he'll dip a sourdough finger into the virgin olive oil and say: 'You're right, Tori. You're right. How does a year sound to you? Let's start trying in a year.' And I'll say, 'How many children do you think we should have?' and he'll say 'Two.' And I'll say, 'Me too.' And we'll beam at one another and smile in disbelief that we ever thought this conversation would be hard.

Oh, I'm depressed now. I get out my compact mirror and look at my post-facial face to cheer myself up.

The two lines on my forehead are back. They vanished for a while because they had so much product in them but, like the real Slim Shady, they are back. No money can apparently erase away these two lines and all the things that have happened to me that caused them.

An idea.

I put my phone on selfie mode to check how flattering the light is. Not bad actually. The fog softens the harshness of the low sunshine.

It would be a shame to waste it, I think.

I screw up my face to make the lines on my forehead more prominent. But I still take at least twenty selfies to ensure I've got one where I look pretty even though I'm pulling a funny face. I lighten it and, well, yes, I blur it ever so slightly so the two lines aren't as bad, but they're still there. That's the point.

Dear F*ckers,

Today is my thirty-second birthday and I've been given two very prominent presents this year.

These f*cking forehead lines.

Look at them. Just look at them.

At first – like any woman growing older in the world we live in – I hated them. I bought creams to hide them. I would only arrange my face into positions that didn't make them worse.

But then I realised something.

These two lines are the equals symbol. They're just '=' rolled gently onto its side.

Because life = wrinkles.

Living = wrinkles.

Having fun and being carefree and travelling the world and going on adventures = wrinkles.

And going through hard times and coming out stronger = wrinkles.

Every moment of my life, both good and bad, over these thirty-two years = these wrinkles on my face.

So, I'm going to stop apologising for these wrinkles. I'm going to embrace them and everything I did in my life that put them there.

What do your wrinkles equal? What have you come through to get such a deserved, brilliant trophy on your face? Let me know below.

Lots of love

Your (older) friend

Tori x x x

I have over a thousand likes by the time I leave the park. I feel a little better.

★

'Mum? Mum! Can you see me? I can see you.'

Mum's nostril is right up in my screen. I can see every pore, every light moustache hair. 'I can hear you Tor.'

'Move your face away from the iPad, yes, that's it. Now, can you see me?'

Mum's whole face lights up like I've just performed a magic trick. 'Oh there you are! Wow. Isn't this clever?'

Every single time we Skype.

Every. Single. Time.

'ARE YOU HAVING A NICE BIRTHDAY?' she shouts. 'I saw your post about wrinkles. It was funny.'

'I'm having a great birthday, thanks. I'm looking forward to seeing you tomorrow.' I'm curled up in bed, all dolled up for my night out, though I'm still not actually dressed. Cat purrs gently on my lap like a white-noise machine. I stroke her long fur with the back of my hand. 'I feel so old though!' I wail.

'Nonsense,' she replies. 'Wait until your sixties. Whenever I go to the GP now, I have to ask him how many ailments I'm allowed to bring up in the ten minute session. The limit is three. So I have to prioritise everything that's going wrong with my body.'

I squeeze up my face. 'Crikey. What's number one?'

'My prolapse.'

'Right.'

'But they're putting this inflatable ring up there to stop it all falling in. It's very clever, but I can't jog any more.'

'Thanks Mum. You can stop now.'

She cackles at me. 'Having you was worth it though, Tori.'

'I can't believe it's my birthday and you're using it to guilt me for your prolapsed vagina.'

Dad arrives in the background, cradling a sleeping Ewan. 'Oh, is she talking about her prolapse again?' he asks. 'Do stop her.'

'Hi Dad,' I wave. 'Aww, hello Ewan. He's so *cute*.'

Dad waves the baby towards the camera so I can see him better and I feel my stomach turn over with genetic love. 'Happy birthday Victoria.' He steps back to a respectable distance so I can see both him and Mum. 'Did you have a lovely day?'

I nod. 'Great, thanks.'

'You're looking very nice. You off somewhere with Tom?'

'Yeah. We're going to that special place where they put chocolate in all the food.'

'Very fancy.'

The tinkling sound of Tom showering stops and I look to the clock at the top of the screen. 'I have to go,' I tell them. 'We're leaving in a minute and I'm not dressed yet.'

'Well, happy birthday poppet,' Dad says. 'We can't wait to see you tomorrow.'

It takes Mum two full minutes to disconnect from me while I laugh at her confused wrinkled neck trying to find the right button. Then the screen goes black and I can see my reflection in it. I can smell Tom's aftershave through the en-suite door. He hardly ever wears it any more, tonight must be a special occasion. I step into my dress and wiggle the straps over my arm. It's blue and expensive and I'm not quite sure my shoes match.

Tom emerges in a cloud of steam, like he's just been through the makeover part of *Stars In Their Eyes*. He raises both eyebrows. 'You almost ready?'

'I just need to get my bag.'

Objectively, he looks handsome. His suit is well cut because I was there when he bought it. His skin is soft, his dark stubble the right length to be considered designer. He's not currently smiling but, when he does, he only gets one dimple which is cuter than two dimples. He's tall enough and just broad enough to be considered manly. He is an attractive man.

I do not fancy this attractive man in my bedroom. I'm having to intellectualise myself into finding him sexy.

'You look nice,' I tell him. Because he does.

'Thank you.'

I wait for him to say 'you too'. I have shaved and mois-turised, primed and foundationed, plucked and highlighted, washed and blow-dried, dieted and squatted for this man, this one man, to tell me I look nice.

'There's a ten past train we might just catch if we leave now.'

He doesn't.

We power-walk to the station, heads down against the cold, hands stuffed safely into our own pockets. We catch the train because it's one minute late. There are seats and we fall into them, opposite one another. We are on our phones before the train has pulled away.

Sandy: You having a nice birthday? I'm so jealous you're going to that chocolate restaurant. I'm desperate to try it out.

I smile as I compose a reply. We've been messaging back and forth since the baby shower, and I find I'm talking to her more than Dee these days.

Tori: Yes, thank you. Although I went for a facial and I think the beauty therapist negged me.
Sandy: At least you weren't negged during a facial using the sexual sense of the word. That really would ruin a birthday.

I burst out laughing and Tom looks up briefly, irritation lacing his face. He doesn't ask me what's funny. He just returns to his phone and me to mine. My post is doing really well. It annoys me that the ones where I'm honest about ageing do so much better than the others. I refresh my feed over twenty times in the fifteen-minute journey to Blackfriars. I get annoyed at Tom for being glued to his phone even though that is exactly what I am doing. I secretly think I'm not as bad about being on my phone as he is about being on his phone. I also know he secretly thinks the opposite.

'Ready, Birthday Girl?' Tom asks.

We step off the train and put our phones back into our pockets. The glass walls of Blackfriars reveal the city all around us – lit up against the night sky, showing off all the big rides in this theme park of a capital. I get a rush of embarrassment, remembering when Tom and I were last here together. All the things I said. All the ways he ignored them. How can it be that it's winter now and yet nothing has changed?

We walk with bowed heads through the Dickensian streets which have felt significantly less Dickensian since Nando's has installed its flagship restaurant here. You can smell the chocolate restaurant before you get to it. And we're engulfed by the heady warm scent of it when we push through the doors, the cold clinging to our coats. We're led upstairs and seated at a good table near a radiator with a view of the empty market below us.

'Look!' I say, in delight, excited by all the things in this restaurant I am supposed to be excited by. 'The pepper grinder is full of chocolate beans instead of pepper.' I pick it up and shake it in Tom's face, scattering cocoa dust over the table.

'Cool,' Tom replies, although he could be more excited about it.

'And there's chocolate beans for us to eat! Look! Here in a bowl!' I gesture towards it but Tom isn't looking. Tom is checking his phone. I defiantly pick one up and try it. It bursts like bitter chalk in my mouth and, when the waiter arrives with menus, I'm coughing and spitting it out into the napkin.

'Sorry, I didn't explain,' he says. 'You don't eat the beans whole. You roll them between your fingers to break the shell, and then eat the middle.'

I grin up at him, probably with bits of kernel all stuck in my teeth. He is young, cute. Probably waiting tables here until London gives him the break he's sure he deserves – much like everyone else in this city. 'Whoops, my bad.'

He smiles. 'Happens every day. Now, can I get you some drinks?'

'I'll just have a beer,' Tom says to his phone.

'Tom, it's a chocolate restaurant. We should get chocolate cocktails.'

The waiter opens up the menu and points out the ones that are the best. 'Ooo, yes, one of those,' I say, when he points to one made of molten chocolate.

'Just a beer mate, thanks.'

The waiter leaves just as Tom puts his phone down and smiles at me. 'Chocolate cocktails. Exciting!'

'Why are you getting a beer?'

'Because I feel like a beer.'

'But don't you want to order something chocolatey if we're in a specialist restaurant?'

'Not particularly.'

'OK.'

We can't argue because it's my birthday and because we're both making an effort because it's my birthday and you can't argue on your birthday because what does that mean? But I'm annoyed that he's getting a beer. Even though it's his life and he can get a beer if he wants one. But it *really* annoys me that he's got a beer.

The drinks arrive and we smile at each other.

'That looks great, Tor,' Tom says of my drink, swigging from his bottle. 'What does it taste like?'

I take a small sip and the thick milkshake-like liquid clings around my lips. It tastes delicious, like Willy Wonka childhood dreams come true mixed with guilt about the calories. 'Amazing,' I squeal. 'You should've got one.'

'I might try a bit of yours.'

This annoys me because I don't want to share, but that will make me sound childish so I sidestep into a different row instead. 'I think we should ban our phones through the meal,' I say, out of the blue. 'Whoever picks theirs up first has to pay for dinner.'

Tom's mouth is a thin line. 'But we're paying for dinner using the joint account.'

I sip my drink. 'You know what I mean.'

'Fair enough.' Tom tucks his phone back into his pocket then he stares at me.

'What? What is it?'

He points with his eyes towards my phone on the table. 'You too.'

There's this really good moment where we both have to look at the menu to decide what to have which gives us a valid reason for why we're not talking. I watch him peruse the menu and try to make myself feel affection towards him. It comes, after a moment or two of effort. I think how kind it is that he's taking me here when he hates novelty restaurants. I picture him nervously asking the shop assistant about what vibrator to buy because he honestly thought it was a good idea. The affection swells and I reach out and take his hand and squeeze it over the table.

'I love you.' I tell him. In that moment it is the truth.

'What's brought this on?' His hand is warm and he squeezes it back. He is happy I have touched him and said that.

'Just you being you. I'm very lucky to have a man like you on my birthday.'

Our shared tenderness is cut short by the re-appearance of the cute waiter. 'Do you know what you'd like?' he holds up his notepad, ready to take it down. I signal with my eyes that Tom can go first.

'Oh, yeah, thanks. I'm going to get the cheeseburger and fries,' he says.

I lower my menu. 'You're not getting a chocolatey meal either?'

He shrugs. 'I feel like a burger.'

'But you can get a burger anywhere.'

The waiter, sensing tension, beams at both of us. 'Our burgers come with cacao mayonnaise.'

'There you go,' Tom says, handing the menu back to him. 'Can't get *that* anywhere.'

'You sure you don't want the lamb?' I press. 'You love lamb. And this one comes in a dark-cacao gravy.'

Tom's voice is now being expelled through gritted teeth that are stretched into a determined smile. 'I. Told you. I. Feel. Like. A. Burger.'

'Suit yourself.'

The waiter expertly turns towards me and asks, with side-helpings of smoothing-over charm, 'And what would the lady like?'

There are only two vegetarian things on the menu. One is a macaroni cheese with chocolate, which is what I really, really want. But I also want another chocolate cocktail and I'm already picturing the cellulite that will form on my arse.

'The cacao vegetarian curry,' I say, feeling a little piece of me die as I say it.

'Excellent choice. Let me know if you need any more drinks.'

Tom and I are left. We drink from our drinks. We smile at one another. We comment on how nice the decor is. We manage two whole minutes of discussion about how Borough Market is so overrated and only tourists go there. I finish my cocktail and order another. Tom orders another beer. Loosened by the first drink, I allow him a sip of my second cocktail and he says, 'Man, this is amazing actually,' and orders one for himself. The sparkplug of my love for him splutters into a flicker of light. The food arrives and that gives us additional conversational fodder while we ask one another what theirs is like. Tom makes a joke about the cacao mayonnaise and it's funny enough that I just about laugh. There are couples all around us, sitting at identical tables, probably having identical conversations. How normal is it to have nothing left to say to the person you're supposed to love more than anyone? Tom and I know every single thing about one another. I've collected his anecdotes, and his memories, and his worries, and his traumas, and his childhood favourites, and his opinions about all of his friends, and I've pocketed them all like

Pokémon. I've completed the set. The only new ones to collect are the things that happen to him when I'm not there. *How was your day? What happened? Did your boss do that annoying thing again? Please tell me because it's new.* I sip at my molten chocolate drink and think about why people have children. Is it simply to give themselves more to talk about? Is the act of procreation merely an exercise in being able to sustain conversation? And, if they are seriously at that point, why are they having a child with someone they are so totally bored of?

Tom is three beers and one cocktail in and he is softening.

'You look pretty tonight,' he finally says. I can smell the beef on his breath from over the table.

'Thank you.'

'I know I'm lucky to have you, Tor.'

'I'm lucky to have you too.'

He wiggles his eyebrows over his burger which is encased in both hands. There is a splodge of artisan mayonnaise on the side of his lip. 'Looking forward to trying out your present later?'

No.

No no no no no no.

I wink at him in what I hope is a seductive way. 'Of course.' I pull up my skirt under the table and flash him the belt of my suspenders. 'And I've got a present for you too.'

He sees the suspenders and he grips my thigh. Just feeling wanted by him, if only for a second, makes me suddenly want him. I push my thighs together so I'm clamping his hand and we smirk at one another. He is still in there. Rock Man. The Man on the Rock. The spark may be like one of those flimsy cheap lighters that takes forever to catch in the wind, but there's still some gasoline left. If I have another drink I'll be just about relaxed enough to not mind the vibrator. It may even be enjoyable. It may even be kinky. I mean, couples use sex toys all the time. We don't. But others do. Maybe we just need date night and sex toys to 'spice things up'. I mean, it wouldn't be trotted out as advice for everything if it didn't work.

My phone starts to vibrate manically.

'No phones.' He removes his hand to wag his finger.

'I know.' I pick up my fork and try another spoonful of curry.

My phone goes again.

And again.

And—

'Oh just get it,' Tom snaps in a tight whisper. 'I know you're dying to.'

'I'm not going to get it.'

'Just get it.'

It vibrates again. Angrily. Urgently. I'm worried now. That someone is hurt. 'I'm not going to get it. A deal's a deal,' I say, though my fingers are itching to pick it up and other tables have started to notice the noise and are shooting us looks.

'This is ridiculous, just check it.'

'Nope.'

He holds eye contact. We're both half-laughing to try to ensure the other one knows we are joking but it is loaded. Atmosphere hangs on every atom in the air between us.

'It's just, whoever it is, they keep messaging. I'm worried something's happened.'

'Tori! Just check your fucking phone already.'

I'm stinging that he has sworn at me as I swipe upwards. Part of me hopes, just for a moment, that something bad has happened so Tom feels guilty.

My hand flies to my mouth.

'What? What is it?!'

'Oh my God!'

'What is it Tor? Is everything OK?' He's panicked now, leaning over towards me, hands gripping the table.

'It's Dee,' I say, looking up from my phone. 'She's gone into labour.'

Month Nine

Nigel Tucker is feeling very blessed!

So, she came earlier than expected, but she's our Christmas miracle. I'm so, so proud to introduce Janice Harper to the world. Weighing only 5lbs and 2oz but perfect and healthy and we're besotted. Dee's been such a trooper and I'm the luckiest man on earth. X x x x x

238 likes

Comments:

Amy Price: Oh my God – congratulations! She looks so much like you Dee. Sending ALL the hugs to your family.

Claire Spears: SHE IS JUST GORGEOUS! I cannot wait to meet her. Congratulations!!

Sally Thomson: What beautiful news and what a beautiful baby. Wishing you all the best on this most special of days.

82 more comments ...

★

Christmas is everywhere by the time I'm allowed to see her.

The air crackles with frenzied energy. Everyone is driving badly or walking without looking or pushing with their elbows. The bus to Nigel's flat is heaving – the windows

331

fogged and sodden with condensation. At least five different people sneeze on me. It's too hot but there's not enough room to take off my coat. I sweat into it, getting annoyed because my fringe will look all separated in the photos I'll take when I meet the baby.

I've never actually been to Nigel's flat before and it takes me a while to find it on Google maps. I go down a few wrong roads and retrace my steps. But, eventually, I am here. Outside. Looking at the flat and thinking how very Nigel. It has a security-gate code thing to stop even pedestrians getting in. It must've cost a fortune. I check Dee's message on my phone to remind myself what number they are and press the appropriate button. There's a ring and a buzz. Her voice crackles out of the speaker.

'Tor? That you?' She sounds like Dee. Her voice is the same. I'm not sure why I thought it would be different, but I'm relieved that her voice is the same.

'Rumour has it that YOU'VE HAD A BABY,' I yell into the intercom. 'I'm coming to check these unsubstantiated claims.' Her laughter crackles as the gate buzzes and slowly swings open.

Dee's waiting for me at the door to her flat and seeing her breaks something inside me. 'Dee!' I go to hug her but she steps back.

'Ooo careful! I'm still all stitched up down there.' She pats me tenderly on the back though as I walk through to her new home.

I can smell the baby before I see her.

The scent of baby lingers and casts its usual hypnotic spell. It makes the air in this flat feel calm and serene.

'Where is she then?' I ask. 'I'm not here to see you.'

Dee laughs, holding her stomach. 'Don't make me laugh again. She's in the living room. Here, I'll show you.' We follow the scent through the flat that Dee hasn't quite managed to de-bachelorise yet. The walls are all still cream, the furniture all still black. But framed photos of them hang on the wall in the hallway. Snapshots of their life, cementing their time together – though this time last year they didn't know the other existed. I pad after her, instinctively taking off my boots, and there, there in the corner, is her baby.

I walk over to the Moses basket and look down at my best friend's baby. She's tiny. I've never seen one this tiny before but Dee's auburn hair grows aggressively out of her head.

'Dee,' I whisper, feeling her beside me. 'She's beautiful. She's got your hair.'

We stand there quietly. Janice sleeps, head on one side, little fists clenched, lost in whatever unconsciousness newborns have.

'She's something, right? I was always worried my baby wouldn't be cute, but she really is, isn't she?'

'She's so small.'

'Well, she was so very early.'

I stare at her a while longer. I crouch down and hold out my little finger, pressing it into her palm. Janice grabs hold of it in her sleep. I turn and grin back at Dee. She smiles at me, tired, from where she's gently lowering herself onto the sofa.

'I'll make tea,' I say.

'I love you.'

I deftly remove my pinkie and work out my way around Nigel's kitchen. It's all steel and shiny and everything you would expect. The teabags are in a special jar. The fridge takes a while to find because it's invisibly built into the units. I return with two steaming mugs. Dee reaches out gratefully.

'So . . .' I say.

'So.'

'Dee, you've had a baby.'

She shakes her head, like she can't believe it either. 'I know. What's that about?' She looks so different. Her face is whiter. Her hair is limper. And yet, there's something about the way she carries herself. She seems wiser, older, like a grown-up.

I sip from my mug. 'How are you? Really?'

She shakes her head, a smile creeping across her freckles. 'Happy. So so tired, yet so so happy. She's just . . . it's so weird, Tor. It's totally fucking surreal. I can't even explain it.'

I smile at her. I am happy for her. I can manage that, and that makes me proud of myself. 'And how are you after . . . everything?'

Dee blows her fringe up and shakes her head again. 'For God's sake, Tor. Everyone tells you how awful it is, but

they don't actually ever get across *how* awful it is. I thought
I was going to die. I actually thought I was dying.'

My heart rate picks up at even the thought of it. My
palms clamming. If I ever have a baby, I will have to do
this too. It's the fear that creeps up on you sometimes, out
of the blue. A bit like those moments when you realise,
when you're doing the washing up or something, that you're
going to die and there is absolutely nothing you can do
about it. If you want to give birth to a baby, you will have
to go through labour. And not one person has anything
good to say about that. 'You're OK though?'

'Yes. And it's worth it. It is. I mean, look at her.'

We both peer over the top of the Moses basket again.
The baby is still just as absorbing. Her smell wafts over us.
The house is so still. Dee is so still. I've never seen her like
this. All . . . chill. I ask how Nigel is doing and she grins
so widely as she explains how in love he is. How cute he
is when he changes a nappy. How amazing he was during
the labour. There is so much love in this room. It ripples
out of the walls; it looks down on me from the framed
photographs. Dee is wrapped in multiple duvets of love.
She's just explaining how hot the male midwife was when
I notice it.

The glint on her finger.

'Dee? You're engaged!'

She goes red, her cheeks flooding with blood, camou-
flaging her freckles. She looks down, bashful. 'Took you
long enough to notice!'

I'm kneeling at her feet, sinking into the plush cream carpet. I am gasping. I am holding the ring closer so I can see it properly. 'Oh my God,' I say. 'Oh my God.'

'I wanted to tell you in person. You know how much I hate it when people post it online.'

I rub the diamond between my fingers, playing the role of caring what it's like. It's a large cuboid diamond on white silver. Generic, but still quite Dee. 'You're not tempted to take a photo of your hand and add a comment saying "he liked it so . . ."?'

'Tor! No! Although Nigel is desperate to. He's so insecure, bless him. He wants to post everything all the time.'

I am blinking more than I should, and that's probably because I'm feeling sadder than I should. Sad at this happy news. But I'm smiling and I'm managing. I ask her all the questions I am so well-trained in asking. And I ask them without strain in my voice, as I am well-trained in doing. 'How did he do it?' 'Were you surprised?' 'Do you have a date?' But she is still Dee. Thankfully she is still Dee.

'He didn't get down on one knee, thank fuck. Because I'd banned him from doing so. I wasn't that surprised. It's Nigel. He kept saying "this will be a *very special* mini break" in the lead up to Norwich. He wasn't expecting me to go into labour two hours later. And, no, we won't get married for ages. Childbirth was the worst thing that's ever happened to me and that's all his fault. It's going to take me two years to forgive him enough to marry him.'

But she is still getting married.

And I am not.

The baby wakes. She gurgles, she cries. Dee winces as she crouches down to pick her up. She winces as she sits back down with her on the sofa. 'What's up baby? Are you hungry my darling? Are you?'

She is a natural. I don't even have to lie as I tell her that. Janice finds her nipple quickly and falls quiet again. Her little blue alien eyes are open and staring up with so much love, and Dee is looking down at her with so much love. There is so much love in this room, did I tell you?

'I can't move for forty-five minutes now,' Dee says. 'Please stay and talk to me.'

'What do you want to talk about?' I artfully move my eyes away from Dee's breast.

'You! What's going on with *you*. How's the book? How's Tom? I will *not* be one of those mothers who can't talk about anything other than the baby.'

I am so grateful that she's asked after me. I am so grateful even though her asking means I now have to lie. To her. To myself. Because if I tell the truth now about how well things are going I will fall apart and I'm not sure I'll be able to put myself back together again. I start gabbling. Insecurity lacing every gurgle of nonsense that streams from my mouth. This is Dee. *Dee.* And yet suddenly I want her to think I'm doing great. To maybe even be slightly jealous of me. I need her to think my life is good, so *I* can maybe think my life is good. 'Book is going slowly. They've extended my deadline . . .' I sip my tea from a black shiny mug. 'Tom is still Tom. He's off again on a business trip next week. You know us. Oh, yeah, we still have our little fights. Oh, yeah, the same old. "Why can't we talk about children?" etc. etc. But, you know, I've been thinking about it, Dee, really thinking about it.'

'Oh, yes?' she asks, smiling down as Janice tugs at her nipple.

'Yeah, I have. And, well, I'm just not sure if I'm maternal, you know? I've not, like, got that ache to reproduce. I'm . . . ambivalent.' My hands are throwing shapes around me as I speak – like I'm making balloon animals of lies out of the surrounding air. 'And, well, maybe I don't have the urge to have kids because I'm so fulfilled by my job, you know? Like, I'm so lucky that I have a career where I'm essentially leaving a part of myself behind on the world. I make a difference. I feel like I have such a *purpose* already. So maybe that's what's scratching that itch, you know? So maybe I don't need to have children . . .'

I tail off because Dee has pulled a face. A very involuntary face. She looks up from her baby and is still pulling the face. 'Oh, Tor,' she says, readjusting her arms so the baby's head is even more comfortable.

'What? What is it?' I ask.

She presses her lips together and gives just the slightest hint of a head shake. 'It just makes me sad to hear you say that, that's all.'

I pause. I tiptoe into this conversation, scared to go any closer to the cliff edge of it.

'Why?'

Dee stares at her baby again. Shhing her, whispering she is a good girl. She manages to look back up, sorrow in her eyes. Sympathy. Maybe. Maybe, a hint of judgement? No. No it won't be that. It can't be . . .

'I'm sure you *think* right now that your career is as fulfilling as having a baby,' she starts to say. Starts to say what will ruin everything. She keeps speaking. In this patronising voice I never knew existed. 'But, honestly, Tor. They're incomparable. You won't understand until you have one yourself, but it's just so much bigger than anything else . . . a career just can't compete. I'm sorry hon, but it just can't. I'm not saying this to upset you, I'm just saying it because . . . well . . . because I'm worried about you and Tom. I don't want him to talk you out of anything. I think you know your books aren't the same as a baby . . .'

And that.

That is when.

The veil falls down between us.

Janice, maybe sensing my tension, falls off the boob and starts wailing. Dee tries to push her back on.

I stand up. 'I have to go.'

'Shh, shh, come on. You've not finished with this one yet.' She looks up. 'Stay!' Dee says. 'I'll get her reattached in a moment. You're not upset, are you? I only said it because I care about you, Tor.'

'I really do have to go.'

If I don't leave within twenty seconds, I will explode into

ash. I will leave chunks of myself, of our friendship, all over the cream walls of this flat.

I cannot believe.

Cannot.

Believe.

She has just said what she has just said.

'I'm not upset.' I smile as I lie. And she falls for it. I don't know how, but she does. 'Please, don't stand up. Get her settled,' I put my hands up. 'I can see myself out.'

Dee seems slightly disappointed that I'm leaving before she wants me to, but more distracted by the baby and what the baby needs. And you know what? I am OK with that part. I am used to that part. I accept that it is normal and natural and part of how friendships change when one of you brings a new life into this world. I am not a monster. I am not selfish. I am not unwilling to adapt. I'm not even letting my jealousy cloud this – though I am sure I would be accused of such if I ever dared bring this up.

'Take care, yeah?' I tell her. I reach out and stroke Dee's red, glowing hair that burns like fire in the low winter sun streaming through the windows. 'I'll call you soon.'

'You sure you have to go?' She sounds needy now. Maybe Nigel is not due back for a while. But she has just told me how fulfilling all this is so she'll be fine by herself.

'Yes. Christmas. Career stuff.' Poison leaks from my tongue as I say the word 'career' but she doesn't notice because Janice is reattaching. I put my coat on and pull on my boots and say goodbye over my shoulder. Just as I'm about to push through the front door, I stop and look at the photographs. There is one here that I took – of Dee and Nigel on the dance floor at the wedding I brought her to. The wedding that changed her life. Nigel's got Dee hoisted on his shoulders, her head is thrown back with laughter. She fell off his shoulders moments later, then dragged me to the loo to tell me she really liked him.

That Dee. That Dee who was with me only months ago. That Dee who sang 'Elephant Love Medley' with me in the car. Who always took my calls. Who understood it. Who could see the wall and the hurt it causes.

She is gone.

Because that Dee would never say what that woman in the living room just said to me.

Maybe she's right. Maybe my career isn't the same. Not that she would know, she is only a teacher. And I have never had that thought – that bitter, superior thought – until this moment. Maybe she is saying it because she cares. But, what was clear, what was so clear from what she just said, was this: *Having a baby is better*. It is the better option. It is the option with the most depth. The most meaning. The most significance.

. . . and you couldn't possibly understand, hon, because you simply have not had one.

I shake my head at the photo. If I allow myself to get angry, maybe it will stop me from crying. It's hard enough, feeling the clock ticking and yet life not obliging to give you the things others have. To feel defunct and left behind and scared as hell about it – and the more nervous you get about it, the more you give off some smell that makes it less likely to happen. I did not ask for there to be walls. I swear I do not want them. I don't want to feel like this. Why is Dee making me feel like this? Why would you make anyone feel like this about something they cannot help?

I tried to tell myself Dee's baby wouldn't change anything.

But it has changed everything.

I push through the door and it slams behind me.

★

I decide to walk home. It is crisp and the sun is bright and golden. Christmas taints the air and it will be good for me, after all that. I mosey along back streets, discovering pockets of pretty houses I've never seen before, a small park I never knew existed. When I get to Brixton, I stop and look at the lights and try to make myself feel festive. Which is hard because it's still daylight and some random yells at me to accept God into my life.

I'm surprised by how unshocked I am.

Instead I'm resigned. My soul has settled comfortably into the inevitability of what just happened.

I decide to surprise Tom with some special sandwiches. How he will like that. I stop at the artisan bakery that used to be a KFC and order two Christmas sandwiches with everything on them – one meat, one veggie. I tell them to put extra cranberry sauce on Tom's because he really likes it. I hardly get any change from a tenner. I cradle the giant sandwiches in my arms and plan the rest of my day. I will surprise Tom and he'll be in a good mood because he loves it when I surprise him. Then I guess I should at least try and write some chapters. I might do some Christmas shopping online.

'I'm home,' I call, stepping over the threshold of our flat. Our home. Cat is the first to acknowledge me. She pads over, the bell on her collar ringing, and meows until I bend down to stroke her. Once I oblige, she flounces off in the direction of the kitchen.

'In the living room!' Tom's voice calls back.

I shrug out of my coat and gloves and hat and other winter paraphernalia and take the sandwiches in. He's set up a workstation on the sofa – papers spread everywhere, both his laptop and his iPad set up.

'Hey Tor,' he says to his screen, fingers blurring over his keyboard. 'How was Dee?'

'She was fine. The baby is cute.' I hold up my parcel. 'I got us Christmas sandwiches from Flour Pottery.'

Tom looks up at that and I gesture to the sandwiches like a magician's assistant. He closes the top of his laptop with a click. 'Have I ever told you how much I love you? How very very much?'

I curtsy. 'Shall we eat them at the table? I don't want you getting cranberry sauce on the sofa.'

I get out some plates with a clatter and ask him if he wants tea. He does, so I boil the kettle and plate up the sandwiches as I wait for it. I find a bag of Kettle chips and pour half into a bowl. When everything is arranged, I bring it to the table, where Tom is sitting, eyes wide with adoration. He beckons me to him, and gives me a backwards hug from where he sits in his chair. 'This is just what I needed. Thank you! I love it when you surprise me.'

I sit down and pick up my sandwich. 'I know.'

We eat in companionable silence. The bread's gone slightly soggy from where the mayonnaise has bled into it on the walk home. I rip that bit off but enjoy the rest of it. The combination of tastes you only eat one month of the year. The tang of cranberry with the velvet crunch of nut roast between bread. Tom's face is buried in his, small animal-like grunts emanating from him every five or six bites. I look over at him and I smile.

And I say, 'Tom, I want to have a baby.'

I'm not even sure if it's true as it falls out of my mouth. But I say it anyway. I put it out there. I was not planning to say it, but it's there now.

Tom puts down the last part of his sandwich. 'What's brought this on?'

His face has changed, the smile has gone. His nose is wrinkled.

I am so calm. I am holding my sandwich and I feel nothing but calm and certainty, like I've been switched on to autopilot. 'I want a baby,' I repeat, still not even sure if that's true. Still saying it though. I reach out and poke the invisible boundaries of our relationship, then I flatten my palm and I push.

344

He shakes his head, like I've let him down. 'I knew you'd be like this after seeing Dee. I knew it.'

'That's beside the point. Do you want a baby, Tom?'

He leans back, throws his arms up. 'Of course I want a baby. At some point.'

'At *what* point?' I press, putting down the remains of my sandwich. 'When, Tom? In a year? In two? In ten?' I cannot believe I am saying all this. *Why am I saying all this?* I am breaking all the rules of us. I have picked up a pointy stick and I'm gesticulating madly to the pink elephant. I've even made a neon sign for the pink elephant. I'm relaxed, I'm not even angry. I'm just . . . finally saying it.

'Is this why you bought sandwiches? To butter me up?' he asks.

'I didn't know I was going to bring it up until I did.'

'I don't believe you.'

'Well, it's the truth.'

'Do you really think *now* is a good time? I'm on deadline. You know I'm on deadline.'

Cat jumps up onto my lap and tries to eat some of my soggy discarded bread. We don't even acknowledge it. All my voices, the voices that usually keep me in check, scream *What are you doing? Why are you ruining this? He was so pleased with you about the sandwiches! You could've had a nice day!* But there is a new voice, an older voice. A wiser one. One that has been getting louder since I've started seeing Anne. One that has come back to this one life of mine after being away so long, and looked at the mess all the other voices have made, and that voice is saying *No, what the fuck have* you *done?*

'We're not happy Tom.' I am just saying it. It is all falling out of me. 'We've not been happy for so long.'

The hysterical voices yell, *Tor, what the hell are you doing to us?!*

The wiser voice whispers, *Tor, finally.*

'Where is this coming from?' Tom's face is stretched into ugly defiance, like he's ashamed of me, like I am a cat who just shat outside its litter tray. 'Look, it's not fair for you to get upset about Dee and take it all out on me. You've got to stop doing this, Tor. This is not about me and you, this is about Dee and her having a baby and making you insecure and . . .'

The calm shatters. I stand. I yell. 'IT IS FUCKING ABOUT ME AND YOU.' My fists are curled into balls. 'WHAT ARE WE DOING? WHY WON'T YOU LET ME TALK ABOUT US?'

Tom kicks back his chair and leaves the room. 'I'm not going to talk to you when you're like this. You're being hysterical.'

Cat follows him into the kitchen, thinking he's going to feed her. I stand with my fists still clenched and have no idea what I'm feeling, but know it's a miracle I'm not yet crying. So many parts of me beg me to stop. To smooth this over. To apologise. To tell Tom I didn't mean it. He will punish me for a few days, sure. He'll be crabby and silent and he will make a few jokes at my expense. But soon it will be forgotten and we can get back to normal. Our life. Our togetherness. The only thing I have really that everyone else has. The only tick I've got in the right box.

The wiser voice tells me to follow him into the kitchen. Anne is in my head too, joining forces. She is saying, *'It's not unreasonable to want these things, Tori. It's not needy. They are natural things to want. Do not let Tom think you are the problem. Not any more.'*

'You can't just walk out,' I call to him in the kitchen. I sigh and follow him in.

He's boiling the kettle again and making a cup of tea. *How can he be making a cup of tea?*

'I told you,' he says, his back to me. 'I'm not willing to talk to you when you're this upset. I can't get any sense out of you.'

'I'M NOT EVEN CRYING! I'M JUST ASKING YOU A SIMPLE QUESTION!'

He turns with his arms already crossed and a silent '*a-ha*'. 'Don't yell at me, Tor. Don't raise your voice to me.'

'DON'T GIVE ME A REASON TO YELL AT YOU THEN!'

'Tori,' he warns. He turns his back again. He gets out mugs and he puts teabags into them.

'Tom,' I plead. Oh, this is where the tears come. The tears he always uses against me. 'What are we doing?'

He pauses. He turns. He looks at me. And I'm expecting more flames, more insults, more deflection. He gets so annoyed at me whenever I cry. Instead he meets my eye, and his, his are watering too.

347

'I don't know, Tori,' he replies quietly. 'I don't know.'

The kettle is bubbling but we ignore it. We look at one another. It clicks itself off.

'We don't make each other happy,' I say. I say the truth. The truth that, for whatever reason, woke up in this moment and refused to go unsaid a second longer. 'We haven't in years. We don't have sex any more. We argue all the time. We keep delaying the future and I think we're doing that for a reason.' A bubble of grief pops and erupts and the tears really come then. I bury my face into my hands and the sobs start ripping through me. This is it. We are breaking up. I know this. This is what is happening here. Because it must.

Tom, unable to ignore my pain any longer, steps over and hugs me. He hugs me so tight. His smell, I've always loved his smell. 'But I love you, Tor,' he whispers into my ear. 'I love you so much.'

'I love you too.' The grief makes it come out like a whistle, one you can hardly hear. My heart, it hurts so much. It's twisting in my body like it's been stabbed with a flaming torch. I say, 'But I'm not sure if loving each other is enough.'

He's shaking his head into my shoulder. 'I wasn't expecting this,' he mutters. 'I wasn't expecting any of this.'

'I wasn't either.'

He has to believe this. He has to. We were going to eat some sandwiches and I was going to write some chapters. Maybe we could have gone for a walk around the park together before it got dark. Somehow, for reasons it will take a lifetime to truly understand, I changed everything.

I feel the words falling out of my mouth before I realise I've even said them.

'Tom? I think we need to break up.'

I can't believe I've said it. I'm in as much shock as he is. He goes stiff in my arms. We lay suspended, together, in the shared wretched agony of what I've just said.

Then, then he lets go.

'If that's what you've decided to do,' he says, 'I'm not going to humiliate myself by begging you to change your mind.' He turns from me, goes back to making the tea. I blink at him, my mouth open, my insides collapsing in on themselves.

He's not fighting for us.

I blink away the tears so I can still see him. He's getting out the milk now. He's only making the one cup of tea.

Tom was never going to let go. I realise that in this moment. It was always going to be me. He would cling on while never giving me what I needed. He's been just as unhappy as I have but he was never going to be the one to give up. He broke my heart every day he didn't love me in the way I needed to be loved. Every day he looked at me in disappointment that the reality of me hadn't quite lived up to his fantasy. Every day he changed the subject or made me feel silenced at a wedding. But he was never going to be the one to end this. He is the good guy and I'm the villain. That's how it's always been, playing out, right until the music stops.

The calm has returned, or maybe now it's just numbness. 'I'll pack some things and go to my parents,' I tell his back.

'Tor, if you walk out that door, you can't just walk back in again.' He puts the milk back into the fridge. He slams the door shut. Then he grips the handle and leans into it, like he can't stand without support.

This is the moment. The moment where, after months, after years, of dillying and dallying, of putting it off and getting on with it, of suppressing and hoping it will be better tomorrow. This is the moment where the choice I've been avoiding stands right in front of me, gets up in my face, and demands to be made. I'm not ready to make it. But I don't think I ever will be.

My gut though. It knows. It's known for so long now.

And my gut says, 'I love you, Tom. Goodbye.'

★

I pack up my moisturiser and retinoid cream and the plans Tom and I were making to go to Greece in the summer. I chuck some bras and a few pairs of knickers into a wheelie suitcase, alongside the names I'd secretly picked out for our unborn children. Children that will never exist now. I'm not sure how many pairs of shoes to take, or how many of Tom's most private feelings and memories. Things only I know, after years of careful extraction during gorgeous moments talking under the duvet. I pick up that one time he told me about a childhood holiday to France, where his dad cried because he trod on a sea urchin and where Tom's childhood ended with the realisation that his parents were fallible. I pack it in with my alarm clock. I wrap up the electrical cord of my travel hairdryer and place it in the suitcase next to that feeling that, no matter how bad a party is, you can still return home to someone who loves you.

I flinch as the front door slams. The sound of Tom leaving.

I do not know when I will ever see him again.

And, just moments ago, we were smiling at one another and eating Christmas sandwiches.

You can build a relationship for so many years. You can grow it and nurture it, give it foundations and walls, and tinker with how you want it decorated. Then in just one moment, you can blow at it gently by telling the truth and the relationship collapses like a teetering house of cards. Years of careful craftsmanship. One conversation to undo it all.

There's not space for everything in my suitcase. I'll need to come back for the furniture that we will argue about. The cat who both of us will want. The flat will need to be put on the market and sold. I can't get all my clothes in, and there's no longer room for that safe feeling of being a woman with a long-term partner, even if that partner has sucked you dry. All the memories we've made, all the memories we had yet to make – this is all they are now. Memories. I fit in what I can and I zip it all up.

I do not cry as I bend down to say goodbye to Cat. I

do not cry as I stand with the handle of my wheelie suitcase in one hand and look around our flat – our life – and know it has already become a museum.

Our ornamental wall clock ticks loudly and persistently. It tells me it's only quarter to three. It tells me I'm thirty-two. The clock goes tick, the clock goes tock.

I am alone.

The clock goes tick, the clock goes tock.

I may have just ruined my one chance at having it.

The clock goes tick, the clock goes tock.

I'm walking away from a man who says he loves me, and there is nothing or no one here to catch me.

The clock goes tick, the clock goes tock.

Being unhappy with Tom may be the happiest I will ever be.

The clock goes tick, the clock goes tock.

But I'm still leaving.

Because I know that it's the right thing to do. Because, somehow, somewhere deep inside me, I know it's going to be OK. Maybe even better than OK. Maybe, in time, I could even be happy.

I sigh and feel relief – yes *relief* – ripple through me.

I close the door.

I lock it behind me.

I trudge along with my wheelie suitcase to the train station, the wheels getting stuck in cracks in the pavement. My lungs are not working properly, they will not let air in. It's hard to breathe. I am gasping instead of inhaling. I keep thinking, *I should go back, I should go back, I need to go back*. But my legs keep walking away. Away from the life I've spent six years building. The sky is dull. Christmas songs blast from the open doors of shops selling silver ornaments in the shape of festive owls. 'It's the most wonderful time of the year', the music says. I stop and Londoners collide into the back of me and swear.

I cannot breathe.

My lungs. My lungs will not let in oxygen. Everything swims; I feel my knees weaken. *What have I done? What have I done? What have I done?*

And then the cloud breaks, only for a moment.

The winter sunshine finds its way to my face and I turn up towards it. My face feels warmer, if only for a second. This sunshine feels just for me. The universe's way of telling me, *Tori, you have made the right decision. You deserve to be happier than you have been. It is going to be all right.*

I'm not crying.

There will be tears, I know this. There will be pain. Doubts. Endless questions about who was to blame and could I have done more and did I leave too soon and is it actually all my fault, as I turn my face into my pillow at 2a.m. to try to muffle the endless sobs. There will be the missing him that creeps up at the most unexpected moments. Tiny things that I will remember will make me cry. As I hold a cucumber in the supermarket because he always said they were overrated. People I meet that I know he wouldn't like and I'm so desperate to tell him about. I'll worry about him constantly – about his happiness, his job, the health of his mother – and yet I will not be able to call. I'll mourn the in-jokes and pet names that died when Us died. I'll have the surreal pain of knowing there's someone out there, under the same sky, who knows me better than any other human, yet I can't speak to him again. There'll be annoying moments, like not having the good vegetable peeler any more, or not being able to nick his deodorant when I run out. For the rest of my life, whenever I go to a restaurant, I will be able to look at the menu and know what Tom would've ordered. So many imprints of agonising, useless, information. There'll be moments where I will look at this period of my life with true fondness, and moments where I will look at it with only anger at the senseless waste of time.

But not now.

Now there is only the sun on my face, and putting one foot in front of the other, and wheeling myself forward into the chance of happiness. The pain is coming. Oh, how it is coming, but not right now.

I have to change at Victoria and the connecting train is delayed.

How can it be? I think. *Do they not know I've just ruined my life? That I am moments away from falling apart and need to get home so very quickly before I disintegrate in public.* I stand against a wall, waiting for them to say the train is here and breathe and breathe and breathe. People are laughing and sipping coffee from red disposable cups. People have shopping bags filled with Christmas gifts for the ones they love. People are on their way to meetings in business suits and playing games on their phones or listening to music through cupped headphones. None of them see me. Here. With my heart scattered all over the floor in pieces. I ring my parents' house, my fingers shaking on the keys. No answer. I wilt with relief when my mum picks up her mobile.

'Tori?' She is somewhere loud and echoey.

'Mum.' My voice cracks. 'It's me. I've . . . I've left Tom, Mum.' Saying it out loud makes it real. Telling another human that isn't Tom confirms it.

'Hang on, Tor. It's noisy here. You've left Tom? Is that what you said?'

I nod, tears shooting down my face. I am hardly able to speak. 'Oh God, I've left him. What have I done, Mum? What have I done?'

I hear her panic down the line. She's talking to Dad. 'Yes, it's Victoria. She's saying she's left Tom. I know! I don't know! Hang on. Tor? Tor are you still there? We're out Christmas shopping.'

'Mum,' I wail. 'What have I done? I've just left him. I don't understand. We were eating sandwiches and I just . . . oh God . . .' She's telling me it will be OK. She says the word *'Finally'*. She says well done for being so brave.

'The train's arriving,' I manage to get out. 'I'll be there in forty minutes.'

355

'You may be home before us, love. We'll leave now. But you may get back before us. Are you OK to let yourself in?'

I nod. I stumble through the ticket barrier with my phone pressed to my ear.

'You know where the key is?'

'Yes.'

'It's going to be all right, Tori.' There's a long pause down the line. 'You've made the right decision,' she says. 'I promise you. You will look back on today in time and realise it was the best thing you've ever done. We'll see you soon. Stay strong.'

You've made the right decision.

I manage to get through the sliding doors and put my suitcase in the section for luggage. I weave into a duo of seats with no seats opposite and slump my breaking body by the window. The train's automated message welcomes me. It tells me where we are going and where we are stopping. It pulls out of the station and chugs slowly over the river. The city is grey and busy and Christmas is almost here and my world is ending my world is ending my world is ending, but my mother has just told me I've made the right decision.

Her words, her opinion, trickle into me. My fingers stop trembling. I think of how my parents never really approved of Tom. How they carefully toed the line of never slagging him off, but never, ever, saying his behaviour was OK. I could *feel* my mother's relief down the line. She wasn't worrying that I've suddenly made myself single even though I'm thirty-two and there may be no one else, and even though Tom and I have invested so much already, and that he looks so good on paper. I think of other people's opinions I trust and value. Dee always checking if things were all right between us. Sandy seeing straight through my attempts to pretend we were happy. Anne refusing to accept Tom's story and making me realise maybe I'm not so crazy after all, that maybe he's the one with the problem. Even Taylor Faithful rejecting the perfect narrative and walking away from all the stuff she hadn't told us. I've been so obsessed with how it looks that I've not been worrying about how it looks to *whom*. Whose opinions matter and whose don't. And, most of all, how it looks to myself. I watch the city whizz past outside my window and start to feel the grief hit. My heart is not listening to my head, it is determined to break. I will not be able to escape the pain of this. Even if it's right, the agony will demand to be felt. I need to try to hold on until I get back to my parents' house. I know it's going to be hard to stop once I start. A tear spills over and I wipe it away. Another one escapes from my other eye as I do this. And, just as I'm on the brink of total annihilation, my phone goes.

Dee: I'm worried I upset you earlier and I'm really sorry if I did. Can I blame it on sleep deprivation and being off my tits on hormones? Anyway, I hope you and Tom are OK. Call me anytime x

My thumb traces the screen as I read and re-read her

message. This morning was a lifetime ago, but for Dee it was only this morning. I tip my head back to try to stop the tears. My phone beeps again.

Mum: We're on our way home and traffic's OK so we should get back the same time as you. Hang on in there, Victoria. We both love you xx

The tears start to fall quicker, streaming down into my scarf. I turn my face towards the window so no one in the train carriage can see. I open an app to try to distract myself and scroll through the updates of other people's days. I have notifications from the post I wrote yesterday. People have begun to decorate their Christmas trees and are keen to show the world what they look like.

Then I see it.

Jessica Thornton

What an amazing year it's been! I married my best friend, went on the honeymoon of a lifetime, bought my first flat. And now, Tim and I are so, so happy to announce we are expecting our first baby!!!!!!

There is a black and white photo of the inside of her uterus with a blodge in it. There are already eighty-two likes and people saying congratulations underneath. They like it. Everyone likes it. Well done you on your amazing year. How happy you must be so well done. I'm so glad you told me. Validate validate validate, like like like, favourite favourite favourite. Here you go. Here you fucking go. If

I click on this heart will you feel less empty? OK then. As you fucking wish. Like like. Well done you. Congratulations. Oh, haven't you done it right. Clever thing. Oh, how lucky you are. Congratulations. I can't believe the good news. Like like like like like like like.

I find I am laughing.

I am laughing, and I am typing.

Into my own box. Into my own status update. The truth. I've finally remembered how to tell the truth.

I write:

I don't know what the fuck I am doing.

I hit send. I feel free. Oh, how free I feel. I cannot even tell you. I will not lie any more. I will not pretend it's OK when it isn't. I no longer care what it looks like on paper. It does not work. I want to care about how it feels, not how it looks. And it has to feel good.

Tori: I really appreciate the message, hon. Sorry I ran off like that. Speak soon x

I send off my reply to Dee and then I hold down the top button of my phone until it turns off. I'm smiling as I watch the screen fade to black.

Postscript

From: Tori@WhoTheFckAmI.com
To: Marni@Hawkpublishing.com
CC: Kate@Nightingaleagents.com
Subject: New book

Dear Marni

How are you? Good I hope. Sorry it's been a while since we last spoke. I want to thank you again for all the support you have given me over this difficult period and giving me the time I needed to process everything. And sorry again that we've had to push back my next book.

About that however . . . I've had some ideas. I've started to realise that, when it's come to my life over the past half-a-decade, things haven't always been what they seemed. And I want to maybe write something about it. What are your thoughts on 'What The Actual F*ck?' as a title? If you buy me lunch, I can fill you in on the details. ;)

Can't wait to hear back from you.
Tori x

Acknowledgements

Sometimes good things come out of bad places. Thank you to everyone who made it as such. To Maddy, for once again, changing my life in the most positive, empowering way – and to Alice, Hayley, Anna and Giles. Words will never be an adequate thank-you, but they're all I've got.

I'm now fortunate enough to have not one, but two, kick-ass editors in my life. Thank you to Emily, for totally and utterly getting this book and whipping it into shape. And to Rebecca at Usborne, for believing I could do this and being such a champion. Even though there's no way the publishers of *That's Not My Unicorn* could publish a book with a non-consensual blow-job and multiple uses of the c-word in it. It meant so much to have you there throughout this journey.

Thank you to everyone at Hodder, for supporting the book and being so amazing – especially Melissa, who has been such a cheerleader for me from way back when. I can't believe we now technically work together. It's beyond awesome.

Thank you to the brave women I spoke to for this book

about their experiences of emotional abuse and living with narcissists. You're all superheroes and I hope I've done your stories proud. I also hope, in a small way, this book can help more Toris leave Toms. You really do deserve better, and Tom's behaviour really isn't OK. A huge thank you to Women's Aid – just for existing and for the invaluable work you do.

I couldn't have got through this book if it wasn't for the most brilliant friends and family. So thank you to Holly S, Lucy, Sara, Mel, Christi, Lexi, Rachel, Lisa G, Emma, Ruth, Emily S, Non, Lisa W, Josh, Harriet, Jess, Eleanor, Louie, and Carina. And, as always – Mum, Dad, Eryn and Willow. I am the luckiest person alive to have you guys.